ALL BACK TO YOURS

Tales From Woodbridge: Part II

ROBERT HELLIER

Pete
To the Ding!.

To everyone that read and enjoyed All Back To Mine: Tales From Woodbridge Part I and, of course, still to Helen and my two girls.....

CHAPTER 1

Cool Breeze in Summer

S till fucked. Still trapped. Still engulfed in a cloak of fear, panic and terror. There is still a crew of Dam Dem Kingz, the DDK, gangsters trying to get to him, to kill him. His brain still turned over with thoughts of his love, Stacey, his best mate Craig's ex-girlfriend. How the fuck did that happen? He had often pondered the twisting, turning, drug fuelled road that lead to this place but it still did not make much sense.

Still trapped, no longer in that enclosed kitchen but here in this bedroom. He had outfoxed and, surprisingly, out-fought his opponents and tormentors so far but they were coming for him. Any glimmer of a mercifull outcome now extinguished after he threw that scalding oil into the face of Glib, one of the DDK gangsters. He had managed to quietly hack through the wall from the kitchen retrieved something from the wardrobe that could be his salvation.

Stevie turned, eyes wild, flitting around the small bedroom, desperately seeking an alternative escape route but there was only one answer. Out the window, the slimmest possibilty of extracting himself away from the clutches and knifes of DDK. He tip-toed over to the window and carefully opened it, the breeze instantly cooling his sweat drenched face and neck. He poked his head out looking up, then down, the realisation of his predicament once again making vomit rise in his throat and his legs twitch and wobble.

Below, a Intercity 125 train snaked its way from the west into Paddington station, slowing its approach as it rattled past Ladbroke Grove. To his right was the Homefield housing estate, its large courtyard bursting with green from the trees, bushes and grass in stark contrast to the grey of the surrounding housing blocks. Directly below him, the pedestrian bridge connecting the tower entrance with the road glistened in the sunlight above the bleak, gloomy darkness of the underground car parking and garages below.

He had, over the years, fallen in love with the view, the place. The Trentstone Tower in North West London was one of those places you either loathed or loved. Craig was not a fan, never had been, only staying when he really had to or when business called, only once a month at most. Stevie on the other hand found himself there more and more even though it was a little dangerous to be seen too much by the neighbours. It was likely that one day or another the Police may visit but they never kept drugs there for any more than a day or so, only as long as it took to cut up and repackage. So, it would likely be clean and probably empty but Stevie's DNA and fingerprints would be all over the place. He had never been arrested so there would be no trace yet he remained careful, keeping well away from the neighbours and only came and went under cover of darkness.

How many times had he sat there on the windowsill in the evening breathing in the sights and smells of West London occasionally smoking a joint. A bit of old school Moroccan black, none of that super skunk mind fuck stuff, listening to a chill out compilation whilst enjoying the panorama at dusk on his own. Normally someone perfectly happy in their own company, he had often looked forward to those quiet contemplative moments when he could simply sit and think of nothing or everything, the past, the present and the future.

His eyes rapidly scanned below as he heaved himself onto his knees on the windowsill, licking his lips constantly, his hands gripping the window frame. Even if he could get out, he was not sure if his hands could be pried from those white plastic edges. He was prompted back into action as he heard a new voice from inside the flat.

"Where the fuck is he? Where the fuck is that little cunt?"

"In there" replied the whimpering voice of Glib, nursing third degree oil burns to his face.

He could not tell who it was. Thankfully it was not Kaiser. He braced himself for one of them to come flying through the bedroom door but breathed a sigh of relief as he heard their efforts were still concentrated on the kitchen door. It solidified his need to get out of there quick.

Still gripping the window frame he turned his head. He saw the green clipper cigarette lighter on the side cabinet. His eyes dropped down towards the small wooden structure on the bedroom floor housing those giant fireworks, originally designed to despatch any product high into the sky should they recieve an unwanted visit from the old bill.

"Fuck it" he murmured before stepping down from the window back into the bedroom.

CHAPTER 2

Pure Nirvana

1 15 miles to the west of London on the outskirts of Bristol, Scott was not having a good day. All week both of the girls had been sick with chicken pox, effectively quarantined at home, no chance of them going to school. Somehow Ester had got it into her head she could not take time off from her part-time job and Scott needed to look after them. This had of course gone down like a fart in a lift at his work.

His manager Rhys, like many of his fellow colleagues, done very well out of the company share scheme in the 90s, nearly quadrupling their money, especially those who had been there for a long time. This meant nearly all their mortgages were paid off, the wife's did not need to work and the kids were packed up and shipped out to public schools. So, Scott was not surprised at the sneering reaction by Rhys to taking time off to help out with the kids but rules were rules. However, Scott knew it was another little unrecorded black mark against his name.

The two days off simply meant his work would continue to stack up in his in-tray. Not only that, as he prepared to leave in the morning, Ester told him she was off for another girlie night at the Pure Nirvana spa. She mentioned in a sort of off-the-cuff way as she busily went about sorting the girl's breakfasts.

"Who you going with?"

"The mums" she answered abruptly.

"Ester's snobby fucking stuck up cunty mates from the school" Scott thought darkly.

"Every fucking single one of them living in a fantasy bubble where they do fuck all except organise for a house cleaner and drink coffee. Oooh those fucking coffee mornings must be a fucking joy to attend. Swanning around the high street decimating the husbands credit cards with wanton abandon before descending on some poncey organic coffee house. Fucking parasites, the lot of them, well the ones Ester chose to hang around with anyway" he mused as he looked on at his wife sweeping around the kitchen acting like Supermum.

Lately Scott had noticed the mums were all getting pissed up on Friday afternoons, which was okay but normally meant Ester did less than usual around the house, which was next to nothing anyway. On more than one occasion he had returned home to find kids still in school uniform, Ester sprawled out on the coach watching some reality shite on TV in the midst of a hangover from the afternoon's session. The last time he returned enquiring about dinner she exploded.

"This ain't the fucking 1950s you know, swanning in here demanding grub. You cook it."

"I would not use the word 'ain't', 'fucking' or 'grub' in front of your beloved mums Ester, you do not want them getting wind of your working class roots. You might be banished to the outer reaches of Chipping Sudbury."

"Ha ha very fucking funny" Ester snarled back in response.

"Just because I have friends more sophisticated than you are used to. I don't know why you can't make more of an effort, how about going out for a few drinks with the hubbies?"

"The hubbies? The hubbies? You do know what you sound like don't you? I have made an effort with the 'hubbies' but to be frank with you, darling, they bore the hell out of me, plain and simple. Half of them have inherited a shit load of cash and live in cloud cuckoo land. All it's about is the Caribbean, Cowes week, Cheltenham, Royal Ascot and Wimbledon. What the hell do these people think the rest of population do? Swan around drinking Pimm's, eating caviar and fucking their cousins."

"Don't be so crass" Ester replied in a fake haughty toff accent before Scott continued.

"And the half, the other half, are all new money. At least the other lot aren't crude and vulgar with it, bragging about their new Range Rover this, six bedroom that, Rolex this, in your face every fucking five minutes, making everyone in the vicinity feel as inadequate and insignificant...."

Ester cut him off.

"Well at least they have made something of their lives rather than coasting along like you, pining after your scumbag mates back in Woodbridge."

"I don't fucking pine over anyone, when have I ever mentioned them lot back at the Ridge?"

"The Ridge? You sad little man! You haven't mentioned them once, but I know, I know alright, bunch of fucking no hopers. Bet they are still hanging around in that shit hole pub that you used to drink in day in day out blasting away the few brain cells they have got left smoking weed and sniffing coke."

"Errr excuse me, the first night I ever went out with you and your mates, you got smashed out of your face on weed! You threw a whitey and puked over Kelly Amores head. What the hell are you talking about?"

"Yes, but that was when I was in my 20s. Them lot are well into their 30s by now and no doubt still at it, it's quite pathetic" she sniffed.

"How do you know? You haven't seen them once since we have been married."

"Fuck. Why did I mention the wedding, oh fuck here it comes...."

"Oh the wedding! The wedding! Oh yes, and look how that turned out. Fucking shambles, fucking embarrassed by the lot of them. Shit in the bed!! Fucking glad we haven't seen them since. And like I said don't even think about inviting any of them out west."

"Out west? Out west? What on earth are you talking about?"

"You know what I am talking about, Scott, you know exactly what I am talking about."

Scott analysed her face, so hard and cruel but she was not always like this. It was just the stress and pressure she is under living in this environment with her new friends. She had a smile that could melt the heart of a statue on a cold winter's day. How he missed that smile of hers; he had to look at the old photographs on the computer these days to even remember what that smile was like. Beautiful. Stunning, so warm, so inclusive that made his heart race thinking about it. But somehow it had all changed. And how to change her back he did not know. How on earth could he alter the current trajectory their marriage was taking? It seemed impossible to stop. Five years they have been married with two beautiful kids, which Scott thought would bind and so-lidify them into one.

He would keep trying as he still loved her but he loved his two little girls more and had to keep the family unit together for their sake. He had seen all too often how single-parented children had struggled in life after parents breaking up and divorcing. He thought about his old friend Craig, his mum dying when he was seven, and although his dad had been a provider for a time and his brother, Shaun, helped out as best he could, the lack of a mother's love and warmth had most definitely affected him, set-ting him on a path to god knows where. He had heard from China, on that new Facebook website thing, that Craig and Stevie had a massive row about something, something dodgy probably and Craig was last seen looking a right mess. He hoped they were both alright.

Scott did not have the energy to argue with her anymore, they had fought too much recently.

"I'm sure that will fun" he muttered quietly as he ushered the two girls upstairs to brush their teeth. He heard Ester leave for work the door slamming without saying goodbye.

Later that night, and as Ester got herself changed to go out, Scott sat with his two beautiful daughters to read them a story. As it was Friday he then let them watch a DVD in the master bedroom, both snuggled up under the duvet gawping at the latest ani-mated offering from DreamWorks studio.

"Bet that DVD was nearly £20; doesn't she know I can download them for free off the internet? Maybe if Ester stopped spending so much money on premium supermarkets and organic fucking grocers she might have a chance of giving up work and joining the Chipping Sudbury set" thought Scott as he walked downstairs to micro-wave his ready meal.

"As soon as she leaves tonight and the kids are in tucked up bed and I

am going to have a good long hard wank."

With that thought resonating in his head he sunk into a low dark depressive mood.

"Is that all I can do as an act of defiance? Wank over some freely available pornography on the Internet. Fuck me is that what my life now boils down to?"

Scott grimaced at the thought as he collapsed on the sofa as the microwave blasted his sad meal for one.

He had acquaintances but no real friends in his life anymore. His real friends were god knows where, doing god knows what. Okay, so he did not want his old life back, it was a bit too dirty, too much drinking, partying but he would have liked it if his mates had grown up and matured in the same way he had. He would have relished the odd night out here and there but what he would have loved more than anything would be growing up together, having all their kids at school and playing together, going on holidays together and all that. That would have been brilliant. Not living in each other's pockets or anything but at least some interaction, being able to laugh at the good old days.

Later and after she had kissed the girls good night, Ester packed her overnight bag back gave Scott a cold unloving kiss on the cheek and left.

CHAPTER 3

It's a London Ting..

R uby Edwards looked up from the file she was reading spotting Stevie walking towards her, their eyes meeting briefly as he sauntered between the banks of desks in the open plan office. She waited a few seconds after he passed her desk before rising from her chair and walking in the direction from which Stevie had just come. The post trays at the end of the office were organised alphabetically. The D&C post room in the basement remained busy even though the volume was gradually beginning to decline as the rise in email and digital based communications took off. There was now one postal delivery every month that she nervously anticipated, one that would not be routed via the post room. She scanned the other trays for signs of any important looking envelopes, those embossed with law firm or government stamps, those for her fellow peers that provided an indication of important high-profile client engagements they were involved in. Nothing caught her eyes as she looked towards the letter 'E' tray. A bulging internal post envelope took up most of the tray.

She picked it up feeling the weight as always it was heavy. She retreated to the fourth floor of the D&C offices, half of which was still under renovation meaning that the female toilets would likely be empty. Stooping down scanning the tiled floor she checked no one else was in the stalls before entering and locking the door behind her.

She unwound the fabric tie that held the envelope together. Inside was a second envelope containing 1.2 kilos of glistening white cocaine. It was a tradition of hers to sample each and every new delivery. Retrieving a small D&C branded letter opener, pilfered long ago from the barren desk of Tristram Martyn, she slid it through the plastic wrapping and out again, the long groove in the blade now brimming with white powder. After sealing the package with Sellotape and repackaging the envelopes, she turned it over on her lap tapping and scraping off the white dust. Racking out two large lines she chuckled to herself, they were a little on the large side. She would have to watch her step bumping into anyone in the office in the next 30 minutes or so.

Pausing to listen, double checking she was still alone, she banged both lines back in quick succession. Her heart raced as the drug hit home, the rush hitting her jaw and she breathed out slowly to calm herself. Remaining seated she stared at the inside of the toilet door. There was some old graffiti from when D&C took over a smaller firm. A disgruntled legacy employee had written *'Orange Army Forever! Fuck the Greens'* a reference to the brand colours of the old company and that of D&C.

Normally Ruby would be scamming away as her brain galloped and raced, urged on by the coke but instead she began to reflect on what had brought her to this place, in this little cubicle doing drugs in the glass and steel interior of D&C.

She grew up in the outskirts of Derby, a fairly normal and stable upbringing near the beautiful yet sometimes creepy moors of the Peak District. She had been a bright articulate child who excelled academically through primary and secondary schools, college and university. She was single minded and determined, knew exactly what and when she wanted it. Her persona was often harsh, often lacking warmth and empathy. These traits developed during her early school days where conversations often turned towards her achievements, views and outlook. As a result she had never formed true close friendships. Moreover, she found herself gravitating from one set of friends to the next as she grew up and moved through the educational institutions. She stayed in touch with many but never experienced those deep ties that some friendships endured.

One bond, bordering on obsession, however, was with London. It was her place, her calling, all confirmed during a family trip in her early teens. As soon as she stepped off the train the buzz of the place hit her. The tube, the shops, the red buses, the black cabs, the buildings, all infected and excited her. But mostly it was the people. She was fascinated and in awe of them. All kinds of races, religions, colours and creed.

Punks, goths, suits, ravers, indie kids, families, alkies, loners but most of all it was the professionals.

As a gawky teenager she rode the Piccadilly underground for the first time. Her mum and dad smiling at her as her eyes darted from one person to the next as she stood rocking from side to side. Holding the handrail, she swayed, riding the subtle bumps and clatter of the tube train that reverberated up through her young body. A woman coolly hopped onto the train just as the train doors were closing shut. She was dressed in a suit that hugged her tall slim body cut in sharply at the hips, the subtle pin stripes emphasising her physique. Ruby had never seen a woman in a suit before and she stared at her in wonderment. She could not help herself and simply gawped open mouthed at the woman. Her style was somehow both masculine and feminine, something that Ruby would emulate in the years to come. The tailored trousers seemed at odds with the off-cream high heeled designer shoes yet strangely also complimented each other. An unusual sliver of self-doubt and embarrassment cut through the young Ruby as the woman looked at her up and down, coldly analysing the northern interloper in her stone washed jeans, high top copy converse and red checked shirt. Ruby was a bit of a tomboy, never a girly girl and on that day in the big smoke she was dressed like Madonna in the film *Desperately Seeking Susan*.

Ruby staring coldly back at her, a slight smirk curled on her lips, her mind already made up even at that young age thinking.

"Don't worry about me my love, don't you pity me, no not one bit, one day I will be like you."

All those years ago she hoped off the tube train with her family at Piccadilly Circus and five minutes later was staring up at the Eros. She smiled to herself because she knew her calling, knew what she was going to do. She was going to go through University and move to London to dress and live just like that woman she had just seen on that tube train.

And that is exactly what she did. She sat on the toilet rattling from the drugs as her thoughts skipped from her childhood to the unfortunate events surrounding her ex-boss and mentor Tristram.

"Tristram. My goodness. Tristram."

He had effectively handpicked Ruby during the annual graduate intake process at D&C. All new recruits were assigned to a senior manager who would show them the ropes, teach them the protocols, the ways of working, how to act and how to dress at D&C. They would coach and mentor them for 18 months by assigning training programmes and client assignments all whilst monitoring performance and behaviours. Tristram knew getting the right candidate was important. Some 40% of graduates would fail to be retained by D&C after the two-year trial period, 20% of those not making it past another year. The process in D&C was always progress or get out. Graduates were no exception and Tristram knew that the senior managers mentoring them would be responsible and judged on their success or failure. The CVs of the new recruits had already been subject to rigorous vetting, that together with a challenging interview and competency assessment process meant that the intake was already the best of the best. The graduate coaching role enforced on nearly all senior managers was another small yet important piece of the puzzle needed to be slotted into place, all required for progression and promotion to that nirvana, that utopia; making D&C equity Partner.

Tristram as always planned well in this regard by organising separate lunches with the hiring Partner and the HR Director responsible for the graduate intake process. He subtly pummelled them for information on who was who, the top performers, the flaky, the troublesome, the cocky but most importantly the strong, those with high potential to succeed. There were five that appeared to be stand out, with Ruby being the only female. Tristram liked working with women, thought he could boss them around a bit more and generally be a bit of a twat and get away with it. Ruby surprised him when they first met; very impressed by her approach, she was like him to a degree, single minded and focused. Self-centred, driven, clear. She would fuck over anyone to get where she wanted to go. He liked that. Well only if it was not him that was being fucked over, other than that he liked that a lot.

Likewise, and in return, Ruby was also impressed with Tristram, she could tell he had what it took, knew how to operate and in the first few weeks at D&C she kept a keen eye on him, noting who he worked, lunched, drank and importantly who he grated against. She knew she needed someone to latch onto, follow and progress in their slipstream. He was obviously well liked and respected in D&C, not a single Partner cold shouldered him. So, she selected him as much as he selected her.

She recalled their first meeting where Tristram laid it out, leaving no stone unturned in terms of his expectations and what she would gain if she met those expectations. She would work hard, she would work all hours, she would only book a maximum of six hours a day to his client engagement accounts no matter how many she actually worked. Her phone would be on 24 hours a day and over weekends. Not required whilst on holidays. That was nice of him. She would receive bonuses for a good job done. She would also be awarded development opportunities to lead engagements for some of the smaller clients. He promised she would develop and ratchet up her experience by being with Tristram. But only if she did what he said and worked fucking hard. He wanted his pound of flesh. She could counsel him, that was fine, he did not need a yes man (or woman in this case). However, once he had decided on a course of action Ruby would shut the fuck up and would not say anything again on the subject, no matter what the outcome, whether she was right or wrong. She will get promoted from senior associate to senior manager in time if she did all that and more.

"If you stick with me that is what I'll give you" he said smiling at her. Ruby recalled looking at him as he pressed his fingers together, he looked slimy. She wanted to make sure this was kept in a professional level only.

"I am happy with that arrangement. I am yours. I do the work, I do the graft and get rewarded. But let me make one thing perfectly clear. Just so we get off on the right foot with no misinterpretations. You will never fuck me. Okay? Never. If you ever try that is it. Over. Understand?"

There was a flicker of disappointment in his eyes but he kept grinning.

"Sure" he replied leaning back in his chair.

"You're not my type anyway."

It was a few months before she witnessed his true colours on the narcotics front. They were at a client conference in Lisbon, a notoriously easy place to score. Tristram together with a client from a large automotive company were nosing it up all night. She did not partake, refusing all offers before going to bed at a respectable 2 am. The following morning, she could not believe it. As the conference opened Tristram walked in looking as fresh as a daisy as though he had an early night. He greeted clients and D&C folk with his usual cheery bashful self. Up close, however, it was a different story. The greasy remnants of alcohol oozed from his pores; his red eyes were like piss holes in the snow. Nevertheless, he looked pretty damn good for someone who had been up all night on the sauce and snow.

As she sat on the toilet, the gear continuing to speed through her veins, she unrolled the note in her hand. She was not entirely sure how the drug thing had all came about. She had never needed much sleep and could out party the best of them without it. She could do an all-nighter easily just on drink. She first took coke in London with some friends whilst back at someone's house after they had been out drinking. She liked it, she did not love it and had never developed a problem. She could take it or leave it. Yet she could see a lot of people LOVED it. She began to see that many could not have a night out without it. But it was not until Stevie Chambers started work at D&C that she sensed she could make something out of that opportunity.

She liked Stevie from the first moment she met him, but at first did not quite know why. Could not put her finger on it. Tall, modestly handsome, quite funny with a glint in his eye but was not outwardly arrogant or cocky. It took her a few weeks to notice what it was. Stevie for some unknown reason was the only person that rattled Tristram. It was bizarre. To begin with Tristram shrank when Stevie was around, he became quiet rather than brash, inverted rather than extraverted. She could not figure out the connection between the two. Jonathan Bland was the hiring partner and by all accounts had been recommended by Tristram yet there was an uneasy vibe between the two.

And then the drug dealing started. Stevie caught Ruby and two other senior associates red handed. It was then that Ruby saw what Stevie all was about, devious little fucker but not necessarily nasty. He blew off the other two associates immediately and proceeded to get his hooks into Ruby. He mentioned he could always get great coke, insinuated that Tristram bought a tonne of nose bag every month and that Ruby could make a nice little earner on top of her D&C salary. She probed why he did not go straight to Tristram but he changed the subject. Ruby did not take him up on the offer straight away but after one of her friends asked her if she could get any coke she realised what he was all about. She met Stevie's friend Craig who arrived at a house party where they privately sorted out the deal in an upstairs bedroom. It snowballed from there going from a few grams to buying ounces and selling individual grams to her wide circle of associates. She finally plucked up the courage with Tristram, slipping him a wrap in a pub where they were debriefing on a client meeting. He liked the gear and she said she can get it whenever he wanted. He became by far her biggest customer, for a while anyway, all before the IRA blew him up that London bus all those years ago.

In the toilet she pulled out a bottle of nasal spray from her Chanel handbag squirting it up both nostrils. Her position scared her a little. She was now a big drug dealer in central London and she had read enough newspaper stories and seen enough films to realise what happened to most. Even though it unnerved her, she trusted Stevie who had coached her well in the dark arts of dealing. She was careful, laundered and hid the excess money where it could not be found, all courtesy of her contact in the City, Nathaniel Gray. She swapped phones regularly and had recently been assured by Stevie that she was, in fact, protected. Who by she did not know? She did not want to know. He had given her a number to call if she was ever arrested. She was not sure if she believed him but he seemed to be genuine.

One evening she was in the Minstry of Sound, head down grooving at 5 am, Stefan Stockdale headlining, working the crowd into a frenzy. She looked up at the raised DJ booth, packed with people, celebrities and the like. As she looked across the crowded booth trying to spot gurning A or Z listers, there was Stevie, eyeballing her from above, a small smile on his face as he raised a glass of champagne at her.

There in the middle of the packed sweaty dancefloor she realised who Stevie was. The penny dropped. Many saw him as the office dogs body, the junior manager that did the detailed client work, churning out the advisory notes and guidance to the clients, never seemingly ambitious or career driven, someone to do the work and simply go home at night. Never pursued the glory of winning new clients or rising the ranks. An anomaly in D&C but accepted by all, nevertheless. This was how others viewed him but not Ruby. She knew all right. That fucker was a drug dealer, a fucking big drug dealer.

She liked him and he seemed to like her and in that there was a certain level of comfort. Yet it still sent a shiver up her spine as she left the toilets planning her deliveries to her eager clients throughout the great city of London.

CHAPTER 4

Willow The Wisp

I feel alone and isolated in this weird, creepy, claggy mist. Feels like I am on a film set, not that I have ever been on one. Everything feels fake: the sludgy ground, the dead rotting trees without leaves, but most of all that mist looks too heavy. Looks like it was definitely spewed out of some sort of dry-ice machine off to the side somewhere. If it were a film set then there would be an end wall of some sort, maybe a little green illuminated exit sign so all the jobbing actors knew how to get out of here in case of a fire or a half-crazed gun toting director fucked off with fluffed lines or a lack of fluffed cocks in his trailer. Always fancied being an actor but my old man put me off that one alongside my juvenile aspirations of being a marine biologist or a stuntman. As I walk further I cannot find a wall, nothing so fuck it I just keep walking.

Where the fuck am I?

And where is that fucker Craig?

That prick has not really left my side since we left school. Wish he was here now; could do with some back-up. Beginning to start to feel a little uneasy here, a little bit fucking twitchy if the truth be told. Maybe it's the drugs; does shit to your head, makes you think weird, a bit off kilter. Never does nothing to mine much though, nerves like steel. Yep, no fucking problem on that front.

Definitely feeling a bit thingy and para about all this gloom though. I squint my eyes peering through the fog and there is nothing but a dull grey light surrounding everything. I walk up to a rotting tree and I touch it, expecting it to be cold and wet but it's warm and although it looks damp it is actually covered in a hard clear plastic that makes it glisten like it is supposed to be soaked in moisture. Yep all fake. Just to be sure I give it a sniff. Nothing. No odour, nothing.

I keep walking through the mud, but again it's not real mud only two inches deep and I can feel a solid even floor beneath it. I raise my foot, appalled at the dark brown mud covering my brand new white Adidas shell toes. I reach down wiping the sludge away and it falls off like a clump of jelly not leaving a single mark on my trainers. Fake.

"Fake like you, maybe" says a voice echoing and reverberating around this odd place.

I spin around at the words which come out of the mist but not from any discernible direction. It was a statement not a question, definitely someone getting wide. Where is fucking Craig when you need him. Always quite enjoyed unleashing him in such situations, so called hard cunts giving it the big one, in my face, giving it this and giving it that. I secretly quite enjoy it; watching their expressions change from a confident snarl into a "Ohh fuck what have I done" face when they are faced with that prospect. A prospect that is gonna fuck their shit up. Ha, ha, yes, yes, Craig is a good lad, a good lad, one of the best. Fucking love it. Right, let's get out of here.

I see a light far away, like you would see if you were in a tunnel. It's my way out of here so I put in a bit of purpose to my stroll, keen to get out. Not sure what is happening at the moment but there are things to be done, scams to be made and drugs to be consumed. Might ping The Judge see what he is up to. Maybe even Scott, although think he has his head in the books. Always has his head in the books, got his uni final exams on the horizon, hmm, well after should get his fucking head in amongst the nose bag, ooh yes.

I pick up the pace in my stride as the urge to get out of this weird place increases. As I start to jog I see something out of the corner of my eye. There is someone about twenty metres away, exactly the same size and build as me running in parallel also towards the light and eventual freedom. A stab of panic jabs at my chest, right around the heart as I realise me and this other bloke are vying to get out here first. I pump my legs harder as I break into a sprint but this fucker also starts to give it some. I grit my teeth as I run looking over to get a good look at him but he is not really a real person, a dark shape of a man, well a boy, no face, more of a sentient being than an actual, real person. I see him looking over, checking, validating whether I can keep up this pace. Of course I fucking can! I am getting out of here mate, not you, you weird cunt.

I knuckle down, giving it some extra effort as the exit gets nearer but I panic as the walls begin to close in, getting narrower with every step, bringing me and this fella ever closer. Only a few metres to the brightly lit exit now and we are neck and neck. With a metre to go, lungs straining, legs and arms furiously pumping I do what I always do. I fuck the cunt over.

I smash my elbow into his face just as I burst out into the light. I briefly hear him yell out as the door slams shut locking him in that place. For a split second I am elated at the underhand victory but the sweat smell of success evaporates as I hear a pitying cry from within.

I slam my hands against the door crying out, pleading with whoever to let him out. Please, please let him out. I am sorry. I am sorry. I am so sorry.

CHAPTER 5

A Gulf in Class

S tevie was busily taking the meeting minutes in his branded D&C notebook whilst trying to keep up with the dialogue and comments being aired in the room but his mind kept wandering. He was excited, really excited, off after work down the C&C to meet Scott but mostly about impending three weeks in Thailand. Scott and two friends from university were off traveling and Stevie, Craig, Tanner and China would be meeting them in Phuket. Today was Scott's send-off drinks starting at 2pm so the sooner this meeting was over the better.

The meeting concerned one of the more interesting assignments at D&C. He was sat in a grandiose boardroom of a large multinational pharmaceutical company whose UK headquarters were based near Weybridge, Surrey. They originally operated a huge factory in the north of England employing nearly 3,000 people producing a wide variety of medicines and consumer products, pills, creams and the like. Nearly five years ago they began to gradually move the operation to Poland taking advantage of the cheap labour and the free trade agreement in place. Poland would soon be joining the European Union in 2004 and many businesses were eyeing up the cheap manufacturing opportunities in Eastern Europe plus the influx of a cheaper workforce that would soon be arriving in the UK.

Unfortunately, they did not have a consultancy firm like D&C to help the transition from the UK to Poland. They had gone for the cheap option using a cheap boutique management consultancy firm that did not have the holistic multiple country, multi-department network like D&C. They were in trouble due to this lack of due diligence and thorough analysis of the intricacies of Europe and the free trade agreement rules. Most of the raw materials used in Poland were sourced in the UK and other EU Member State's. As part of the move overseas they had been fatally advised to *"just sign the EUR1 Customs form for each and every shipment"*. So that is what the company did, day in day out for nearly five years.

UK HM Customs & Excise in the UK received a request from Polish Customs to validate the authenticity of EUR1 forms under the mutual assistance clause within the EU/Poland free trade agreement. The EUR1 documents stated the goods meet the rules of origin criteria in the agreement. Sadly, in most cases the goods did not, resulting in hundreds of false Customs declarations thus claiming zero rates of import tax in Poland. The company immediately understood the consequences so parachuted D&C in to help facilitate the audit that would surely follow.

It was a big meeting. Customs had turned up mob handed so the entire senior management team from the company attended including the managing and finance directors plus a sheepish looking operations manager who had overseen the transition from the start. On the D&C side Stevie was accompanied by his boss plus a consultant from the international trade tax team that specialised in Customs issues. As they went through the introductions Stevie noticed one of the Customs officers did not provide details other than his name and he was based in the Customs office on the south bank of London. Stevie immediately smelt a rat but kept quiet knowing his time would come and if his hunch was correct would give D&C a lucrative client engagement.

Customs outlined the scope of their enquiries centred on the issuance of the EUR1 forms. The Managing Director then provided a long and protracted overview of the company attempting to be seen in the best light possible including how socially responsible they were and how much tax they paid. Stevie noticed most of the tax mentioned was VAT not corporate tax which the company paid little due to the tax optimization structure D&C put in place shifting profits to low tax jurisdictions via inter-company transfer pricing framework. The Managing Director was stalling for time and Stevie could see that the Customs officers were getting annoyed at the delaying tactics. They interrupted him announcing a full audit at the Durham factory which was now nothing more than a vacant shell. Stevie froze hoping the audit start date would not interfere with his holiday plans.

Luckily, they would start the week after he returned from Thailand. The meeting began to wind down after they had outlined what and who they would like to see during the audit. Before the meeting closed Stevie spoke up.

"I think I have all the discussion points noted and the associated agreed action points. I will distribute them around to everyone tomorrow on email if that is okay so we are clear on the way forward. Apologies but I did not capture what Customs team you are part of, I would like it for my notes?" he said looking directly at the officer who had remained more or less silent for the entire meeting even though he was busily taking notes. The Customs team looked nervously at each other and there was an awkward silence in the room. Stevie readied his pen, hovering it over the notepad raising his eyebrows slightly whilst looking at him pushing for an answer. The officer finally gave in and after clearing his throat he clearly announced:

"I am from the National Investigation Service."

"Bingo!"

Stevie had been spot on, clocked him as soon as he clapped eyes on him; leather jacket, jeans, he could literally hear the handcuffs clanging around in his pockets. The client was fucked. Potential criminal proceedings. D and fucking C to the rescue! This was now a full-blown fraud investigation, a slam dunk for D&C who would reap the rewards for their clients ignorance. No multinational wants their name dragged through the mud in the newspapers especially in a situation like this. They had closed down a UK factory at a loss of nearly 2,500 jobs and it would appear that they have tried to defraud the Tax Authorities whilst doing so. Even if the fraud aspect went away, Customs would hammer them with penalties and interest and tie up staff for months on end with the audit.

The Managing Director was shocked at the revelation but managed to remain calm as the officers left.

"I knew he was Investigation as soon as I saw him but I wanted to get it out in the open just so we are all clear, apologies if you thought I was putting pressure on them. I realise we need to get them on side but it is best we all know."

"No it is fine, I am very glad you did Steven and precisely why we brought you in on this" said the Managing Director.

"Gotcha!" he thought as his boss nodded sagely in agreement.

"What would you advise we do next?" he said looking at him directly, ignoring the operations manager who was clearly in for a gigantic bollocking when they left.

Stevie kept quiet deferring the question to his boss who proceeded to clearly outline what they should do and how D&C could help. Stevie just wanted to finish as early as possible knowing his mates were back in the C&C getting stuck into the beers and catching up with Scott.

After the meeting wrapped up, his boss congratulated him on a good job before tasking him with drafting the formal proposal for D&C's services. Stevie then jumped into his car, a BMW 330 M Sport, slotted in a mini disc into the player and drove back to Woodbridge. He drove quickly covering the 40 miles in under an hour. He parked at his parents' house where he was still living, shouting a hello as he bounded up the stairs but no one was in. He changed quickly from his corporate attire, into baggy clobber deciding on jeans and a retro Atari logo t-shirt. He pulled on some white Adidas shell toes and a lightweight beige Carharrt jacket for the short walk to the pub. He arrived just after 2pm and as soon as he entered, he noticed there was a strange vibe in the pub not one he was expecting at all.

On the televisions in three corners of the pub the screens jumped from the news readers in their studios to vivid live pictures of a tall building on fire, smoke billowing out from the white and black steel and cement structures. The C&C was busy even though it was early but was quiet as everyone took in the events occurring over the pond in New York.

"Hello Scottie boy long time, long time, how you doing fella, what's all this going on?" said Stevie as he hugged his old friend.

"World Trade Center Towers in New York, a couple of planes went into them, they reckon it is a terrorist attack."

"In planes? Into both towers?"

"Yes mate you wait until you see the footage, big arse passenger jets as well."

"Fuuuuuuck meeeeee" he replied in shock knowing D&C had an office in the Trade Center precinct but not in the main towers.

During the afternoon the scale and magnitude of the disaster played out on the screens as one after the other the towers collapsed as millions of people around the world watched on.

Craig arrived completing the core group of friends and even though the terrorist attacks cast a cloud over proceedings they drank through the afternoon making sure Scott had a good send off. He was travelling to Egypt, Cairo then Dahab on the Red Sea for three weeks learning to dive in and around the famous Blue Hole. The destination selected due to the world class diving and tales of cheap weed that could be smoked openly on the beaches and bars. Afterwards Thailand where they would meet the Woodbridge lads for three weeks partying and more diving. Stevie had already learnt to dive in Australia and was looking forward to getting back under the water, in amongst the quiet and unexplainable beauty.

A few days later and after failing to get the images from the Twin Towers attacks out of his mind, Stevie went on-line and made a rather odd purchase. The item arrived and he secreted it in the bedroom wardrobe at the flat in Trentstone Towers.

CHAPTER 6

P2P, OTC & R2R

So, Connor was gone and just like that it seemed their world would turn upside down. A week after Connor's brutal sacking at the hands of DDK Stevie emerged from the new campus buildings at D&C, the cold chill in the air mixing with nerves at the prospect of the first DDK pickup. In his rucksack was a green and white Marks & Spencer plastic carrier bag containing the cash for DDK. He walked the short distance to Holborn tube disappearing down onto the central line for the short journey to Bank where he would need to walk up through the vast underground expanse linking the Central, Northern, Circle, District and DLR railway lines. He recalled doing a drop here with Connor on one of the giant moving walkways. It all seemed a bit of a laugh with him, an underlying sense of mischief and schoolboy naughtiness even though they were always nervous and twitchy. Now with DDK it was all business, dark veiled threats with a distinct undercurrent of menace.

He needed to time it right and be on the Northern line northbound platform at exactly midday. As he checked his watch noting he was a shade too early he slowed his pace stopping to tie his shoelace on his expensive New & Lingwood brogues taking the opportunity to check for any unwanted attention. There was no one behind him although the enclosed harshly lit space of the underground was not helping his constitution as he moved on, the money in his bag weighing heavily in many senses of the word on his shoulders.

He emerged halfway down the platform and briefly panicked as he could not work out in his mind which end of the platform he should be standing to ensure that he was at the back of the train and not the front. The signs indicated the next train was four minutes away for which he was thankful and after a frantic couple of minutes he noticed a man peer to his right into the darkness of the tunnel. He felt the air pressure change, the strong breeze being pushed down the tunnel before he could hear or see the bright lights of the train approaching.

As the train roared into the station Stevie instinctively stepped back checking behind him for anyone who looked like a pusher. Urban myth or a real life occupational hazard of commuting he did not care as the train screamed into the station. As the train slowed to a standstill Stevie spotted the DDK contact, they maintained protocol, Stevie rubbing his eyebrow twice and the lad responded by touching his earlobe. There were only a couple of other passengers in the carriage, a builder fast asleep under a baseball cap in his paint splattered jeans and a fifty something professional woman deep into paperwork in a red folder. Stevie sat down next to the lad and placed his laptop bag on his lap. He quickly removed the M&S bag with the cash and placed it between them and it was quickly whisked away. The gear was the exchanged in a similar manner as they approached the next station where the DDK gangster left without a hint of a fare-well or recognition. The doors closed and Stevie remained on the train until Kings Cross before jumping on the Bakerloo line. All the while he was wondering what the future held this combined with the sheer terror of walking around with three kilos of cocaine.

The landscape and infrastructure of London meant that there were infinite possibilities for how to get product from A to B and onto C and D. Boat, car, barge, tube, bus, bicycle, foot and taxi were all used to good effect at some point since 1997. During his commutes to work he was constantly thinking about ways and methods to keep the logistics and supply chain simple yet invisible and importantly risk free.

He had a close call at Brixton underground station during 2000 where he was due to meet Connor at a mutual friends flat near where David Bowie was born. As he ascended the escalators he saw a Police cordon complete with a sniffer dog. He was not carrying any drugs he was picking them up but the bag he was holding had been used on several occasions between him and Connor and not doubt had traces which could be detected. He knew dogs were also trained to pick out the odour of cash of which he was carrying plenty. He was in a smart suit so not the usual type that maybe stopped at random, but that fucking dog could be serious trouble. He could not turn back; Brixton was a final destination station at the end of the line so he could not divert to another tube line and anyone coming up and going straight back down would be spotted. So he nonchalantly drifted towards the turnstiles but subtly away from the dog. As he approached a queue formed but the one nearest the dog was less busy, maybe his fellow commuters had the same idea but it would have looked odd if Stevie did not head for the barrier that was less busy so he went for it. He was about fifteen metres from the dog and the way the station funnelled towards the doors he would have to walk within at least five metres of the highly trained fucking mutt.

Luck was however on his side as a young black kid immediately caught the attention of the dog as its ears pricked up and began snuffling around his ankles and his front pockets. The Police sprang into action and cajoled the protesting lad against a wall for a thorough search. Stevie kept walking and gave the one of the officers a look as he glanced over to the search that was ongoing. This was one of the many times that would become an important lesson. Stay well clear of high crime areas with a high Police presence. Another was to ensure that you thoroughly washed or disposed of bags used for transporting drugs or money.

CHAPTER 7

Never Turn Right

T he day of their holiday to Thailand finally arrived. Craig was late meeting at Terminal 3, Heathrow, looking sheepish and guilty. A late night and misplaced passport was the excuse. Stevie eyed him up suspiciously but let it slide.

As soon as he arrived he was berated by China and Tanner who soon changed their tune when Craig pulled out the business class tickets bought for them as a surprise. These were the days you could still get away with large cash purchases before the Proceeds of Crime Act 2002 and the 2007 Money Laundering regulations. They had visited a travel agents in the Uxbridge high street booking four flights and three nights at the end of the holiday at a five star hotel in Bangkok. It was quite risky shelling out thousands of pounds in cash when their names were all over the tickets but the agency in question looked in need of funds and they were sure not all of it would find its way onto the books.

The events of the New York attacks were fresh in everyone's minds, so Stevie reminded everyone that mucking around too much near airplanes was not a good idea.

"We are going to exposed to free booze, I am all over it but just think about what you are doing and what you are saying. I don't want anyone fucking about in front of any airline staff or security whether it is here in Heathrow or in Thailand. You will get banged up, end of. Don't mention New York, Al Qaeda or anything related alright? Do you remember when Stefan Stockdale said there was a bomb in his record box when he was going to Poland? That was pre

9/11 and he was arrested and interviewed for 8 fucking hours and banned from EasyJet for life. Funny as fuck at the time but this is now and I have been looking forward to this and don't want it fucked up by anyone."

"Don't look at me like that. God, you always do it don't ya?" Craig replied.

"Do what?"

"Party fucking pooper."

"I'm not a party pooper, I just know what you are like and him" Stevie said pointing a finger accusingly at Tanner.

"Oi, what did I do?"

"Well what about two weekends ago, you got smashed, fell asleep, woke up and pissed all over China's mum and dads coffee table? You do that on a BA flight you'll get us lot nicked."

China was glaring at Tanner.

"Yeah well I said sorry about that, that was a one-off, anyway I understand and will be on best behaviour. But let me clarify when you say free booze, is there a limit or a cap on it?"

Stevie simply punched him on the arm in reply before heading to the fast-track security checks which were as thorough and rigorous as expected. Stevie kept a watch on his traveling companions who all behaved impeccably. The business class section was full, mostly business travellers and one family. They quickly settled into the flight and each got stuck into the films on offer. Stevie chose *Jay and Silent Bob Strikes Back* the others following suit as Stevie laughed and sniggered from the opening titles.

Arriving in Bangkok they were instantly hit with a wall of heat as they stepped down out of the plane, making the short walk to the terminal building. After clearing immigration and Customs without any dramas they followed Stevie who headed to the domestic flight desks booking flights taking off an hour later to Phuket. The joys of Bangkok would have to wait a couple of weeks. They were bussed out onto the tarmac worryingly past a plane that had been blown up the previous week in a terrorist attack aimed at a member of parliament. A cleaner on board had been killed after the take-off was delayed. The sight of their two propeller plane next to the burnt-out shell set them all on edge reminding them foreign countries were often a very different proposition to the UK and they endured a bumpy nerve racking flight to the Islands in the south.

A day later they met Scott and his university buddies at their hotel in Patong Beach and then proceeded three weeks of boys on tour bliss. They spent four days in Phuket initially revelling in the neon infused party resort full of night clubs, restaurants and hostess bars housing prostitutes of all shapes, sizes, ages and genders. Tanner ended up in hospital for a night after drunkenly coming off his moped when a dog allegedly ran out in front of him causing him to crash. Stevie and Craig were roaring drunk in a small bar when they found out, as a panic-stricken Scott arrived frantically telling them of the incident. They quickly visited the hospital but ended up ignoring the bandaged Tanner favouring a pair of wheelchairs that they tore down corridors racing each other. The doctors and nurses loved it placing bets on the pair as a bandaged Tanner could only listen to the noise out in the corridor. He shrugged off his injuries the next day which looked better once all the dried cracked blood had been removed and continued partying in earnest. No one in the group, except Craig that is, openly admitted to sleeping with any ladies of the night but on numerous occasions many performed excellent Houdini impressions disappearing into the night. The accusations would begin like clockwork the following morning with everyone except Craig keeping quiet about any such liaisons.

One morning one of Scott's university friends had rigorously denied engaging in any whoring activity after being spotted wandering in the opposite direction to the hotel. He even went into a bit of a strop and a sulk about the relentless banter so the group stopped ribbing him. However that very evening as they were all walking past the bars on their way to a restaurant a Thai girl came flying out of a bar and jumped on his back shouting.

"My little hairy gibbon!"

Everyone cracked up with laughter as he tried in vain to protest his innocence whilst trying to literally shake off the attentions of the lady.

"What happens in Thailand stays in Thailand you fuckers" he muttered.

"And the fact you like fat birds?" sneered Craig unhappy at his disingenuous attitude all day.

"She's not fat, she's fit as" he argued as they watched her sashay back to the bar telling him to pop back later. Craig as he often did when he had a target in his sights, keep up the relentless piss taking.

"Like fuck she is fit! If she jumped on a bus the driver would charge her two fares. A rice only diet this lot are meant to be on? Not her! A side order of fucking kebab I reckon. I bet your knob is red, not cause its sore, it's just fucking embarrassed."

He glared back at Craig who was firing into him hard, he was not used to this and did not quite know how to take it. He could not even give him shit back as Craig revelled in the sex tourism literally having a different prostitute in his bed every night.

As the argument wore on Stevie lost interest scanning the scene around him. It now all seemed a bit sordid and seedy; dozens of bars, loud awful pop music, bright lights and several overweight Germans firing into teenage hookers made him feel uncomfortable. At the nearest bar he saw a very young, very pretty hooker, sat on a bar stool with a huge fat man who was busy trying to order a round of drinks. He could tell he was German by the way he was dressed, light blue shirt probably an XXL size with light brown chino shorts, black socks with sandals topped off with lobster pink sunburn after sweltering on the beach all day. The girl noticed Stevie looking over at her and she smiled slightly, not the beaming fake, grab your money and run Thai smile but a smile that said something else entirely and he could not wait to get out of there.

On the final morning in Phuket Craig arrived at around 11am at the usual spot by the pool, everyone nursing raging hangovers trying to eat cheese toasties for breakfast.

"Top of the morning to you lads. Fuck me you lot look like extras from a fucking zombie film" he chirped in greeting, a smug grin spread across his face as he sat down pinching one of China's sandwiches.

"Yeah go-ahead mate, my fucking head is in bits, think I am going to boff. Them fucking buckets are brutal and that Red Bull, I think it's well dodgy, it's like doing a line of nosebag. Come on then spit it out."

"Spit what out."

"Piss off mate, every morning you come down here and give us the run down on the previous night's activities and you clearly are bursting to spill, so I ask you again, spit it out."

"Love you China you can read me like a book, you are not going to believe what happened last night, this is too fucking funny. Remember we were in the Tiger Club last night and I was firing into that Thai bird with the dreads."

"The whore with the dreads you mean?"

"Yes the whore. With the fucking dreads, whatever fuck wad. Anyway whatever. She obviously does all right, she gave me a lift back to hers and she had a fucking R1."

"An R1, what's that?.. An STD?" laughed Tanner.

"No dickhead a Yamaha R1 motorbike, one litre one hundred and twenty fucking seven brake horse power, fucking bad boy, and she was only little, anyway I jumped on the back of it and she fucking booted it down the coast to Karon Beach, next resort down to the south. Fucking mental, damn good driver. I was shitting it though big time, no helmet, was fucking battered as well on that Samsong whiskey. Anyway that's not the story. Fucking hell this is funny as. So, she had a half decent gaff, I was expecting a shack in a paddy field but it was smart apartment set back off the main road overlooking the beach, three bed gaff and that. Anyway we started getting it on, she's giving me a nosh, fucking fingered my bum hole, as well right dirty bitch."

"Aaaaah and who said romance was dead" smiled Stevie having heard stories like these time and time again although he secretly enjoyed them.

"Anyway she pulls out a polaroid camera, you know the old ones where the photo pops out the bottom straight away and she goes in that horrible high pitched squeal they do. Me take photo of you, you my favourite boy and all this nonsense in pidgin English."

"So, I am up for a photo shoot so I grab my cock and squeeze the base between my thumb and index finger like a cock ring, making it look a bit bigger an that. If by the way that is at all fucking possible. She takes my photo, flaps it to dry it off and pulls out this massive fucking photo album with all these geezers in it. And she goes 'Here my album; it called my favrite farang' Ha, ha. Anyway I fuck her, cracking little ride an all."

"Hope you doinked up" stated Stevie.

"Cause I did, hope you fucking did as well riding them ladyboys you fancy. Right so when we finish we are in bed and she pulls out some weed and we have a smoke and that, decent puff as well, got a bit back in my room if anyone fancies a blaze later. I grab the book and start looking through it. All these fellas, most in the buff, all pissed up, grinning for the camera, maybe about 50 or 60 geezers I don't know maybe more. There I am going through and guess who I see? Guess who I fucking see?" squealed Craig who could barely contain his excitement.

"Fuck off, who?"

"Guess!"

"Fuck off who?"

"Only fucking Bedswell!"

Stevie, Scott, Tanner and China mouths dropped open before bursting out laughing.

"Piss off you're lying! No fucking way."

Bedswell was one of the main reasons they had chosen Patong Beach in Phuket as their first destination. He had raved about the place persuading them to go.

"No way, no way you're fucking lying."

"Bet you any money."

"Bollocks."

"Come on, I'll bet you and I will prove it."

"Alright, a score" said Stevie holding out his hand to Craig.

"Okay mister" replied Craig still mimicking his Thai romance from the night before shaking his hand roughly.

"I will prove it cause when the Rastafarian, Woodbridge dick loving petrol head nodded off I fucking nicked the photo waaaaa, ha ha."

Craig jumped up from his chair and began bouncing from foot to foot loving being the centre of the story before delving into his back pocket. He whipped out the photo. And there he was, one of their best friends from back home, Bedswell, lying on the bed, naked, one leg straight, one leg cocked, dick in hand. He looked a bit like Brain from East 17 snarling at the camera.

"Ooooh my goooood, no no" spluttered Stevie, crying with laughter. China and Tanner were snatching at the photo trying to get a look.

"I cannot wait to hit him with that down the C&C" roared Craig with laughter.

"Oi behave, you can't do that mate he's got a bird now hasn't he?"

"I know only kidding, only in private you pleb. What goes in Thailand, stays in Thailand. Still taking it home though, wind the fucker up big time."

After they calmed down from Craig's jaw dropping tale and Stevie had coughed up the 1,500 baht bet they packed up to travel the short distance to Ko Phi Phi Don. The boat journey was glorious the sea breeze keeping the temperature in the mid-twenties, they marvelled at the huge limestone islands and rock formations that emerged from the crystal blue waters. They passed Ko Phi Phi Leh where the Leonardo Di Caprio film *The Beach* had been filmed in 1999 and quickly arrived at the small jetty on Phi Phi Don. The island consisted of two limestone peaks joined by a thin spit of land only a few feet above the sea level where the main village was located. Here they spent a more relaxed week, fed up with the brash neon and hookers plus the arrival of loud, aggressive American Navy personnel in Phuket. Craig nearly received a proper hiding after enthusiastically launching into a song and dance routine of YMCA's *In the Navy* at a hooker bar.

Stevie loved Phi Phi, although the resort was geared towards tourism the small island had a delightful peaceful charm to it, no cars, so very quiet. They stayed in basic shacks close to the beach, the local food varied and tasty plus excellent beach bars for evening lavations. The highlight was the diving. Stevie and Scott left the rest of the group for 3 days to complete their advanced PADI diving course. The surrounding waters clear with a visibility of 30 metres, diving with Scott next to the huge submerged limestone cliffs. The sea life was incredible even a few metres off-shore where clown fish darted in and out of the anemones, up for a fight even when presented with a Bermuda short cladded snorkelling adversary from Woodbridge. During the dives they saw a huge five-metre-long moray eel, lemon sharks and a highly poisonous black and white sea snake that their Norwegian dive instructor played with as though it were nothing more harmless than a puppy.

After Phi Phi the headed to the islands in the Gulf of Thailand attending the infamous full moon parties on Koh Phang Nang. Tanner and China added magic mushroom lassis to the list of consumed stimulants that were on sale at the bars and chemists near the packed beach and bay. Neither could speak properly yet locked into each-other's wavelength that no-one else could penetrate. They eventually left the others in a bar in each other arms, cackling away at some imaginary concept or plan. Scott, Craig and Stevie stayed overlooking the bay where thousands were partying at the sound systems dotted along the beach.

"The Judge would have loved this eh?" smiled Craig.

"Fucking right but too many rigs and DJ's, he would be in a permanent dilemma and if a tune played he didn't like he would be off to the next one."

They reminisced some more about growing up together, discussed and speculated about who was doing what and who was with who but also about the future.

"So you two still going to be at it for the foreseeable?" queried Scott.

"Mate the money is too good and there hasn't been a sniff of bother really. The odd little heart stopping moment here and there but yeah we are gonna keep going."

"Listen be careful, it's a dodgy fucking business you two are in. Rarely works out."

"You worry too much mate, me and Craigy boy here have it sussed out. Ultra-careful, we are not on any old bills radar guaranteed."

They hit the beach at 2am, stopping at the Purple Orchid bar, DJ BellazRoddaz dropping some heavy growling drum and bass out of the huge speakers. They carried on to the Drop Inn bar that was playing more crowd friendly house and trance, they danced and drank as a light drizzle descended on the party but not enough to dampen the mood or temperature. A huge tree draped in lights was in the middle of the beach front dance floor, the DJ booth perched high in the branches above them. Stevie stopped dancing and reached into his pocket for a cigarette and lit it teeth grinding, eyes darting, foot tapping. The little diet pills procured over the counter from the enterprising chemists were not as pokey as amphetamine they used to bomb back in the day but kept you moving. He smiled as he watched Scott and Craig prowling the dance floor glaring at each other menacingly, twenty metres apart throwing only a couple of subtle dance moves. They kept eyes locked and moved ever closer to each other like boxers in a ring starting off slow sizing each other up. Some party goers noticed thinking there was some serious bad vibes between the two and a fight might break out. One Scandinavian couple tried to pull Craig away and talk to him but he ignored them and simply whispered:

"He's fucking getting it!" to the startled Swedish girl.

Stevie had seen this on many occasions before, he had no idea where they got it from it was just something they did. Craig pointed at Scott shaking his head not taking his eyes of him. Scott opened his hands out wide just like a football hooligan giving him the come on. They slowly edged every closer, some people moving away sensing it could kick off at any moment. As they got to within centimetres of each and as the beat dropped, they broke out into wide grins, hugging each other and screaming as they bounced up and down. As they shifted and grooved up and down egging each other on they began telling people off for cutting across there imagined real estate, the runway they called it.

"Professionals only sir, please vacate the area" Scott would shout is hand raised like a Policeman.

Stevie laughed reaching out to lean against the tree as his head began to feel light from the speed and the drink. As he touched the bark a shot of electricity shot up his arm making him jump backwards.

He ran up to Craig and Scott.

"I've just been fucking zapped by that tree!"

"You what you lunatic?"

"I swear, this rain must be getting into the lights and electrified the fucking thing."

Craig had been electrocuted on numerous occasions and walked up to the tree and put his hand on it. He grit his teeth as he held it there for nearly five seconds before pulling away.

"He's fucking right, owwww shit. You have a go Scotty boy!" he yelled nashing his teeth, amped up by the jolt it had just been given.

"Fuck that pal I believe you."

They had noticed at the previous bar there were a large contingent of very rowdy Israelis partying, too boisterous ruining the vibe. They arrived dancing nearby, pissing people off in seconds. Craig eyed them up with his usual pitying stare.

"Oi oi mate, how's it going?" shouted Craig at one of them.

"Good good lets fucking go!!!" he screamed back in Craig's face.

"Hmm quite" replied Craig in a posh English accent that perplexed the Israeli.

"Have you hugged the Tree of Life yet?"

"The what?"

"The Tree of Life" shouted Craig in reply above the thumping beats throwing a thumb a hand towards the illuminated tree.

"You not heard of it? Wow where have you been living? It's a full moon tradition, gives you good luck, go give it a big hug!"

"Fucking right, wooooahhh" he shouted back before bounding over to the tree putting his long arms around it. He jerked and twitched and fell backwards, holding his right wrist. The three Woodbridge lads pissed themselves laughing.

"Smelly yid cunt" whispered Craig to Scott who screwed his face up not impressed at the comment.

Craig waved at him on the floor bent over crying with laughter but to be fair to the Israeli lad after he got over the shock he came over and gave Craig a hug.

"Wait here I'll get a few of my mates."

They then spent half an hour tricking people into getting zapped before getting bored moving off towards the next bar, bouncing away as they went.

"Funny that but pretty fucking dangerous, that tree has about three hundred volts going through it. Could fucking kill someone, easy" deadpanned Craig.

Scott and Stevie looked at each other in amazement before immediately bumping into China and Tanner who were without doubt the most fucked up pair at the entire party. Both were wearing thin glow sticks that had been fashioned into glasses making their wide amphetamine infused eyes even larger, both were soaking wet and had obviously been in the sea at some point. Tanner was, as usual, bleeding but they could not work out from where, both were holding metal buckets, the standard full moon drink of Thai whiskey and red ball. China took a huge swig through his straw and instantly vomited, puking his guts up and splashing Scott's trainers. China looked into his bucket. It was full of sea water. Without looking he flung it behind him high into the air and in amongst the dancing crowd.

"Who does he think he is, Begbie?" laughed Stevie referencing the classic pub fight scene in 1996 film *Trainspotting.*

They stayed at the party until 9am before catching their speedboat taxi back to Ko Samui and their beachside accommodation, another Woodbridge favourite haunt; Charly Huts on Chaweng Beach. They stayed up for the rest of the day drinking, trying and failing to play volleyball eventually succumbing to sleep.

Before long it was time for the Woodbridge lads to depart back to the UK leaving Scott and his friends to continue their travels to Malaysia, Indonesia and finally Australia. Stevie and Craig loved spending time with Scott again and it was a sad moment when they left in the back of a pick-up truck for the start of long journey by boat and bus back to Bangkok. They were looking forward to spending three days in the capital city, shopping and seeing the sights. They had booked a 5-star hotel which after living in beach shacks for two weeks it would be a welcome break.

CHAPTER 8

Mountains Out of Mole Hills

S kully called an emergency meeting with his crew at a safe house deep in Walthamstow.

During the first seven months of 2010 Dam Dem Kingz, the DDK, gradually took control of large swathes of ground and associated drug trade in the north east of the capital. It had held its territory in Tottenham, Hackney and Walthamstow for over ten years but since 2000 the rise of other gangs in East London, specifically the Burgess Street Crew, the BSC, from Tower Hamlets had begun to push for a slice of the drug trade to the north. It brought the two gangs directly into conflict for the first time. Rather than hold its position DDK went on the offensive pushing into new areas it normally stayed out of. They managed to do this by aligning with smaller street gangs, supplying them nearly pure coke and crack at introductory highly incentivised prices combined with providing extra muscle and weapons when needed.

Skully had originally attempted to find out if some sort of deal could be struck with BSC. As was protocol he put in a call to Lord Lawton but his reply was vague and obtrusive, telling Skully not to bother him with little squabbles. So, he forged ahead, BSC were fair game and not connected, had no protection or back-up. It should have been easy with strength and decisive action to nip the beef in the bud. BSC were an emerging outfit no way near as big as DDK but were dangerous young opponents having grown up on the wild estates and streets of Tower Hamlets, fighting and winning the battle for supremacy against the many other street gangs in the area. Once they had gotten a taste for the money, respect and power that came with the drug trade, BSC wanted more, much more and so began the probe into areas that were traditionally outside of their geography, reach and ambition.

In response, DDK had targeted Poplar in east London quickly subsuming a small local crew into the DDK network. The area was up and coming as the bar and club scene continued its slow move east and south away from the traditional west end, which had become stale, uncool and expensive since the early acid house years. Getting a foothold in Poplar to push the cocaine trade was a key objective for Skully as he surveyed the map of London during those early months of 2010. He knew it would be a profitable market but also an opportunity to step on the toes of BSC, let them know DDK was not going to sit on its laurels and let the young uns take the piss. It would signal the start of an uncompromising brutal turf war in London.

The opening salvoes in the early months of 2010 were nothing more than intelligence gathering operations; akin to probing reconnaissance platoons during wartime, getting a feel for oppositions numbers, firepower and importantly their will and resolve. DDK coached its new gang members from Poplar well, providing training, planning and operational support on the street. They started taxing BSC dealers, waiting in the shadows of the huge housing tenements for the evening's dealings to be complete before ambushing them. The initial victims were subjected to fists, baseball bats and a couple of stab wounds to the legs and backsides. The physical ramifications were mostly minor but to those wannabee ambitious street thugs what hurt the most was they had let BSC down. Without strength, power and respect they were nothing. The simmering thirst for revenge was caste. Dam Dem Kingz would pay.

In response BSC petrol bombed a DDK stash house and although the petrol filled bottle did not make it through the lounge window the house lit up like a Christmas tree. In the end it was only cosmetic damage to the external walls but a tit for tat campaign of violence followed in and around the streets of east and north London between the two gangs.

On a warm evening, Faxman, one of Skully's most trusted lieutenants, now ensconced with the Poplar DDK affiliates, prepared to head out for the evening. One of the main areas of the clandestine drug trade was the Poplar high street, which on a Thursday, Friday and Saturday night was packed with people out for a good time until the early hours, many wanting a bit of narcotic assistance to help them enjoy the evenings activities. Faxman was well doctrined in setting up the drug trade with the mostly white consumers. They could not simply set up a couple of black dealers on a street corner and hope for the best. No, they did what Stevie and Craig had done many, many years before, let loose a couple of dealers into the masses who would become regular trusted faces in the crowd.

The bigger longer-term investment opportunity for Faxman, however, was the small but busy nightclub on the high street which, after the pubs closed, would be busy with those eager to continue the party. To control the drug trade inside you needed to control the door. As bouncers needed to be licensed it was no longer possible to simply take the door through force. This is where Skully and Lord Lawton came into their own. All it took was a couple of phone calls, a couple of greased palms and DDK was quickly in business as the sole exclusive drug suppliers to the nightclub clientele.

This was not obvious to those on the outside looking in but it did not take BSC long to figure out the score after a couple of its dealers were accosted at the club, beaten and had their drugs and cash lifted. The club was now DDK territory and now a legitimate target for the BSC gang.

Faxman visited the club at 1am, which he did each and every Saturday night, staying for a couple of hours collecting the take from the dealers. Coming from the street, Faxman revelled in his relatively new elevated status in this area of London. The club on a Saturday night was the place to be seen and he particularly enjoyed soaking up the club's VIP area. There were always women attracted to his flagrant acts of apparent wealth and power. He would buy Hennessey and magnums of champagne and rack up large lines of coke only partially hidden behind the cocktail menus, to the annoyance of the powerless security and bar staff. He would act the gangster rap star from behind the velvet rope, two blondes on either side of him, flashing cash, gold teeth and chains, grabbing his crotch through his baggy jeans, always feeling safe in this little bolthole. However, as with many before and after, complacency would take its toll and Faxman would pay the price.

The club was packed so going well for both the club owners in terms of the bar takings and the DDK dealers patrolling the outskirts of the dance floor. He was greeted warmly by the door staff who ushered him and his small crew quickly through much to the chagrin and annoyance of the queueing (and paying) punters unhappy with the preferential treatment being dished out. As was usual they had a small section of the VIP section allocated, not quite big enough for all of Faxman's entourage and crew but suited him as it signalled who was in and who was on the sidelines of the gang; who was doing well and who needed to pull their weight. The VIP area was usually reserved for celebrities, A list was the desire, Z list was the norm. It was also a money spinner for the club as it offered tables in the VIP for hire for non-celebrities, those either foolish or rich enough to buy the privilege via an minimum spend on bottles of spirits at vastly inflated prices. One of the tables was occupied by two contestants from the reality TV show *Big Brother,* a screeching flaming gay lad, the other a fake breasted, fake tanned wannabe footballer's WAG/ glamour model. Faxman tolerated the gay celeb for all of four minutes before roughly grabbing him round the neck and pinning him up against the glass wall, threatening all sorts of ultra-violence if he did not leave immediately, which he duly did.

Unbeknown to Faxman, three BSC members were keeping an eye on proceedings, stalking him, waiting for the right moment. They were all effectively undercover; smartly dressed, no street wear and therefore unnoticed by Faxman's crew in the VIP area or those dealing in the large main room. All were wearing white shirts, single ear studs, no bling on show and nothing to suggest they were street urchins hellbent on taking out a rival. There were no toilets in the VIP area, something that the new club owners were trying to resolve, but for the time being that meant pissing, shitting, snorting and fucking with the plebs. Faxman was not completely naive to the dangers he faced but he felt relatively safe in the club knowing his crew had his back, keeping an eye on whether any opposition were in the venue. He nodded to one of his crew leant against the bar throwing his head to the side in the direction of the toilet. He responded with a nod before following him to the toilets at the back of the club.

The dance floor was packed with a young crowd, dancing and grinding to hip hop and mainstream R&B. Many noticed the movement from the VIP area and strained their heads to see who was either going in or coming out. A couple of young girls in tight fitting all in one dresses instantly moved towards Faxman either knowing his was a top boy in DDK or simply wanting in on the VIP action. Faxman kissed his teeth, taking a step back holding his chin before nodding up and down as if he was assessing some work of art.

"Wassup dere girlie, ya wanna hang wid da Faxman in a da place eh?"

"Ow bout you n ya sista get up dere an take a drink n me an my boy ere be back in a lickle while seen?"

He waved a hand at the security guard pointing down at the two girls indicating to let them in. They were a bit rough for Faxman, he normally liked to fuck Essex girls from the outer reaches of London rather than inner city scruffs. However, they looked game and sometimes the Essex girls did not appreciate finding themselves in the middle of a spit roast with the DDK crew who had suddenly appeared. On more than one occasion the Police had been called to investigate complaints but Faxman normally did not participate; he would fuck them first in private and then his boys would have a sample, simple as that.

"Nothing to do with me officer. Dat bitch was fuckin gaggin for it, she loves a bit black an all I did was duly oblige officer but maybe she wanted more off mandem and tings got out of hand, I don't know seen? I was at home by then. No, no I did not know who was there officer, you know what it's like all these black folk all look the same innit."

The two girls looked pleased with themselves as Faxman watched them ascend the couple of steps into the VIP.

"Dey wouldn't be smirking like dat later when they got fifteen black snakes to deal wid" he sneered to his boy who chuckled into his fist.

As they approached the toilets a young white ginger haired lad emerged from the busy dance floor, a steely determined look in his eyes. In his pocket his hand clenched around a smooth canister. He was followed discreetly behind by another two, both black and both with a similar look of menace etched on their faces. The toilet was painted black but lit up by fierce fluorescent lighting on the ceiling. As was usual in many clubs, there was a toilet attendant with a tray of after shave scents, deodorant and lollipops, attempting to earn some cash from the inebriated customers. Faxman went to the end of the urinals as his soldier lent up against the row of sinks engaging in small talk with the attendant. The ginger haired BSC gang member entered and immediately approached the DDK gangster by the sinks, counting to ten before turning to him.

"Hello mate you got any powder?"

"What da fuck u askin me for cracker, ya see a fuckin black man and fink I gonna serve up fucking ching eh? U gonna fuckin ask my African brotha ere as well?"

On hearing the exchange Faxman leant back from the urinals looking back laughing at the abuse the white boy was getting.

"Sorry mate I was just wondering" he said weakly. There was an uncomfortable few seconds of silence which was broken by the in-swinging toilet door that was opening. He took this as his cue whipping out the small black canister before putting a long squirt of pepper spray into the eyes of his opponent. The other BSC assailants burst into the toilets covering their eyes as they quickly rushed towards Faxman pulling out long kitchen knives from their waistbands. The DDK soldier yelped in agony instinctively grabbing for the taps in an attempt to wash the fire from his eyes. Before he could, the white BSC gangster grabbed the lapels of his shirt, kneeing him solidly twice just below the ribs before throwing him towards the cubicles and away from the stinging mist that was still lingering in the air. He fell on his side and tried to get to his feet but his opponent was on him again, instantly directing a well-placed kick in the kidneys before following up with two more to the face as his hands went down to protect his sides. He stomped his head with the heel of his right foot like De Niro in those gangster films he had seen.

Faxman instantly recognised the danger, there was no escape in the small room and he was not tooled up, his lock knife was in his jacket pocket hanging on the back of a chair in the VIP area. He dived to his left towards an unoccupied toilet cubicle just as one of the BSC struck out at him with the knife. Faxman smashed open the door with his left hand but the sharp point of the blade caught his trailing right arm, just below his elbow, cutting deep along the underside of his arm towards his hand. The whole momentum of his body diving into the cubicle one way and the slashing motion of the knife the other way adding to the damage. He fell through the cubicle screaming at the intense pain in his arm and collapsed onto the floor but managing slam the door shut with his feet. A huge flap of skin dangled from his right forearm, blood now steadily flowing out but even in his panicked state he could see a main vein or artery had not been severed. With his left hand he managed to hold the flapping skin around his arm whilst continuing to keep a brace of the door with his feet.

One of the BSC boys began kicking the door in trying to get access. They were here to do the complete job. After two solid kicks that produced a small crack in the flimsy MDF door he nodded to his companion to get into the next cubicle to see if he could get access or within striking distance that way. He hopped up onto the toilet and carefully peered over, he saw Faxman on the floor squeezed in next to the toilet and wall with his legs up firmly against the cubicle door. He slipped down and laid on the floor the length of the cubicle but the opposite way to Faxman, gripping his blade he arched his arm under the cubicle partition and began manically stabbing towards where he thought Faxman legs would be. He felt a couple of contacts with his legs and adjusted his aim, hacking furiously. He felt the knife hit something and then a little bit of give, heard a yell from the other side realising he had made a decent contact he pulled his hand back under the cubicle. A second later he heard the door give in under a furious kick from his comrade. Faxman tried to fend off his attacker as he pounced through the door with his legs but the BSC lad grabbed his foot lifting his leg high and then in a underarm motion brutally stabbed him three times in quick succession in the back of his thigh, deep and hard. Faxman groaned at the impacts before throwing up.

The white ginger haired BSC lad was guarding the now unconscious DDK gang member on the floor whilst keeping any unwarranted attention away, a few people had tried to get into the toilet from the main club. He saw them off by letting off a couple of squirts of pepper spray around the door which did the trick but also alerted security and DDK something happening and Faxman was missing.

The white ginger haired boy shouted.

"Get it done, we're gonna have company!"

Faxman was dragged on his back from the toilet cubicle, he made an effort to hang on to the toilet bowl with his left hand but it was greasy with his own blood. He was pulled out under the harsh bright lights. The two BSC attackers did not waste any time, no prolonged speeches detailing the reasons why, no playing with the victim like a cat with an injured bird, they silently went at him with their glistening sharp blades, fast, brutal and without mercy.

They rushed out of the toilet into the main club causing panic and mayhem as they went, pepper spray going off, blades were being thrust at anyone that tried to get near. Even the door staff were a little taken aback by the ferocious trio deciding the best place for them was outside rather than containing them inside where they could do more damage. They burst out of the club making the lengthy queue shrink against the wall, most deciding there and then they would find an alternative venue for the evening's entertainment. The BSC boys sprinted across the street pilling into the back of a waiting BMW that screeched off into the night.

Inside on the toilet floor Faxman was still alive but only just. In the space of three minutes he had been stabbed twenty-seven times, most in the body and chest but also in the legs, neck and face. He was bleeding out steadily on the tiled white floor, his breaths short and painful as his ruptured pierced lungs attempted to get the oxygen he needed but they were filling up with blood and could not function properly. The bright fluorescent lights were burning into his eyes as he lay there attempting to settle himself down, concentrating on trying to breath to give him the best chance of surviving until an ambulance turned up. He thought that it should not take long as this was a decent area of London, not like Tottenham where he grew up, where ambulances could take ages to arrive even in the most serious of circumstances.

He was only twenty-two years old. He thought of his mum and only his mum even as a familiar face from his beloved DDK crew appeared in his vision who ripped off his shirt to apply first aid. His mum. His mum.

"Sorry mum this is not how he had intended it to be.." he muttered almost silently to himself.

As he laid there dying on the cold floor he remembered his mum taking two cleaning jobs to scrimp and save so she could take him and his younger brother to meet their grandparents in Barbados when he was twelve. Back to the homeland his mum had said, away from the cold and the naughty boys on the estate. What a two weeks that was, him and his brother swimming in the bath warm sea, eating delicious spiced chicken and rice and listening to stories about the island from his granddad who up until then they had never met. She had been determined for them to meet her two little boys before they died. She was so proud of them when they were younger. Faxman thought about those times when his mum used to look at him with love in her eyes not worry. In those days they both performed well at school, were respectful to their elders, interested in sports, music and art. But then came the inevitable inner-city housing estate trap; getting in with the wrong crowd which often was the only crowd, peer pressure, the street gangs where you were either in or you were out, protected and respected or exposed, alone and reviled.

"Sorry momma, sorry grandma, sorry grandpa but it turned out those London streets were not paved with gold and opportunity. No it turns out they were tarmac and concrete splattered and soaked in blood."

"Sorry mu………."

Those were his last thoughts. His hushed murmured words that were forming on his lips froze as the bright lights above him began to fade to black. There was silence, the faces above him appeared to be shouting but he could not hear them anymore. They became blurred and Faxman felt his lungs and heart stop just before noth-ingness enveloped him.

Days later at the emergency meeting in Walthamstow, Codey Buggan aka Cee Bugg was screaming blue murder. Skully was trying to calm him down but decided to let him vent off. Cee Bugg had found out the names of the BSC assailants that had slaughtered his cousin and best friend Faxman. He wanted to hit them that very night and was demanding a shooter from Skully who would not give in, would not let emotion dictate action. He looked over at Kaiser, his councillor, who ever so slightly shook his head which solidified Skully's owns thoughts on the situation. Getting caught with a firearm meant an automatic five year stretch at her Majesty's leisure which meant you had to be very careful about how to go about gun related business. This was why in 2010 knife crime was at an all-time high, the Police and courts just did not seem to care about carrying a blade even though it could do as much damage as a handgun.

"Listen, we will wreck vengeance on Burgess Street, Cee Bugg, you have my word on that Bruv but steaming in unprepared will get us all killed or nicked. You can have a shootah no problem but you are not going to be using it like you are in the wild west. Ya ere me fam? Give Kaiser a week, tell him what you know about these fellas and he will lay it out for you properly. A proper plan of attack rather than going in guns blazing. You do the shooting though bruv yeah?"

"Fuck yeah. Dem BSC boys are going down for wat day did ta de Faxman."

Skully stood up grabbing Cee Bugg by the shoulders.

"Business as usual until the Kaiser says otherwise, seen?"

Cee Bugg looked over at Kaiser who stared back emotionless, a stoic, beady eyed look etched on his face.

"A week yeah?"

"Week will be fine, if it goes like I think I wouldn't organise a hot date on Thursday, yeah?"

"This Thursday. Arright."

CHAPTER 9

Trident

Across London, Jarvis, now head of SO16, the Metropolitan Police armed response unit, took off his headphones and looked over to his counterpart, the head of Operation Trident.

"What do you think?" he said to Jarvis.

"Well, you heard the man. No hot dates next Thursday."

"Alright, let me have the report on these lot by tomorrow morning and I will give the lads a briefing."

Jarvis then went to a private office pulling out a personal mobile phone as he closed the door, eyeing the vicinity ensuring he was alone and would not be overheard. The call was answered quickly.

"The fellows from up in the north look like they are going to rethink their strategy over that disagreement in the east. The one that happened on Saturday. It might just be that we might be in conference with them later in the week. You want me to cut them loose?"

"Will the CEO and Head of Strategy and Operations be there?"

"No probably not, highly unlikely. Probably just a couple of the senior managers."

"Hmmm.....Well we cannot have elements of the conglomerate acting like this, so I think that we need to remind them who is really in charge. It will send a message both to him and indeed the public that we are not going to let these sorts of things happen out there."

He then broke the loose code language surprising Jarvis.

"Listen, everyone is fed up with these god dammed gangs running amok all the time. The stop and search policy is not working and winding the natives up even more. Law abiding citizens are getting mugged, happy slapped or whatever it is they bloody well call it. And above all people just do not feel safe anymore, maybe sticking one of these animals in the gutter might actually improve things. So, get it done and I will call the CEO afterwards and tell him what is what. Alright? We clear?"

"Yes sir, we are clear. Crystal clear."

"Do me a favour, can you speak to you know who and get me an updated report of who is who in the channels of trade. Things have been happening so quickly it is jolly well difficult to keep up these days. This little episode may well force a change and I would like to see who else is out there that we could use. Might have to have a bit of a shuffle round, you know keep everyone on their toes. Alright, good luck and I will look forward to reading about it in the papers."

Jarvis hung up considering the task in hand. The SO16 team had to appear to do everything by the book and act in accordance with the Metropolitan Police code of conduct. His team had royally fucked things up a couple of years ago in the aftermath of the July 2007 London Underground bombings. Everyone was super twitchy, that plus some very iffy intelligence resulted in his team blowing away an innocent member of the public on the tube. However, everyone understood the situation London was facing during those scary days, so it was brushed under the carpet, compensation was paid, and his team had gotten back to business. This situation brewing on the streets of east, south and north London was similar, and he knew that in the end, in the cold light of day when faced with armed criminals, hardened gang members things were different. All he had to do was wind the fellas up tight, get his most trusted to shout something like *"He's got a gun!!!!"*

And that will be that. Pop. Pop. Pop. Job done.

Later that evening he retrieved the file on the computer for Cee Bugg.

"This is one nasty little fucker" he mused as he looked through the rather impressive file.

He had an arrest sheet as long as his arm since the age of thirteen. Prone to violence, robbery with intent plus all the usual, drug dealing, aggravated assault, the list went on and on. This stuff was gold dust and would be used at the pre-operational meeting to hype up the team even more. Make sure they knew this was a dangerous man, likely to be armed and that they should take all known precautions to protect themselves and the public.

You did not have to be a genius to read between the lines; shoot the fucker and do not miss.

He then called his counterpart and long-time partner in crime in the drug squad.

"Hello Dave, the big boss has asked for an updated organisational structure if you don't mind. Think he might be looking to shift some of the chess pieces around."

"Ah, not a problem Mr Jarvis. I had it updated the other day as it goes. We nicked some fucking music supremo, Christiano Pittelli, up in Camden last week and it turns out he is in the frame. Two fucking coppers strolling the beat caught him red handed sniffing lines in his fucking Porsche. Fucking twat. Only went and found a 200-gram block on him. Anyway, I got stuck into him and this hipster squawked like a parrot as soon as I placed my hands on the table and he gave us a couple of names. Steven Chambers and Craig Winters."

"Never heard of them, any previous?"

"Nope, aside from a small marijuana charge back in the day for the Craig fellow they are as clean as a whistle."

"Odd thing though is they seem to be from well out of town, place called Woodbridge."

"Woodbridge...Woodbridge..." Jarvis sloshed the name around in his mind.

"Oh Woodbridge! Jesus Christ yeah I know Woodbridge. Fucking hell, Woodbridge. You sure?"

"Yep"

Jarvis thought back to the night over ten years ago when he nicked the nonce drug dealer bloke Christopher Baines. It had been a great pull and a decent payday courtesy of the blow and pills he had stuffed down his trousers.

He recalled phoning Lord Lawton about the score and the information that Bainsey had provided, stating that the supplier was an Irish fella. As usual The Lord hung up, called back to warn him off pursuing the line of enquiry.

Jarvis tried to connect the dots in his head but kept quiet on the matter.

"Yeah okay I think I get the picture now. You sure these Woodbridge chaps are hooked in with the Tottenham DDK boys?" replied Jarvis.

"Yep, The Lord confirmed it. As soon as that Christiano fella was pinched I put the call in. I gave The Lord the names Christiano had sung; Steven Chambers and Craig Winters. As usual he hung up. He then obviously put a call into DDK at N17 and he called back within the hour and told me it was hands off those two and listen to this! The Lord said go easy on the fucking music mogul. Typical ball-ache though as the two beat coppers that pulled him won't fucking let it lie, keep phoning me up wanting to know progress and whether it would be going to trial and would they be giving evidence and all that shit. Typical newbies desperate for it to appear on their fucking arrest sheets. I fucked them off a few days later with some bollocks that he is a secret Police informer blah, blah, bollocks, bollocks."

Jarvis finished the call. Sipping on a coffee he thought about the two lads, Steven and Craig from green, leafy Woodbridge.

CHAPTER 10

Peaking

Enter Nathaniel Gray aka The City Hammer.

Ruby Edwards introduced him to Stevie in 2006 after mentioning she had employed his services in washing her drug money. She had met him at some point via her dealing in amongst the square mile and Canary Wharf. Initially he was just another venture capitalist / commodity trader with a ton of cash and a habit but as they bonded, he began dropping snippets about his true profession; money laundering. Ruby knew Stevie would probably be interested in meeting him but she was nervous about losing out on his custom. She negotiated a finder's fee with Stevie after explaining what he could potentially do for him and Craig who were in dire need of another avenue to wash their cash. Two years of working for the fiercesome Skully and DDK had actually been a breeze, business was on the up, making far more money than before. They even appreciated how professional the DDK organisation were, rarely having to deal with hoodie wearing, gold teethed strutting gangsters.

By the end of 2006 they had consolidated operations to their four primary customers/distributors. Christiano Pittelli supplied north London/Camden celebs, musicians and associated hangers on. He was the key to the ongoing viability of the operation buying the most weight. There was Ruby Edwards in central London who had now left D&C to become a full-time cocaine dealer. Stefan Stockdale was still buying a shit load of gear and still paying late. His DJ career was on the wane though. Stevie was watching him carefully. Craig's old comrade in arms, Jon Weldon, continued to be their home counties supplier who had evolved to become one of the biggest dealers in the Thames Valley. He operated an open all hours delivery service via his taxi and courier companies with a little crew of drivers that did his dirty work. Not only did he charge the customers for drugs but also for the taxi/courier fares, double bubble!

So, they had more cash than they knew what to do with. Salon owner, Alison Hiles was getting nervous, the scam had been going on too long for her liking and began making noises about getting out. She was grateful but she now had kids and was scared witless about going to prison. Stevie tried to reassure her but he knew the days of pushing cash through the salon were numbered. They needed another way to get rid of their cash and the emergence of this Nathaniel Gray character seemed to be a god-send.

Stevie was dazzled by him within minutes of meeting him, cutting through the niceties and bullshit getting down to the point at hand. Nathaniel was astute though initially choosing his words carefully but eventually jumping to the theme. He wanted in on the cocaine thing, it was a solid business model and he had a wide network in the city who he could sell it to. He knew from Ruby that Stevie was different. He used his knowledge of laundering as leverage to get a good deal. Stevie and Craig agreed a lower price per kilo in exchange for what Nathaniel claimed would be an airtight laundering and investment set up.

The underlying details and mechanics of the laundering scheme were kept from Stevie and Craig but basically involved them setting up several investment companies dotted around the usual tax havens, all purely involved in overseas investment out of sight of the UK authorities. They would invest minimal clean capital via Nathaniel's brokerage firm. The rest of the investment was cash, delivered to Nathaniel often by one of Jon Weldon's couriers. Somehow the cash and clean funds would be invested in property developments overseas mostly in the Middle East places like Abu Dhabi and Dubai but also in Ireland. Via greased palms, back handers and pay off's the land was purchased under market value making the eventual returns very attractive. Nathaniel advised them to keep pumping cash into the investment companies and he would do the rest. It was win-win as the Middle East and

Europe were both undergoing huge property booms. He also advised the lads to switch all UK bank accounts to Iceland where they would benefit from huge interest rates, nearly double those offered in the UK.

Craig was not keen. He met with Nathaniel a couple of times, both times in the midst of gigantic hangovers which did not help his outlook. He didn't like him. He thought he was slimy. He did not trust him. He did not even laugh during his tales of bedding pretty young things who patrolled the bars and clubs of London trying to bag a highflyer.

"Any cunt that calls himself the City Hammer, is a cunt" he simply told Stevie as they left a meeting with him.

"Well if a nickname gets him laid fair play to him. Reckons his other nickname is 'stunt-dick' as he stands in for actors too shy to flash the old meat and two veg.   Anyway, he is not my cup of tea either but we've got too much cash. We need him mate."

"Well I trust you to make the right decision, so do whatever but I am not meeting him again. I nearly gave him a slap back there. What we do need to talk about though is the crack thing. Weldon is pushing. He is washing up on his own to meet the demand but he is getting all antsy about it. He wants it ready to go. Mate it is huge money and we don't have to do anything. Just order it in off Skully and job done. Stefan will be in as well."

"Hmmm not Stefan. That fucker is losing it both on and off the dancefloor. I've been keeping an eye on his gigs mate and his days are numbered. Sooner or later he is going to run out of cash and then we are going to run into problems with him paying the tick. Remember what we said all them years ago. No addicts except when they are truly minted. Stefan is not going to be minted for much longer the way he is going."

"I think he is okay, he is still playing and paying. Bit loose sometimes but he has always been like that. Managed to persuade him to DJ at mine and Stace's New Year's Eve bash."

"Well there is a sign of the times if there ever was one. No DJ's play at house parties on new year, it's their biggest payday. That means he is tainted. The promoters see him as too much of a risk to book. Watch him mate. We cut him loose if we have to. I know your good mates but this is business at the end of the day."

Craig breathed in deeply not liking where this discussion was going.

"Alright so I keep an eye on the superstar DJ, we'll order the rocks off Skully for Weldon and you set up that bollocks with that Nathaniel stunt dick hammer twat fella."

"All right. Done. See you New Year's yeah?"

CHAPTER 11

Innocent questions

W hy was it that I was an only child? I had always wondered growing up. My mum and dad are, when I really think and analyse it, fucking awesome parents. The drugs may have robbed me of some of my memories but there are things that stick out, lodged in a vivid colourful yet almost rose-tinted view in the brighter recesses of my mind. Seven years old, not a care in the world and on holiday in Devon, swimming out to that raft at Dartmoor Country Park, my dad needing to give me a hand for the last few metres as I struggled with my still developing unwieldy swimming technique. I collapsed up onto the raft gasping for breath before letting out a riotous belching burp after seemingly swallowing half the river during the lengthy crossing. I made instant friends out there on that raft as all the boys and girls cracked up laughing and started burping together as if to celebrate my arrival and epic first open water achievement. Two friends I made on that holiday were brothers aged seven and eight. They looked like twins yet acted like best friends. As we hung out, played, climbed and swam I recall marvelling at their relationship, their bond, through my young pair of eyes. I think about them sometimes even now.

We were camping in an enormous tent that was partly attached to a trailer that provided a very sturdy double bed as comfy as you would find at home. Me, mum and dad all slept together in that big bed, me squished between the two of them putting paid to any notions of any al fresco action no doubt. But the three of us were like that, closer than any other family I knew but as I grew older, they and I began to realise I was missing out on some elements of family life that *others had. I had no siblings; my cousins were far away in Ireland and I craved something other than the all-encompassing love of my parents. Apparently according to mum as a toddler I was a nervous little boy who kept close to her, forever holding onto the hem of her dress for dear life. But over time a yearning for comradeship and friends, maybe even a girlfriend forced me into being more proactively social than others. Maybe it started out on that raft who knows? Certainly helped out in later life by making contacts, you know networking and such. Maybe this is why Craig and I bonded in those early years during secondary school, we both had something similar missing in our lives and maybe our friendship filled that void. Having said that I was always okay being in my own company, letting my dreams and imagination be my confidante. This also maybe why I did not have a proper girlfriend until I was in my mid 30's and that situation was not exactly conventional.*

One morning during that camping trip and after spending a day with those two brothers from Wallasey in Liverpool I asked my mum something, something which years later I would always regret asking. I told her I wished that I had a brother or sister. A brother or sister that I could play with and then asked; Why I could not have one? I was too young at the time to really notice the impact of my words, but I soon realised and even to this day I remember her expression. Mum is strong, one of the strongest women I have ever known. And remember that includes some impressive professionals who fought and clawed their way to the top of big Corporates against a tidal wave of prejudice and inequality. She's a rock alright. But that day I saw my mum crumple, her tough yet happy go lucky exterior collapsed a little in a wave of emotion and sadness. I didn't clock it properly though at the time. I just sat there waiting for an answer to a very reasonable question.

"You never know Steven, maybe one day but it's not as simple as just having a baby whenever you want one you know" she replied quietly, her head down not making eye contact.

"What about the storks mama? You could get one from the storks!" I innocently asked recalling a cartoon where the babies were delivered in white towels in the mouths of the flapping birds.

I was still at an age where anything was possible and all was innocent but if I had looked closely I would have seen a thin layer of tears wel-

ling up on her bottom eye lids. But I was too young, too interested in playing, too interested in the Coco Pops, the cereal I was only ever allowed to have on holidays. Holiday treat my dad would say as he also tucked into a bowl of the sugary breakfast. After I had unintentionally slammed an arrow through my mother's heart with my ignorant adolescent questioning she slowly rose from the table and stated she was going for a walk. I looked at my dad wondering why she was going alone, she would always ask me to go on walks with her, it was what we did. My dad gave me a tight smile and ruffled my hair.

"How about we go find them two scousers."

It was not be for some time, several years later in my early teens that I learned the truth, the awfully sad truth why I never would have a brother or sister to play with as I was growing up.

CHAPTER 12

Tally Ho

S tevie looked at the green clipper on the bedside table, then down to the large fireworks settled into the wooden frame pointing up towards the window. A bead of sweat trickled down from his eyebrow into his right eye, the saltiness making it sting as he wiped it away with his hand. He heard more shouting coming from within the depths of his flat on the opposite side of the bedroom door and he looked out the window again straight down. Not up, just down.

"Fuck me it's high" he thought as the fear and adrenaline continued to fizz through him.

He looked back at the fireworks, his brain calculating what might happen but he received no answer. This was no simple or complex maths puzzle, like that sudoku that everyone seemed to be playing. He doubted whether anyone in the history of the planet had been in this exact situation and he could not possibly predict the outcome of anything.

"Fuck it" he said out loud as he stepped down from the window ledge reaching out for the cigarette lighter. He rubbed his thumb over the top feeling the familiar rough edges and the finer sandpapery texture of the inner wheel. He took the wooden frame that housed the rockets and laid it down on its back, the rockets now pointed inward towards the bedroom door. He reached down, his hand trembling as he lit the lighter, the small flame sparking to life, the blue and yellow flame flickering in the breeze coming through the open window. At that point Stevie heard a rhythmic banging sound as his enemies once again attacked the kitchen door. He heard the fridge give way as it crashed to the floor. It made Stevie jump and he let go of the small switch on the lighter and the flame died, the lighter slipping from his sweaty palm.

He was now no longer in two minds as he scrambled for the lighter on the floor. Picking it up he now desperately tried to light the rocket. He struck the lighter twice, the flame coming to life on the second time just as he heard a voice shout.

"Fuck, fucking cunt, he fucking got out. Go, go, go."

They had spotted the hole in the wall.

He lit the blue touch paper. It sizzled a little, just like all those years ago out on the moors in Kent with Craig. Stevie knew it was enough, dropping the lighter he jumped onto the bed and levered his left leg onto the windowsill. As he grabbed both edges of the window frame with both hands the bedroom door came crashing open. Stevie instinctively looked around, the noise again making him jump and jerk with fright. In the doorway was one of Skully's crew, a gun in hand but lowered at his side, not how you expect a Policeman or soldier to enter a room. The DDK gunman looked at the rockets gently sizzling and fizzing in their wooden frame on the floor and then raised his head to Stevie. Again, he looked down at the rockets and then quizzically back at Stevie trying to compute what on earth was going on; fireworks and Stevie half hanging out the window on the 31st floor of a tower block.

It took just under a second for him to realise what was going on. Their eyes met; a snarl squashed up his lips revealing gold plated teeth. He raised the gun, a slender matt black pistol with a long grip. He squeezed the trigger, firing at Stevie from point blank range.

It was the second time Stevie had been shot at, but this time was worse. Last time it had been from afar but now it was close, so very close and this time everything seemed to happen in slow motion. As he squeezed the trigger the blue touch paper on the rocket met the main ignition thread that runs from the centre of the firework to the base. The rocket fired to life. It did not move forward but pulsed out sparks and fire from the base whilst emitting a high-pitched screeching that pierced through the previous ambience of the small room.

This is what probably saved Stevie's life, the noise shredded the nerves of the gunman making him flinch away from the sound just as he pulled the trigger sending the bullet screeching just to the right of its intended target. The metal projectile smashed into the wall inches from Stevie's head showering him with plaster and dust. Then all hell broke loose in the bedroom as the rocket erupted out of the wooden frame, it screamed towards the gunman at over eighty miles an hour just missing his head. It bounced off the bedroom door frame and back towards Stevie hitting the main window causing a huge crack. At this point Stevie did not need any more motivation. He jumped out of the open window.

Through the din and wailing of the firework ricocheting around the inside of his flat he heard another gunshot go off. His heart seemed to jump into his mouth as Stevie fell downward.

CHAPTER 13

No Fully Comp

T he screen glowed in the dim light of the office; the new environmentally friendly low-level lighting automatically switched on at 20:30. The night owls at D&C clicked on desk lamps to continue beavering away to meet their all-important client deadlines. In normal times anyone looking would have assumed Stevie was doing exactly that, working late, the dedicated employee sacrificing his Thursday evening all for the good of D&C. However, this was not the case and was probably not the case for thousands of others in London, New York, Frankfurt and Hong Kong. The crash had happened. The good times were over. Stevie did not care about D&C. Fuck them. Their army of consultants would flock like vultures as businesses began to struggle, swoop in on those in danger of folding, D&C eager to provide expensive consultancy advice on how to cut costs, restructure, slim down and optimise tax positions. He stared blankly at his screen, the BBC website headline 'GLOBAL FINANCIAL MELTDOWN' accompanied with a picture of an unemployed city trader carrying a plastic bin-liner heading into the guts of Canary Wharf tube station. A thousand thoughts milling around in his mind, all questions and no answers.

Early 2007 had been good in many respects. Businesses had been booming, the money flooding in and out again into the grubby little mitts of Nathaniel Gray. Craig bought himself a grey convertible Ferrari and a brilliant white Range Rover for Stacey. Stevie tried to ignore them, Craig said they were happy but he had heard the rumours. Stevie had since flown the parents' nest in Woodbridge buying a house in Hampstead Heath with access to central London and the D&C offices. He had a housewarming party in the spring. Craig had not shown up. The next morning, he was greeted to a swathe of incoherent voicemail messages at various hours that could not be deciphered. Another warning sign that seemed to buzz and flash in Stevie's mind.

In the summer the seeds of the impending global economic disaster were sown thousands of miles away in the United States of America. The seemingly unstoppable real estate market hit its peak and then the bubble spectacularly burst. Banks had loaned money using sub-prime mortgage mechanisms which were catastrophically designed on the premise that house prices would continue to increase. The banker's short term financial targets were the be all and end all, longer term value creation was never on the agenda. Reckless risk taking for immediate returns, a complete lack of corporate governance coupled with next to zero regulation. All of a sudden the banks were left horribly exposed as they were left with billions of dollars' worth of debt held against a flabby, overvalued, crashing housing market. Capitalist greed in all its glory. It was not limited to within the confines of the US and as the common allegory went, the US sneezed and the rest of the world caught a cold.

The creeping spectre of negative equity real estate quietly grew until all hell broke loose in the spring of 2008. Three of the biggest financial institutions in the US went bankrupt, overseas banks quickly followed including an Icelandic bank where Stevie and Craig held nearly £3.5 million pounds. They were caught with their pants down, lured into the buoyed housing markets via their overseas property businesses all juiced by the highly illegal money laundering operation put in place by Nathaniel Gray. Those Icelandic interest rates of nearly 15% turned out to be too good to be true and their money seemed to be lost forever. UK banks then went to the wall, Northern Rock, Royal Bank of Scotland and Lloyds, all had to be rescued by the taxpayer and with it came the end of New Labour.

Tony Blair, golden boy to war criminal, got out just at the right time, leaving Gordon Brown, the scapegoat. The UK public wanted answers, they knew it was the bankers, but they were faceless, they needed someone to vent their anger on. Step forward Gordon who must have wondered how he was dealt this shitty hand. As the Chancellor of the Exchequer he had often quoted *"fiscal prudence"* but this mess happened on his watch. Just weeks before the crash he was extolling the virtues of the financial sector and how all businesses should look towards the square mile for inspiration. He was made the patsy for everything, rightly or wrongly.

"How things had changed since those heady days of the 90's" thought Stevie as he clicked onto another article.

Stevie had tried to extract themselves as best he could but all their finances were organised and tied up via Nathaniel Gray. He had been difficult to track down. Craig would surely kill him if ever got his hands on him. Stevie visited his flat near Chelsea harbour but one of his neighbours said he had not seen him for weeks. So, he had watched through his fingers at the financial disaster that was unfolding in front of him. Stevie was paralysed, stuck, frozen like a rabbit in the headlights of recession of epic proportions, an out of control juggernaut about to wipe him out.

D&C suffered like many others, yet Stevie escaped the redundancy rounds that swept through the company. He secretly thanked his strategy of playing the grey man. Stevie was nothing more than a trusted resource to get work completed whether it was ad-hoc two pages of advice or part of larger projects. So when the downturn happened and the executives met in the top floor grandiose boardroom with the organization structure pinned to the wall, red marker pen in hand, ready to end D&C careers in no more than a flick of the wrist, Stevie was left untouched.

To begin with Stevie was more worried about the rapid decline of cocaine consumption that was seriously impacting sales. As more people were laid off the belts were tightened; the luxury of cocaine for the recreational users was put to the side. Hardest hit was Ruby, whose city clientele was decimated with hundreds losing their jobs. She had to go back to work but because of the huge gap in her CV since leaving D&C plus the sudden huge competition for jobs in the city, she had to take a junior position at one of the accounting firms. Back to working twelve-hour days on dull corporate restructuring and transformation projects. She kept at it though selling gear, working her contacts, squeezing the network.

The previously easy targets set by Skully were impossible to meet as they struggled to sell their stock on hand. However, DDK were also being impacted in a similar fashion. Shit rolls down hill and all their other sales, those to other distributors, on street corners, the estates, pubs and clubs, were also in freefall. The expected pressure, threats and distinct possibility of violence never came even when the monthly orders of nearly three kilos dropped to just one. Skully accepted it and told them to keep pushing, keep seeking new business. There were no beatings, no kidnappings, no knee capping's, no floggings. Thank fuck for that.

With all these issues swamping him Stevie could ill afford any more problems. Yet his biggest challenge was about to rear its all too familiar ugly head.

CHAPTER 14

Descent

The dark days of 2008 dragged on as their dire financial situation became apparent. Unbeknown to Stevie Craig had accelerated his descent into deep, dark drug addiction, his behaviour becoming even more erratic and volatile. Stevie was not oblivious but tried to block it out focussing on retaining control of the finances like he always had done but they were struggling. Stevie kept plenty of capital back on the books so he could still afford to pay them both a dividend payment every other month from ESG Property Ltd and the off-shore companies.

However, the signs were beginning to emerge, subtle to begin with Craig beginning to ask here and there for more advances and also began to negotiate Stefan's debts with Stevie. Unbeknown to Stevie, Stefan was all paid up. Craig was simply lying about the debt and was now blazing headlong through huge quantities of gear and blaming Stefan. He was now trapped in the ever-tightening vice of cocaine and crack addiction, unable to escape its grip. Stories drifted down to Stevie via the Woodbridge and London rumour mills.

Stevie tried to intervene in the autumn of 2009 but realised it was too late as he attempted to pull Craig away from the influences of Stefan, Jon Weldon and god knows who else he was hanging around with.

They met up high in the Trentstone Towers flat. It was now a rare meeting between the two as they chopped up and repackaged one kilo of coke and half a kilo of crack. Craig looked terrible.

He had always been big boned but his torso normally consisted of a fair amount of muscle. His pot belly contrasted with his skinny face and legs. They had always taken the piss out of his 'chicken legs' but his eyes were sucked back into its sockets and although the strong jawline was still there and visible, the skin was stretched across his neck making his Adam's apple protrude like an old mans. His eyes blazed, looking on hungrily at the glistening white powder and rocks laid out before him trying to be cool, trying to resist. Fucking hell did he want to dive in! He knew what Stevie's reaction would be if he did in front of him. He eyed up his old friend with an ever-developing hatred that simmered under his yellow tinged skin.

"Having a taste would come later when that fucking goody too shoes is not about" thought Craig darkly as he chopped, divided and bagged up.

Stevie took a deep breath and tentatively began to explain he wanted to change tactics, shake things up a bit.

"So, listen mate, I was thinking maybe we mix things up a bit. How about I take over the sales to Stefan and Jon. You take on Ruby and Christiano up in the city. You can go and hang around in the winebars and clubs eh?" he explained light heartedly, trying to smile, keep it friendly.

Craig stopped chopping; it took his brain a few seconds to register what he was saying.

"You fucking what?"

"I was thinking I will take over dealing with Stefan and Jon. I will..." Craig cut him off, barking at him.

"You will fucking what? Fuck that mate, I built up the relationship with em, they deal with me and me only. You got that? What's going on? You pushing me to the side, you fucking side-lining me or what? Why? What the fuck have I done?"

"I am not pushing you to the side, it's just that, you know..."

"No, tell me, you know what, you know fucking what?"

Stevie just held out his palms gesturing towards the drugs on the table then to Craig.

Craig exploded.

"Fuck you, you fucking high and mighty fucking cunt. How's

about getting off your fucking high horse and fucking get down and dirty with the fucking troops like me. Ducking, diving, getting more people into the thing. Building sales. No fucking chance you are taking Stef and Jon off me, fuck you. Fuck that you fucking fuck, you AND fucking me need them just like you and me need those fucking pricks Ruby and Christiano, or whatever that cunt's fucking real name is. I deal with my cunts and you deal with your cunts. We take it in turns to meet the fucking savages, the fucking NIGGAS and get the gear, and meet here once a fucking month. End of. So fuck you."

He stared at Stevie, his eyes ablaze with rage, breathing deeply.

"You wanna fucking let your fucking hair down a bit more often mate, look at you, you fucking snobby cunt, looking down your fucking big nose at everyone. I'll fucking smash it across your fucking face if you think you can give it the high and mighty and try and fucking stab me in the back you judas cunt."

"You and your fucking great business insight as well. What the fuck! You know fuck all mate, you've already well and truly fucked me over. Have I ever fucking blamed you for losing most of our fucking graft, have I once fucking blamed you for sticking your cock up that snake Nathaniel Gray's arse, him giving it all that about fucking Abu fucking goat Dabi fucking wherever and Ireland and fucking Iceland. Jesus fucking Christ, fucking Iceland, that great banking nation? Sizable returns due to generating external investments by sky-high fucking interest rates? You fucking fuck up, you fuck. Him turning your head, you sticking all our fucking cash into some fucking bank in fucking Iceland. I mean, fucking Iceland? You fucking moron! Where was your fucking 100% foresight bollocks then, you fucking mug. That Nathaniel fucking Gray fucking stunt cunt whatever, is probably having a right good fucking laugh at you and me now, ain't he?"

"He fucking topped himself you twat."

"Fucking good riddance, fucking lowlife, fucking leech. Anyway, answer me this, did I ever blame you or have a pop?"

"It was a joint partnership decision, simple."

"Oh fucuuuuck off.....Bollocks you were fucking all over it, you wouldn't have let it go you greedy cunt. So, no, I never once blamed you, never questioned you in 10 fucking years. And you fucking repay me by trying to fuck me over."

"I am not trying to fuck you over, I am worried about you."

"Well worry no more. Worry about your fucking self from now on, you need to, you've got fucking issues mate. Right so I think me and you are done. Fucking finished. You are not fucking dealing with Jon and Stefan, they fucking hate your guts anyway. They think you're a fucking snake, and you've pretty much just fucking proved them right an all."

Craig took a breath placing his two hands on the table before looking up at Stevie. He was creeping onto dangerous ground. The addict in him thinking ahead. Don't fuck this up, all this pristine gear will be gone. Lost Stacey but don't lose this. Need to keep the channels of trade open. He eased off but luckily Stevie was also thinking it through, his greed was as equal to Craig's.

"No mate I don't want to split it up, we've got a fucking good thing going on here still. A change is as good as a rest and all that" said Stevie getting into negotiation mode.

Craig thought it through, again looking at the powder and rocks on the table, silently singing to him.

"Alright listen, you've got your bum chums in the city Tweedel Dumb and Tweddle Dee, I've got Stefan and Jon. Your two and my two generally buy the same amount now all those city bankers have reappeared from under their rocks. So we'll go halves based on same quantity from DDK and making sure we fucking pay. One and half to two kilo's a month that's it. You collect and pay one month and I do the next. Meet here, chop it up together but other than that, fucking done. Keep this place, make sense but sell the rest of it all down the middle."

Stevie tried to persuade him otherwise but actually made sense and although he worried about how reliable Craig was, it seemed stupid to dissolve the good thing they had going on. They could never continue going to DDK separately, they liked to deal in weight, they would just replace them and neither wanted to receive a leaving card like the one Connor had received.

They thrashed out an agreement over a couple of hours ending on a handshake. Seemingly the end of their partnership and friendship. They would continue dealing; Stevie would sell to London, Ruby and Christiano and Craig to Stefan and Jon. Stevie was clear with Craig he needed to pay, he said did not care if he stuck half of it up his nose or sucked it from a pipe, he had to pay or they would be on the receiving end of Skully's wrath at the eager hands of Kaiser. Craig nodded away like a dog.

Within three weeks they dissolved all the property businesses, with Alison buying them both out, the salon now completely straight and legitimate. There was a fire sale of their three London rental properties selling for nearly 20% less than the original purchase price. This may not have seemed much to the outside eye but they had pumped a huge amount of unwashed cash into these properties, installing the best materials, technology and fittings. That together with money invested with Nathaniel Gray meant they had lost over an eye watering £5 million in little under 2 years.

CHAPTER 15

South Downs

An 999 emergency call was received requesting an ambulance at an address in the Kempton district of Brighton. When the paramedics arrived they found the front door open, and in the sitting room were 11 men and women naked and unconscious. On the coffee table was two large dildos, a glass butt plug, a loaded handgun, two bottles of GHB and a small mound of cocaine. A girl was dead, all others in bad way and were rushed to hospital. Craig hung up the phone breathing heavy leaning against the plexi-glass side of the phone box oblivious to the smell of stale piss within.

Earlier he had come around after a three-day binge, culminating in what the locals called a 'slamming party' involving huge amounts of Viagra, cocaine, meth and GHB in a weekend-long sex and drugs marathon. Many had been knocked out cold at some point by the GHB, most underestimating its effects when mixed with alcohol.

Craig woke in his usual state, not knowing where he was, what he had done or who he was with but was instantly disturbed by the eerie silence in the room. A bright sliver of light between the drawn curtains sliced a cut through the dusty hot room. His heart jumped with panic as he gingerly touched the girl on the sofa next to him, recoiling in horror upon feeling the cold embrace of death on her skin. Without checking the others, fearing everyone was dead and with his brain pounding in his skull, he fled the scene, pausing to make the call a couple of streets away.

He walked to the beach now brimming with locals, tourists and day trippers alike. The abstract normality of their lives, parents pushing children in buggies, elderly couples taking in the view whilst licking overpriced ice creams, made his paranoia and sense of desolation bubble up within. He tried to remember the events of the weekend but he could not. His brain too slow and fucked. He could hardly remember the sessions anymore, the parties, the bullshit slurring from his mouth, the people he met, the places he went, nothing, it was all a blank. He shivered as he vaguely recollected being viciously fucked in the arse by a leather clad bearded bloke. Craig thought he was what they call a bear. He recalled being face down over the arm of a sofa but he was so wasted he could not do much to resist against the assault which may or may not have been consensual.

"Hmmm, when in Rome" he half-heartedly joked to himself but the vague memory made his heart thump in his chest, which in turn made his brain throb and pound in unison. He crossed the promenade onto the beach before stripping off his clothes to his underpants. Diving into the cold water made him gasp but it felt good, willing the cold seawater to wash away his sins, his addictions and vices. After a few minutes he returned to his pile of clothes shivering as he tried to brush the cold water from his skin with his hands. He pulled on his grimy stained t-shirt and jeans, feeling a little better and once again for probably the 500th time vowed to get clean. But it wasn't just about getting clean, he needed to repair the damage done. To his family, with Stacey, with Stevie.

Stevie. Fuck.

A few weeks ago back in London, Craig picked up the gear from DDK, a tall light skinned black fella on the DLR, he looked a little bit like The Judge. Five fucking kilo's. Craig knew he was not going back to Trentstone Towers where Stevie would be waiting. He headed to Blackfriars buying a first class ticket to Brighton.

"When actually was that?" he pondered as the guilt he was feeling was gradually being replaced by a gnawing sensation in the pit of his stomach. Cooo-eeee. Crack was calling. Just a whisper at the moment not a shout but it was calling alright.

He looked far out to sea as his thoughts turned from Stevie to

Stacey and that beautiful house they had once shared. It should have been perfect. But oh how he had fucked up that one as well. He turned the house into his own private party den. That cellar tailor-made for sessions but the location was not. Too far out in the sticks. That was why Brighton is where it's at. Stacey had been scared off alright. Could not handle it.

He felt sorry for her, all that effort on the house only to be invaded by a load of drugged up tearaways.

"She is better off without me and she now owns the yard lock stock. Gave her a good price to buy me out. Wonder how much I have left of that in my bank. Not much. Have a stash of cash plus a bit of gear. Need to pay DDK. They will be looking. Wonder if somehow Stevie paid them. Hope Stevie boy is okay. But fuck him, always lands on his feet. Need to get clean. Clean."

He reached into his pocket pulling a cigarette packet out, taking one between his lips he lit it with a yellow lighter. Holding the cigarette packet in his left hand he felt a small lump inside the cellophane wrapping.

"Oh hello!" he whispered rubbing the baggy containing around two grams of crack. Dark thoughts instantly began to permeate in his mind as the gnawing in his gut increased in intensity, his arms and back becoming alive and itchy. The thoughts of going straight, getting clean were briskly swept aside as he began to twitch and sweat despite the cold sea water still dripping from his hair and skin.

He looked up out to sea and inhaled the cigarette smoke deep into his lungs.

"No, no, no fucking chance, that's fucking it, no fucking more, none of this bullshit" he muttered, clenching his fists and digging his heels deep into the smooth pebbles.

He smoked the Marlboro until the foam filter collapsed between his fingers before instantly lighting another. A young couple, probably London professionals, with their little girl ran down the steep tiered slopes of the beach before setting up camp for a day.

"Oh just fuck off, will you" he growled darkly under his breath.

"Just fucking leave me the fuck alone."

He rubbed the lump of crack again through the plastic with his thumb. His firm steadfast declaration of sobriety began to wilt under the physical and psychological pressure of withdrawal. His body began craving the drug as the minutes ticked by, his right arm began to itch feeling his skin beginning to crawl as though tiny minuscule bugs were moving just under the top layer of his flesh. He breathed out long and slow as he tried to combat his body's yearning for the yellowy white rocks in his palm. He stood up breathing in and out but the feeling in his right arm was now building in his left, slowly seeping into his hands, the crawling bugs darting towards his wrists.

"No, no get away" he shouted as the parents twenty metres away looked over, concerned at the wellbeing of their daughter playing with pebbles and shells nearby. He glared over at them as he squeezed his hands together and punched his upper thighs to try and rid himself of the bastard skin insects.

He moved away along the beach past the new pier and onwards towards what was left of the old pier, now just a skeletal structure a few hundred metres out in the sea. He eyed up a discarded diet coke can before sitting down at the bottom of one of the natural tiers of the beach, out of sight of the main road. He bent the lower section of the can inward, creating a crease to lay those precious rocks. He reached into his back pocket for his Swiss army knife, he pulled out the small sharp pointed blade and carefully punctured the tin along the crease, making sure there were only the smallest of holes. He sparked another cigarette more out of necessity than desire tapping the ash into the crease creating a cosy bed for the crack. A gust of wind swept in from the sea blowing the ash up into his face.

"Fucking, fuck cunt!" he grimaced in panic as the insects burrowed and turned in his flesh once again. Taking a huge pull on the cigarette he laid the bed of ash down again. He pulled his knees up to his chest trapping the can between his chest and thighs whilst he retrieved the rock from the baggy. He broke it up between his grimy black fingernails carefully laying it out on the ash, careful not to drop any as it would be lost forever amongst the pebbles. Ideally he would have liked to cover his head with his coat to ward off any wind or prying eyes but he was not in the mood. He needed to get it done. He exhaled before lifting

the can to his lips, not caring whose mouth had been there before, sparking the lighter, the flame hovering above the crack. He
sucked long and slow but hard enough for the flame to be pulled
downwards against the rocks. The bitter taste the crack fumes
greedily being drawn into his lungs was delicious. He kept going,
the rocks now glowing a luscious red and white under the flame
as his lungs filled with the noxious lovely smoke. He stopped.

A million little firecrackers set off, little sparks exploding in his
head as he finally exhaled slowly. The insects instantly stopped
squirming as his heart thudded a loud rhythmic drum beat in
his chest. He ground his teeth as a wave rose up in his chest. He
quickly lit the remaining ash again sucking on the minimal resi-
due, not much there, always the consummate pro, he had done an
excellent job on the first pass.

"Mmmmmm fucking get in there sarn, whhoooh, mmmm that's
it. That's it!" he yelled.

He felt like he was instantly back in the game.

"Shit happens. Come on, let's get sorted and let's get back on the
horse and in the race."

He smoked another cigarette looking out to sea and began making
plans to get himself sorted. He was going clean up his act, make
peace and pay back all the money he owed to DDK and/or his old-
est best pal Stevie, hook up with the crew from Woodbridge, get
back together with Stacey and get himself sorted.

He stood, throwing the can on the floor, made a move to walk
off, went back retrieved it before walking towards the main road
running up into town. He never made it off the beach, the remaining rock of crack serenaded him calling his name. He sat and
again fired into the other rock. He now walked at pace up into
town, muttering to himself, his eyes wide and bloodshot, talking
to himself as the crowds began to close in and surround him. The
paranoia thumped in his chest. Every-fucking-one-of-these-fuck-
ing-cunts was looking and talking about him. He barked at people
simply going about their business, just in town for a spot of shopping. They all swerved away as he staggered and jabbered towards
them. Parents steered their kids away from the wide eyed lunatic.
Husbands held their wives tighter as Craig veered and ranted. He
finally flipped, freaking out in panic grabbing hold of a lamppost,

clinging to it for dear life. He held on tight, lashing out, kicking and punching at anyone who came near. If he let go he was sure they were going to get him, swarm him, claw at him, lynch him, destroy him.

He slid onto to his knees babbling like crazy, his arms still firmly wrapped around the steel post. Yet through his crazed mind he somehow saw sense.

"What the fuck are you doing? You are going to get nicked in a minute and you will get implicated in that sex death. Get the fuck out of here. Get the fuck out of here now."

If he did not need any more encouragement, he spotted a Policeman walking up the street. Craig bolted away, off and down the Lanes, the jewellery quarter, barging people out of the way as he went. He crossed the park near the Brighton pavilion. He walked up Carlton Hill and onto Mount Pleasant where each of the houses was painted a different colour, a symbol and beacon of the vibrant gay community. At the top of the rainbow coloured road in a basement flat lived his old party partner and one-time superstar DJ, Stefan Stockdale.

Craig recalled he had been around at the start of the weekend but had disappeared at some point, but he was not sure when or where or who with. Craig's head was a mess; psychosis had settled in as he twitched and jerked his body towards Stefan's flat. He had to get off the street knowing what he needed and that Stefan would be obliging, maybe. He wrapped his knuckles on the old wooden door but there was no answer. He knew he would be in; he always was these days but it would be difficult to raise him from his pit. He tried again and again until he simply kicked the door in. It was barely secured anyway, and it gave way easily. There were a couple of people asleep, a girl on a chair, a bloke on the sofa, both out of it and comatose. It was a one bedroom flat and the main bedroom was downstairs in the basement. He walked down, the stench hitting him immediately. On the main wall was a huge damp patch where the cellar room had not been tanked in properly. There was a huge super king-size bed that took up most of the room and on it Stefan and a rough looking blonde woman who looked about fifty were asleep.

"Should have got East Side Gallery Property Ltd in to do that job you tight cunt" he shouted trying to wake him but Stefan did not move from his slumber.

Craig went to the bedside cabinet on Stefan's side, there was an old tuna tin can used as an ashtray. He pulled open the drawer finding a little teak wooden box well-oiled and shiny to the touch. He took it out before heading upstairs eager to get away from the smell but most importantly the accusations of theft if Stefan ever woke up.

In the living room on the floor was a cushion from Thailand that unfolded to about six foot with a triangular head pillow, a prized asset for anyone returning from the orient. It was perfect for computer gaming but even better for smoking brown.

He set up on the floor and opened the box. Contained within was a layer of foil, a McDonald's straw cut in half, a syringe, a zippo lighter and a paper wrap half full of heroin. He needed to get smacked out, to stop the clogs of insanity turning in his mind as the three days of sleep deprivation and a barrow load of drugs tried to push him ever closer over the edge. Stop the skin ants that again began to sporadically appear and twitch in his arms. He looked at the needle. Again, a voice appeared through the crazy red haze that flooded his mind, it was the voice of reason, the voice of Stevie. He had never mainlined anything, he always thought he might kill himself. So he discarded the syringe throwing it towards the kitchen, hearing it clatter near the overflowing sink full of dirty pans and plates before pulling out the foil. Folding it he made a little trench, similar to what he did with the crack before, but no holes or ash and this time sprinkling a line of the brown opiate in its place.

He looked over at the girl asleep on the chair, she was slightly gothic looking, young with black jeans tight on her legs that stretched out down onto the floor. He could make out the slight bulge and curves between her legs. He looked at the man asleep, then down at the smack and back at her. Grim thoughts percolated again.

"Best way to get kip is to shoot yer load!"

It was an age-old mantra, if you've been on the class A's knock one out before bedtime. His cock began to twitch in a semi state of arousal as the remnants of the Viagra tabs necked over the weekend signalled their presence in his groin.

He sneered as he pressed his semi through his trousers. He stood creeping forwards before peering down to assess in more detail.

"Pretty"

"Dirty goth slut"

"Bet she fucking loves it, fucking dirty fucking whore. Getting fucked by all sorts in Kemptown, queers, straights, trannies anyone is fucking game, fucking slag."

He looked over at the man on the sofa, vaguely wandering if it was her boyfriend. He did not really fucking care either way. He looked down rubbing her hair softly and he thought he heard a little groan and smile in the corner of her dark lipsticked mouth.

"Yes fucking well game this one."

He unbuttoned his jeans and pulled down his trousers releasing his penis, it sprang out and stood to attention, rigid and strong. He had not showered or washed in three days and the stench of his balls wafted up making him grimace. He wanked his cock in her face whilst rubbing her through her jeans. She was out cold, maybe on smack, whatever it was she was not responding, and all the better for him.

"Fucking good, don't want to fucking talk anyway."

He started tapping her on the head with the head of his penis as he masturbated. With his right hand he unbuttoned her jeans, revealing white knickers in stark contrast to the rest of her dark clothing. He stopped rubbing himself and pulled her jeans and knickers down just below her knees. He looked up at her face as he did. Still nothing.

"She's putting it on, she fucking pretending to be a asleep. She fucking loves it!"

He resumed his previous position wanking in her face but now he pawed at her crotch. The insects appeared again in earnest under his skin, his arms began to itch. It felt like there was grain and gravel building up and trying to push through his veins.

"Fuck, running out of time, the ants are fucking coming to get me, need to fucking shoot my load" he thought as he knuckled down and started wanking furiously. He swapped hands and went for it as he stared at her, gritting his teeth.

"Eeergh, erggh.........."

He came right on top of her head, right where the hair parted. It was not much, no super porn star climax that shot through the air. It kind of burped out the end, just a small blob. He barely felt his climax through the pain building in his head and arms.

"What the fuck are you doing?" yelped a high-pitched voice from across the room as Craig was brought out of his filth and drug clogged world back to reality. The man who was asleep on the sofa had been woken up by Craig's antics.

"That's my fucking girlfriend you fucking pervert!" he shouted scrambling to his feet pointing in accusation.

"What does it fucking look like, I am fucking having a wank over your creepy looking bird you fucking clown. What's your fucking problem anyway, it's not like I am fucking her is it?" Craig responded angrily as though he were the wronged party.

At this point the girl woke up face to face with a dripping, smelly semi hard penis. She screamed as she realised her knickers were around her knees. The man took a step towards Craig who instantly backhanded him across the face with his seed covered right hand. It was not like a bitch slap as he kept his fist enclosed and it knocked him flying backwards. This gave the girl the chance to jump up, pulling up her jeans and run to the door, dragging her stricken boyfriend with her, both completely oblivious to the clump of jizz on her head and his cheek. Craig ran to the door bellowing insults at them as they rapidly made their way down the street.

"Yeah that's it you fucking fucks, take your fucking pencil dicked boyfriend with ya you slag, don't you remember you asked me to fuck you, you filthy fucking stop out, remember that if you fancy calling it in you fucking skanky cunt."

The couple were an instant distant memory as the insects were now in his fists and he punched the open palm of his other hand over and over again. Yelping, he returned to the living room noticing the now vacant sofa. He put the wooden box on the coffee table and set himself up for a big brown hit. Before he did he found a piece of paper.

"Stefan - Please don't wake me, I am fucked and need some time out.

*Soz I pinched your bits and bobs, really needed it, cash in my pocket
(maybe). Only wake me if I am choking on my puke.*

Love ya

Craig x

P.S Don't let your grandmother in there suck me off."

He tried to laugh at his wit but was going down into a hole
quickly, half considering going into Stefan's room to hunt for
some powder or rock but decided to hit the H. He lifted the foil
lighting the zippo underneath the smack filled trench. It began
to smoke, emitting a small thin wisp that floated upward. He put
the straw in his mouth and, just as he had done with the crack,
took a long exhale before slowly sucking the smoke into his lungs
moving the flame along the underside of the foil. The smack
jumped and crackled under the heat as he sucked it all up deep
into his lungs. He held it in as long as he could. This time there
were no fireworks. No grand entrance. Fuck no. The opiate high
slower than the crack hit, it seemed to start in his knees, gradually rising up his body in long rippling waves. Very different to
the quick short sharp slap to the head of crack. Subtle. Different
sure. Not as nice as crack but nice enough.

"Smack is the lady, crack is the whore" he muttered as the warm
glow reached his chest. A wave of nausea hit him and he jumped
up from the sofa but did it far too quickly making his head spin,
he lost balance crashing into the wall next to the front door. He
would never make it to the toilet or sink so he puked there on the
carpet. There was not much in his stomach anyway, mostly thick
bubbly bile. He tried to think of the last time he ate but could not
remember. Maybe half a Twix. Could not manage a fucking whole
one though.

The smack did its job beautifully as he staggered back to the sofa;
it massaged his shoulders flooding his brain with a tonic that
seemed to batter down and dilute the crazy thoughts that began
to slow, now only sporadically popping up. A moment ago his
brain was whirring at a million miles an hour, the cogs turning
fast but it was like someone had taken their foot off the pedal.
The insects and gravel were still in his arms but they seemed to
have been picked up and washed around in a syrupy gloop.

He pinned the note to himself and crashed backwards looking at the ceiling, the swirling artex looking like a Michelangelo mural. He sat like this for ages, his brain having a one hell of a fight; crack versus smack, up versus down, Jing versus Yang. He was like a referee clothed in black, whistle in mouth checking for signs of foul play. But he could not really do anything about it, simply a bystander witnessing the war of attrition between the two sides of narcotics. It made him laugh a little as he watched the uppers and downers jostling for position in his cortex.

An hour or two passed. He felt himself going, the smack fug flooding his brain, sending him off into unconsciousness but he wanted to be sure and with a great deal of effort he pulled himself up readying himself for another hit. With eyelids half shut he sucked the smack down into his lungs again and thought of the dead girl a few streets away, probably in the morgue now. He did not know who she was or where she was from. As he wondered about their family and friends, a tear began to appear in his eye bubbling up but not enough to cascade down his cheek. He flopped back on to the sofa pulling his heavy legs up. He closed his eyes as the heady combination of fatigue, grief, guilt and heroin washed over him mercilessly taking him away.

CHAPTER 16

Royal Befokeng

Stacey stayed over at her friends small flat on the Friday night located on the outer edges of the exclusive St Katherine's Dock by Tower Bridge. They went out for a meal at a new Indonesian restaurant near Brick Lane and caught up, having not seen each other for months. Her friend was an old acquaintance from the modelling days, pretty but not pretty enough so became a legs model. At over six foot her pins were amazing, going on forever from the slim ankles all the way up to the near perfect posterior.

For Stacey it had been good to get out of the house. It was lonely. Craig had long since left after paying her off over a year ago. Shit, what a relief that had been. He had nearly trashed the house she had worked so hard for. She had found it, designed it and built it so felt it was more hers even though Craig, through his ill-gotten gains, had paid for most of it. It had been over between them long before this and they both realised this was the case. As the drugs took hold and without the house project to bind them together he had become increasingly obnoxious and rude to her, acting like a complete slob around the house before effectively moving into the basement where he would sniff, drink, smoke and god knows what else. Yet it was not just Craig, the seemingly never-ending stream of lowlifes that appeared at all hours, never far away, leeching onto him, constantly hanging around. She even found one of them upstairs lurking in her en-suite bathroom when Craig was not even in. She was sure he was up to something, looking for something to steal but she could not be sure. He shiftily apologised muttering something about a toilet being blocked. She checked later on that day and all toilets were fine. Craig deteriorated physically, seemingly living off nothing but turkey mince wraps, not a vegetable in sight. Just that, cocaine and alcohol. His drug dealing and drug use was obvious. The constant drip dripping and sniff, sniffing, with one of his eyes seemed to have lost connection with the other.

She had been miserable and scared. Another gripe was she never saw the old Woodbridge, in particular Stevie. She had always liked him, made her laugh and was a good influence on Craig but it seemed like he had also given up on him. She had spoken to him on the phone a couple of times when he was trying to get hold of Craig. It was obvious they had had a big falling out but did not want to ask or pry. She recalled on the last occasion she told Craig that Stevie had called he had grabbed her and screamed at her never to speak to Stevie again and if she ever breathed a word about him or anything, he was up to she was dead. Later in the day he had come grovelling back to her bursting out crying and blubbered how sorry he was, how her loved her and Stevie. The next day he was back to his usual routine, staying up all night, going out returning days later looking completely fucked, acting twitchy and incoherent blaming his mates and trying to laugh it off as a cheeky little party. All bollocks.

It was not long before he came to her offering her the house in exchange for £250k, which she negotiated down to £235k. After visiting the solicitors to sign the paperwork Craig disappeared from her life. It felt like a weight had been lifted but not before changing the locks and putting in a new security system. Just in case.

On that bright summer morning in London, Craig rung her completely out of the blue. He started talking to her as though they were great mates who have not spoken for a while.

"Hello sweetheart, how's it going, sorry haven't called in a while been working on a project on the south coast. Anyway listen all the old Woodbridge lot are meeting up tonight, Stevie, Tanner, China, everyone. We are going to The Globe in Baker Street to watch the footie if you fancy it."

"Err yeah could be fun, I suppose?" she grimaced in reply not really sure what to make of the surprise phone call. He sounded hyper and manic.

"You at our house?"

"My house. You sold your share remember?"

"Yeah I know, old habits eh?"

"Whatever. Not there at the moment heading back in a bit."

"I will get Stevie to pick you up. Spoke to him earlier and he is going to be in Woodbridge with his parents. He is driving down into town later, maybe with a few of the lads, he can pop by and get you if you like."

"Yeah okay, can you let me know what time, don't want to be late and get in the way of the boys and their beloved football."

"Ha ha, it's okay, the game is not on until late but I think everyone wants to get down their early to get a spot. Alright text ya later babe."

"Alright, see you later" she replied cautiously as she cringed at the word 'babe'.

"Ciao."

Stacey started at her phone. If it was just an invite for her and Craig she would have declined but the thought of seeing all the Woodbridge crowd and in particular Stevie intrigued and excited her.

It was the 2010 World Cup and England was, as usual, going football crazy with the false sense of hope that the national team might actually do well in the tournament. Hundreds of cars and houses sporting the St George's flag up and down the country. Stacey generally disliked football. She quite liked the game, it was fast, exciting and full of skill and appreciated the likes of David Beckham for obvious reasons but she hated football fans who would turn from one minute to be fairly nice rounded individuals to complete idiots the next.

The one time she loved football though was when she was abroad. She could not put her finger on why exactly but she loved going to pubs and restaurants in foreign countries always knowing there would be a few English lads watching. She could quite happily sit and watch football for hours in warmer climates and have a few pints, her muck mouth often kicking in joining in the raucous behaviour, something she would never do it on English soil. Except boxing. Boxing was a different matter, she would go fucking bananas if there was a decent fight with a home grown fighter in the ring.

The World Cup was in South Africa meaning excellent viewing times in England and the match that evening was no exception. England were playing the USA in their first group game, the team managed by the Italian Capello. It was their first big tournament in four years after the humiliation of not qualifying for the European championships under the dubious stewardship of Steve Maclaren, now known as the *'Wally with the Brolly'*, after foolishly standing on the side lines on a rainy night with an umbrella as England were dumped out the competition by Croatia.

England were tipped to win the group consisting of the USA, Algeria and Slovenia. Although the Americans had a fairly decent squad, nothing compared to the big-name players of Wayne Rooney and Steven Gerrard. So English football fans were going into the tournament with confidence and a Saturday night out was just what was needed.

Stacey had not been out with the Woodbridge lads for a long time. She liked Craig's old friends like China and Tanner. And then there was Stevie.

"Craig had spoken as though they were still friends. Maybe they had made up?"

She recalled the look Stevie gave her at that wedding, recalling it made her stomach flutter a little. There was something there, something about that boy that intrigued her but had never had the opportunity to explore further. After the wedding he never seemed to be about much and when she did see or speak to him he was always abrupt. Maybe a couple of pleasantries and small talk but that would be it, he more or less blanked her. Odd. When they had all been out together he kept his distance but she could always feel a vibe coming off him and she had caught him looking in her direction on more than one occasion.

So tonight would be interesting. She secretly hoped Stevie would pick her up on his own. Unlikely as he would probably be taking some of his mates down to London from Woodbridge. She felt a little excited, another sensation of butterflies in her stomach. She was due to have lunch with her friend but decided to get back to her house and get ready for the evening.

CHAPTER 17

Low Rider

S tevie was at home in Hampstead, North West London. Stressed. Rattling around the house clasping his mobile phone in hand willing for the fucking thing to ring. He dialled Craig's number for what felt like the 100th time in a matter of days and again infuriatingly it went straight to voice-mail. He had already left several messages and was not going to leave another one. Like he often did in times of stress or when he needed to think, to plan, he went for a run.

He pulled on his running gear, black shorts, long enough to cover his skinny thighs but short enough to allow for his half decent gait, a running vest before finally tying up his aqua blue Asics trainers. Taking the brass front door key off his car keys he punched in the security code on the alarm system before stepping outside nervously. He locked the front door and carefully inspected the wood around the small glass panel in the door. Damp had penetrated behind the wood during winter and he had spent a good few hours sanding it down before repainting it. He had used a light duck egg blue that contrasted nicely with the light beige brickwork. He leant against the house stretching his calf muscles out and completing a couple of torso rotations before turning right from his house running up towards Wells Walk.

Kaiser was sat low in the seat of a silver Mercedes C Class parked up the road. He was hoping that Stevie would stash his front door key under a plant pot or a doormat but he saw Stevie slide the key into a small Velcro pocket in his shorts in the small of his back. For the first time ever Stevie and Craig were late in paying. Skully had sent him round to take a look, not to take any action, just have a look, and make sure they were still living where they were meant to be living. He was to report back, nothing more. He did have something to report, Craig had gone to ground. Disappeared. With the gear?

Maybe. Maybe Craig had sold it and done a runner with the money. Unlikely, the powder had a hold of Craig so Kaiser had been told. Either way Craig was in the wind which left poor old Stevie solely responsible for the debt. The next visit might entail a little more action thought Kaiser excitedly as he watched Stevie run up the road away from him. He would thoroughly enjoy giving this smarmy privileged white kid a good hiding. Before leaving he called a DDK associate to take over surveillance duties for the rest of the day.

Stevie always started very slow, a bimble he called it, for the first kilometre warming up sufficiently before he opened up his stride and locked into his rhythm. A rhythm that was now ingrained in his body. He could run 5k in 22 minutes dead each and every time without looking at a stopwatch. He ran past his local, the Wells Tavern, a great little local pub that he often frequented. It was decked out in St George's flags. It did not usually show football matches but as the World Cup was on the BBC all the pubs in the UK did not have to pay anything extra. Every drinking establishment in the country was taking advantage of the extra business especially if England qualified through the group stages and into the knockouts. The landlord was out front, up early having a cup of tea and a cigarette as he read the back pages of the newspaper in the sunshine.

"Morning Joe, what's our chance then?" yelled Stevie as he bounded past.

"A bloody eye-tie manager and a bunch of overpaid pampered prima-donnas, what could go wrong?"

As he ran on, picking up speed, he turned his thoughts to Craig. Three weeks ago, he had picked up the monthly consignment. Stevie and Craig had begun to use social media to subtly inform each other of whereabouts and progress, a 'like' on a certain ob-scure social media post meant he had picked up the gear and was ready to meet at Trentstone Towers.

Stevie had cycled to the Towers, using a variety of routes on canal paths, main and back roads whilst constantly checking he was not being followed as per agreed protocols. All in order to keep the safe-house safe from the prying eyes of the Police and DDK. He had waited in the flat for over 3 hours and Craig had not shown up. Stevie became more nervous as time went on but refrained from calling his mobile just in case, again as per protocol. He would have to wait a further 4 days before calling the next number in the line of phones that were routinely changed.

It had been 3 weeks now and nothing. Stevie had failed to track him down despite numerous calls to associates, past and present. He knew he had not been nicked as he would have had a call from a lawyer, again, as protocol. He had disappeared along with what he believed to be 2 kilos of cocaine. Stevie then had to let Christiano know he could not deliver an order, which resulted in an ear full of abuse down the phone.

He ended up putting in an emergency request from Skully. Stevie then found out the true depths of Craig treachery. He had done a runner with 5 kilos not 2.

"Business must be good. Five big ones a while back now another two! Good boys."

As the words hit home Stevie froze. Stunned. 5 fucking keys. The fucking stupid, stupid cunt. Stevie recovered not letting Skully know what had occurred. A few days later the 2 extra kilos were delivered, Stevie picking up on the top floor of a packed London bus at eight o'clock in the morning. He then spent a frantic day cutting it up before delivering to Christiano and Ruby in West London. At least that had recouped some of the money quickly.

"Craig! Stitched up by motherfucking Craig!"

The name screamed at Stevie as he ran harder. He glanced to his right down Elgin Road seeing the huge concrete mass of Trentstone Towers looming in the distance, like a giant dystopian obelisk. He considered diverting his run to go there to check if Craig had been but there was no point so he continued southwards under the A40 Westway and past Paddington train station. He ran down to Lancaster Gate stopping twice for traffic but finally entering Hyde Park. It was busy, full of morning runners, parents with children on bikes and roller skates. Many runners disliked busy parks but Stevie loved it.

The run had the desired effect. As the sights, smells and people of London passed he had considered the DDK problem. In all likelihood Craig was gone and he could not rely on him, it was all on Stevie. DDK would want their money, this was clear. After payment Stevie suspected their arrangement would be over. They would sack him in the same way they sacked Connor.

As he opened up his stride around Hyde Park an idea bubbled up, not very original, most definately a long shot but worth investigating.

He had planned to visit his parents' in Woodbridge later that day for probably the last time. They had sold the family home in Woodbridge and were moving to Benahavis in Spain. They had purchased a small villa from one of his dad's friends at the golf club who was now too old to travel and wanted rid of it. They original price, at the height of the property boom, was worth nearly 1.5 million euros but his dad had bought it for a knock down 350,000 euros. They were a little undecided about the move but Stevie had encouraged them to go and said they could stay with him whenever they wanted to come back to the UK. Both his mum and dad worked hard all their lives and Stevie had enjoyed watching them settle into retirement, his dad playing golf 3 days a week and his mum becoming something of a half decent tennis player. They clearly did not enjoy the UK weather during winter and with no grandchildren on the horizon anytime soon there was not much reason to stay.

His idea had been sparked by another little holiday momento that was in a storage box in the loft of his parents house. This time from Thailand, this time a simple business card, not a photo. Stevie did not really need it, he could use google but as he was going to his mum and dad's in Woodbridge he would try and find it anyway.

He did one full lap of Hyde Park before heading north back to Hampstead making the total run a solid 14 miles. For the last mile or so he slowed to a light jog to warm down.

He slipped the key from his shorts and unlocked the door. He went straight to the phone. He had decided to call Skully to fess up, come clean and buy himself some time. Tell him what had happened, beg for clemency and period of grace to get the money he owed sorted out.

He, they, Craig, whatever, now owed Skully just short of £420k but he only had access to about half of that. He hoped Skully would give him time but knew he would levy a hefty interest and possibly a physical charge.

He picked up his mobile phone noticing several missed calls from an unknown number and three voicemail numbers. He rang 121. Unbelievably the voice of Craig sounded through the small speaker of the phone.

"Hello mate, it's me. Listen sorry I've not been about, err, but listen don't worry about things all is in order. All the Woodbridge lot are out tonight. Everyone is going to The Globe on Baker Street to watch the footie. I spoke to Tanner and he thought you were up in Woodbridge this afternoon at your folk's house. Listen, do me a favour, if you are up there can you pick Stacey up from her gaff. I am down in Brighton and will be up later. If that is cool, drop me a text on this number, cannot have phone on and that and we'll catch up tonight, be there about eight. Alright matey, speak to you later."

Stevie hung up fuming with rage.

"Fucking cheeky fucker, phoning me up all fucking matey matey after fucking me over."

He phoned the number but it went straight to voicemail.

"Fuck!"

He pounded up the two flights of stairs to his en-suite hitting the shower. Afterwards he cooked himself a bacon sandwich washed down with a steaming hot cup of coffee. He calmed down trying to think rationally. He had to meet Craig tonight, he had to. How else would he have a chance at getting some money off him.

His mind drifted back to the voicemail. Stacey! That little snippet of the conversation previously evaded him, his focus had been on the 5 kilo's, the debt and DDK gang members. But now Stacey was front and centre of his attention.

He stared through the back-patio doors at the small rectangular garden, he stared at nothing thinking of her. For years he had kept himself away from her for fear of building on those feelings, a slight obsession he had for her, for fear of betraying his best friend. But that reasoning which he had mulled over and over time and time again began to be diluted by Craig's attitude, behaviour and recent duplicity. He decided to pick her up and instantly was hit by nerves at the delicious thought of seeing her.

He texted Craig back and kept it polite and to the point.

"See you at pub, no problem about the lift for Stace, let her know I will be around at 7. Peace out."

Later he opened his wardrobe and selected some Diesel jeans and a long sleeved paisley slim fit shirt. He had always been a casual fan, mostly baggy, but since he hit his 30's he adopted a smarter look, no doubt the Hampstead scene had rubbed off on him. He nearly selected a Hackett linen sports jacket but that would be too much of a target for the Woodbridge boys who would rip the piss out of him solidly all night. Instead he went for a light tan brown vintage golf jacket designed by the legendary Jack Nicholas. He had picked it up at a stall at Portabello Market the year before and was precisely the right mix of smart yet informal and very retro.

As he closed the wardrobe door he caught sight of a man sat in a car down the street wearing dark glasses in a black Mitsubishi Gallant Sport. Stevie squinted at the parking permits in the window and he could not see the light purple sticker that would have indicated he was a local. He was not looking at Stevie's house, just looking down at a paper, a red top it looked like, maybe he was waiting for someone. The thing that worried Stevie was that he was black. He felt a bit ashamed of his racial stereotyping but there were not many black residents in this neck of the woods and he was now very much behind on his payments to DDK.

Was it a DDK gang member sent to take him out? Probably not, they might not get their money if they did. Maybe just keeping an eye on him or maybe warn him, rough him up a bit, give him a kicking. The nerves ratcheted up a notch. He was a passionate football fan but this was nothing to do with the impending game. This was a mix of Stacey, DDK and Craig a volatile, dangerous combination that was for sure. Unlocking his car, a silver Mercedes SL500 AMG, he sat in the driver's seat and pressed the button that retracted the roof. He smirked to himself as he recalled the first day he put the roof down. He was sat at a set of red lights and a little toe-rag on a BMX with his mates yelled "Oi mate you are a fucking faggott!"

Stevie kept an eye on the man in the car who did not look up as he sped past, making sure he gave the car some welly, the 306 horses under the hood making an echoed roar between the tightly packed houses on the street. His aggressive driving disguising the fear rising in him as he felt things were coming to a head in more ways than one.

CHAPTER 18

Been a while..

T he drive down from Woodbridge to London via the M40 was curiously silent yet not as uncomfortable as you would have imagined. The mix playing on the car stereo helped, eclectic Balearic by Ibiza veteran Jose Padilla suited the mood and time of day. As they approached the outer reaches of London Stacey glanced to her left across at a large hill with a fence running along its boundaries. Graffiti written in giant letters; WHY DO I DO THIS EVERYDAY? A hippy derived dig at the 9-5 commuters grinding their way up and down the motorway every day. Stevie smiled as he noticed her looking.

"To provide for their families to try and better themselves you dirty smelly hippy pricks. I would love to go up there and write "I don't I get the tube".

Stacey laughed agreeing although she had never been one to work regular hours.

"So I hear, more of a 11-3 eh?" teased Stevie.

"Piss off. I am a grafter me, you know."

Pulling up at his house in Hampstead he strained his neck to see if any suspected DDK were in the area. All seemed quiet so instead silently cursed the Indian doctor from a couple of houses down who always parked his BMW in *his* car parking spot outside his house.

"Nice spot, have you been living here long?" said Stacey craning her neck to get a look at the houses on either side of the street trying to guess which one was his.

"It's that one there" replied Stevie pointing towards his house.

"About 3 years ago. Was renting for a bit after living with mum and dad for far too long."

"Once a mummy boy...." she giggled.

"Yeah whatever, daddy's girl.........I've heard the stories about you as well you know! Anyway, it was cheap you know but I could not hack the commute into London from Woodbridge anymore. So eventually did the usual, you know, bought the crappest house on the best road and done it up. Fancy grabbing a quick drink before we head off?" Stevie cocked his head towards the house.

"Yeah okay, would like to check out your style, cast my professional opinion on it."

"So you've knocked the modelling on the head completely?"

"Yeah now a full-time interior designer but also do some consultancy with one of the big architecture firms in the city. Too many boys you see and more and more of the clients are female so they roll me out to help with the feminine touches."

Stevie nodded impressed with the way Stacey's life had changed since she split up with Craig.

"Yeah I am also about to launch a little side business on the web selling renovated furniture. Found this old boy, genius carpenter, I buy the stuff, he does it up and I paint it. I just go along to car boot sales or age concern and pick it up for peanuts. He does his thing repairing, sanding down and I apply some chalk paint and job done. I sell a lot to this place over in Henley, they cannot seem to get enough of it."

"Aah nice, well, you should have seen the state of this place when I bought it. See this little front area here? It was so overgrown you could barely see the front door. It was an old boy that lived here and was a bit of a hoarder; the estate agents wanted to just get rid of it and let the new tenant sort it out. Took nearly a year to get it into shape. I was half tempted to give you a call and get some professional advice."

"I wish you would have done" she replied stepping out of the car. Stevie turned.

And there it was. That thing. Something almost physical. For the first time in ten years they looked at each other again, properly face to face, no furtive glances across the room, no sneaky looks at their profile pictures on Facebook, which both had done on more than a few occasions.

Stevie melted, pure and simple. The last two hours at her house plus the drive down to Hampstead had sent him spiralling out of control with emotion, what he was not sure, pure unadulterated unfiltered SOMETHING. She stood looking at him, the rays of light from the sun highlighting and accentuating her soft featured face. She smiled awaiting a response, her white teeth gleaming as she rubbed that slightly crooked incisor with her bottom lip.

"Yeah, well, I was, errr, planning too, but you know, me and Craig had a bit of a falling out around that time so was a bit tricky, you know" he said trailing off as a silence descended between them again.

"Anyways..." he chuckled nervously as he rummaged his pockets for the keys.

"Not only was it a complete shit hole but I bought just at the wrong time. April 2007. Two months before the financial crash and within months it was worth 40% less than what I bought it for. I am playing the long game, property prices are looking a bit better these days so just need to sit it out. Right, here we are, so no criticism is too hard for me to take. Let me give you the grandiose tour."

"Here on the right is the formal sitting room."

"Hmm very nice, solid wood flooring no vinyl, tick, light pastel whites to give the room the illusion of space. I like the two seater sofa, traditional yet....." she stopped her mouth agape pointing at the plastered over fireplace.

"STEVEN!! Why did you do that? Filling in an open fireplace is a crime against humanity, plain and simple" she shrieked aghast.

"Sorry lack of cash on that one at the time. I promise I will get it sorted if it offends you that much."

"Ha ha, it does. Okay, but I will hold you to that."

"The one thing I did spend some money on though is the open plan kitchen, come this way. I ripped off the old flat roof and put in the pitch with the two big Velux windows. Removed a wall that was here and opened it up."

"Now this I do like!" she exclaimed nodding in appreciation.

"I made the kitchen into this L shape with the large island in the middle here with a new convection cooking surface, designed so the chef could either watch television mounted on the wall there or talk to guests on the sofa over there in the sitting room."

Stacey walked slowly pacing through the kitchen, opening cupboards and doors, pushing the drawers to check the slow closing mechanisms.

"I like it. Hand painted I see. Annie Sloane paint, nice. You live here with anyone?" she surreptitiously enquired trying to sound off the cuff, nonchalant in the delivery of the most important question she would ask this day, maybe this month, maybe this year. She nearly pulled it off but was a little too high pitched and her cheeks flushed with embarrassment. Stevie noted it, his heart jumping in his chest as a grin curled upwards on his lips.

"I have the occasional visitor but no I live here alone."

"You see much of the old lot?"

"No not really. I am quite busy most of the time with work but I have been going up to Woodbridge to see the folks on the odd Sunday, so I try and catch up with a few of the lads then, usually for the football. Now that mum and dad are off to Spain I doubt whether I will be going there much from now on."

"They still go to the C&C?"

"No its gone pretty downhill, bit rough now, still get a few of the same old faces down there and it is not too bad for a cheap beer but it's not the same obviously, well nothing is" he said sadly.

Stacey picked up on the vibe and changed the subject quickly.

"How far is it to The Globe pub from here?"

"Not far couple of miles. Why?"

"Can we walk rather than get the tube? It's a nice evening and I am enjoying our catch up. Also not wearing the usual high heels, went for what you would call the casual look."

Stevie looked down at her footwear, a gleaming white with blue trim pair of Adidas samba trainers with white pop socks showing off her brown ankles. He felt the urge to reach out to her, pull her close. Not now. Not yet. Maybe later. The question of reciprocation nagged at his brain. Does Stacey like Stevie after all what has happened? The signals were there, glowing throbbing but his age-old problem of confidence with the opposite sex jabbed away at him.

But it was not just that. He was enjoying himself but the impending prospect of meeting Craig made him feel nervous. He was tempted to suggest they sack The Globe off and go to the Wells Tavern down the road instead but knew he could not. He needed to see Craig, emphasise the trouble they were in and that they needed, absolutely had to pay DDK back.

"Yep that would be good we can get a couple of drinks en-route to keep us going. Shall we?" Stevie replied as they walked towards the front door.

He opened it, it was a narrow hallway and Stacey had to squeeze past Stevie to get out. He was tall, a shade under six foot four, but so was she and she looked at him as she moved past. She had a hungry look on her face, a serious stare with the faintest up-turned smile on her red glossed lips. Her left breast ever so slightly brushed his right forearm sending a shiver through their respective bodies. Again, they seemed to freeze in place, exchanging a look of pure lust and desire as the yearning for each other sparkled and burned in each other's eyes.

Then in Stevie's mind's eye the image of Connor appeared, bound to that chair as he was savagely beaten by the DDK gangsters. The electricity flex whipping across his bare skin, ripping flesh away as his colleague and friend lay metres away unconscious face down in a pool of his own blood.

"Let's go then" he said abruptly cutting off the exchange.

As he primed the alarm and locked the door, he glanced up the road towards where the suspected DDK gangster parked earlier. There was nothing but empty cars lining the road, a mix of high-end Jaguars, Audi's, Land Rovers, BMWs plus the odd small city cars; Fiat 500's and Smart cars. Purchased by the rich WAGS now thinking it's cool to go eco warrior after years of polluting London's air with their Chelsea tractors. They strolled past the Wells Tavern now packed with drinkers making the most of the late kick off for the match.

"Everyone will be well lubricated by the time it kicks off" muttered Stevie thinking about Craig and the Woodbridge associates.

"Looks like a nice pub, what's it like inside?"

"Nice, small but friendly, quite a local's pub which is a change in London. Not too many tourists and the landlord is sound, gives us a lock in every now and again."

"Too early in the journey for a quick one?"

"A little, I know a good place halfway."

"Ok, I will bow to local knowledge" said Stacey with a slight curtsey. She was also very familiar with north west London but was happy to be in Stevie's hands, who equally seemed happy being the guide.

CHAPTER 19

Jonny Wilkinson

With a due sense of dread and apprehension Scott buttoned his shirt as he readied for work. He briefly considered pulling a sickie but spending any time with Ester was not much of a better option. He glanced across the kitchen at the cold hard face of his wife. It was obvious she could not bear to be around him anymore and the feeling was ever so slowly beginning to feel mutual. He had made a promise to himself though, to continue to work at their relationship, mend and flex to her will yet try and be courageous and put his point of view across, all for the sake of his two girls.

The twins were growing up fast, both now six years old and at primary school, finally out of nursery. He no longer had to pay the extortionate fees, nearly on a par with the fucking mortgage payment. He tried to persuade Ester that cheaper childcare was an option but she refused point blank. Most of the anti-natal group parents sent their kids to the expensive place so that was that, end of discussion. He had to be honest with himself, the nursery was class and the kids enjoyed their time there immensely; a huge converted house with big grounds and even an indoor swimming pool where the kids had lessons, all at an extra cost of course. Yet the £80-day rate had put him further into the financial mire. The one small victory he had with his wife was not placing the children on of the day Ester did not work. It had been a battle but he had stuck to his guns, the extra £350 a month was simply not feasible.

He knotted his tie thinking about the alternative to staying at home with the fire breathing dragon; going to work. Fuck. As appealing as a cold sore. Relations with his line manager, Rhys, had hit rock bottom resulting in open warfare between the two. It had come to a head earlier in the year at Scott's annual appraisal. The outcome of the review directly impacting Scott's bonus, which he relied on heavily to chip away at some of the credit card balances. He had always been careful with money and was proud of never having an overdraft on his bank account or missing a payment but that all changed since having kids and a materialistic wife. He could not completely blame her in trying to 'keep up with the Jones's'; there was quite a bit of pressure within her new peer group but she had ended up throwing all common and financial sense out of the window.

"It's what everyone does, everyone has debts, its normal" she would often cite. His response about that very concept causing the financial crisis in 2007 fell on deaf ears. Everyone in British society seemed to be continually saddling themselves with more and more debt, expensive mediocre houses, bigger mediocre houses, new cars, more powerful cars, it was endless. The amazing thing was the banks were not restricting or questioning it, they seemed to approve all applications as long as you had an income. So that is what Scott reluctantly did as well, the biggest hit being the extension that required a re-mortgage. The costs overrun and Scott found himself applying for every credit card under the sun to get it finished. He was sure the builder stitched him up a few grand but once they started they could not stop. Luckily, all the credit cards had long 0% terms but there would come a point where they were finished and he would start to incur the dreaded 18% interest. The annual bonus, if decent, would make a bit of a dent. But it was not to be.

"The rating I have given you for last year's performance is Under Performing" said Rhys smugly.

"Pardon me?" blurted out Scott aghast and shocked.

"Under Performing" he replied.

Scott could not hold it back.

"Are you taking the fucking piss?"

"Scott, I would prefer if you would refrain from using such language in the workplace."

"Fuck you and fuck that mate. Give me the evidence for that rating and I will accept it. However, and as per my written comments, I believe that I have met all objectives and achieved several other successes during the year. Which, I believe, warrants easily an Exceeds rating."

"Well I do not agree. I have received feedback on you from several team members, who have reservations about your performance, particularly in regard to our core values of Trust and Respect."

"What the fucking fuck are you talking about?"

"This was typical" thought Scott. There was no way that the little Welsh cunt could pin anything on him from a technical or project delivery perspective. He was one of the best engineers they had and his work top quality. No, he was going down a wholly fucking different route. Living the corporate values, diversity and inclusion, treating people with respect, health and safety behaviours, energising staff, working as one team and ethical fucking standards. Scott agreed with the majority of these areas but he had a very analytical mind. Some-fucking-times things were simply a yes or no, right or wrong.

"There have been numerous elements of feedback about your Health and Safety behaviours. For example, not working with the designated monitor screen, I have witnessed you hunched over your laptop for hours, not having breaks. This is clearly not in line with our rules regarding office safety."

"Well, excuse me for being a hard worker. Is that all you've got?"

"On another occasion I understand that you were making racist jokes. Again, clearly not allowed under our diversity policy."

Scott cracked a smile, knowing full well what he was talking about. On one of the rare occasions a few of them, including Rhys, went to the pub Scott got stuck into Rhys and provided more than a few digs in his direction. Rhys had told a fairly amusing Englishman, Irishman, Scotsman joke which had the group in fits of laughter. Yes, Rhys told a racist joke and Scott followed up with a cracker about sheep shagging, an unsubtle dig at Rhys's ancestral roots and heritage.

In the end Scott lodged a complaint with Human Resources

about the performance rating and luckily for him it was overturned and given him a *'Delivers'* rating with a slightly better performance factor that nudged his bonus up more. It was a slap in the face for Rhys meaning Scott was now firmly in his crosshairs, always looking for anything he could pin on him, but he was clever and importantly very good at his job.

Yes, Scott was not looking forward to going to work but Ester was in a mood complaining of a migraine and she could not possibly do the school run. This meant it was his responsibility to get them undressed and changed, do their hair, lunch boxes and get them in the car.

Ester was sat at the breakfast bar on a stool in her gym outfit appraising and providing a running commentary on Scott's efforts.

"I thought you had a migraine; shouldn't you be in bed?"

"It is slightly better" she replied holding a hand over her eye pulling a pained expression.

"Why have you got your gym stuff on then?"

"When it gets better I will go to the gym for my usual workout, is that okay master and commander?" she barked back at him.

He had to admit she had done a decent job in getting her weight and shape back since the kids were born, she was probably slimmer than before and she looked pretty hot. Not that Scott had had much of a chance to sample the benefits lately. He actually could not remember the last time they had sex.

"Two ponytails not one!"

"No, not those hair clips they do not match with her socks."

"Don't put their shoes on for them. They need to get the left and rights right themselves."

He finally managed to get the ensemble correct before they noisily left the house. Scott hyped the children up about the weekend by promising to come home with fish and chips.

"No vinegar daddy" pointed one of his girls, reminding him of that little mistake that had earned another bollocking from Ester for messing up the dinner.

"No vinegar indeed, sweet cheeks. That naughty woman at the fish and chip shop, how dare she accidentally put vinegar on my girls' chippies" he chirped back in mock outrage

Following the usual arguments about who was going in the front, Scott reversed out of his drive. Due to the limited amount of parking at a nearby apartment block there were several cars parked on the road and it was tricky to manoeuvre and squeeze through. He slowly and steadily drove the three miles to the school enjoying having some time with his girls singing along to the soundtrack to the latest Disney films. As was usual it was a nightmare to park at the school, every space taken up, mostly by Range Rovers and BMW X5s, making the small amount of spaces even more limited. They parked on a road a few streets away much to the chagrin of the children who moaned and groaned all the way to school. They brightened up when they saw some of their friends, locking arms and skipping merrily past the cast iron gates.

After he made sure their bags and water bottles were in the correct line, he stayed a while watching his kids run around the playground waiting for the whistle that signalled all parents had to leave. He said hello to another dad who just dropped off his girls but he was not hanging around for a chat and was straight off to work. Scott noticed he looked stressed and obviously not happy he was doing the school run. He was dressed sharp and had a huge Breatling watch on his wrist. Scott looked back at his kids, his twin girls laughing and shouting with their friends as they joined in a circle and sang a song while a single girl stood in the middle looking pleased, yet a little embarrassed.

He thought the other dad who had just left, came to their barbecue in the summer and spoke to him a bit. He was the kind of man Ester wanted him to be. A successful senior VP at a US legal firm, big house, expensive suits and a very nice-looking wife apart from that waxy too much botox sheen on her forehead. He recalled him mentioning, well bragging, he travelled all over the world on business, but he also mentioned in passing the immense amount of pressure on him, only 20 days holiday, often working 13 hour days.

Scott looked down at his old chino trousers he had bought from GAP and the cheap work shirt that lost its colour after two washes. He looked back at his girls, without them his world was nothing. It would be pure misery and if he was honest if they had no kids he and Ester would have been finished ages ago. Maybe taken the hit on the house and moved back to Woodbridge and started again. But he kept at it, all for the kids.

As he looked over at them tears welled up in his eyes, but he kept them in, interrupted their little game reminding them that mum was picking them up and received a big cuddle goodbye from both.

"Love you girls."

"Love you too dad" they sang in unison as they sometimes did.

As he walked back to his car, his mind switched, as it often did about plans and strategies to get more money at work and generally how to make home life better. He daydreamed mostly, conjuring up impossible situations like suddenly befriending a top city analyst who would drip feed him inside information about the markets enabling Scott to invest just at the right times. Buy low, sell high. He daydreamed about winning the Lottery but he mostly daydreamed about selling the flat in the Trentstone Tower in west London and pocketing the cash. He thought it was now worth about £200,000. A couple of times when he was in the area with work he drove near to the block just to have a look. As he peered up towards the flat he often wondered about Stevie and Craig. Were they in there? Probably not. Were they still selling drugs? Probably. Still doing drugs? Most likely. Craig still shagging around? Definitely. Stevie still waiting for the right girl to turn up but not actively doing anything about it? Absolutely.

He put his seat belt on and set off on the 30-minute commute to Bristol. He tuned into the local radio first to make sure there were not any traffic delays or accidents which he would need to avoid. After getting confirmation all was clear he turned over to BBC Radio 5 Live, one of his favourite stations, as it gave a nice mix of current affairs and sports news. He listened intently at the unbelievable events that were unfolding in London.

"What on earth is happening to this country?"

He arrived at work, swiping his security card at the car barrier parking towards the back, giving himself the longest walk to the office as possible; delaying the inevitable daily struggle. His work enforced a strict reverse parking policy as per its Health and

Safety guidance. It is safer when leaving in the evening when everyone is rushing to get home, less likely to hit someone. Apparently, it also assisted in not getting car jacked as muggers cannot easily jump you from behind. He still could not figure out the logic in that but could not be bothered to ever question it. Sometimes you just had to nod the head when it came to bureaucracy and rules. He pulled to a stop and began to reverse back into the space, lining up the car with the white lines painted on the car park floor, he put his left hand on the passenger arm rest to make the manoeuvre more comfortable. His eyes looked down.

"Oh fuck, oh for fucks sake!" he muttered.

In the rush to get the children out and because Ester always insisted on tidying his work rucksack away in the cupboard under the stairs every night; he had forgotten his laptop.

"*Shit here comes another bollocking from the Welsh prick*" he thought as he decided to go into the office anyway, explain and grab a quick coffee. Most of the team laughed at his forgetfulness but Rhys stood with his arms crossed.

"I take it you will work later tonight to make the time up. Go on, you better be on your way."

"Yes sir!" Scott sarcastically bellowed whilst giving him a salute as he left the office to drive back home. He could not work without his laptop; it simply was not possible anymore.

He pulled out of the office carpark, through the barriers and out onto the main road that headed out towards the motorway and back towards his home to the east. He switched channels to Talk Sport for a bit but became annoyed with the adverts clearly pitched at labourers in white vans. He switched to a decent pirate station from Bristol, it was a recording and not live but was decent enough playing deep house. He could not ever play house music in front of Ester unless it was chart based. Druggie shit she called it. Silly cunt.

He exited the motorway entering the vast red brick housing estate, their house set deep inside which always proved difficult to find for first timers. It all looked the same with only the road names and numbers the clue to location. Another black mark from Ester. He turned into his road and was pleased that most of the cars that were partially blocking him in earlier were now gone but then saw that a car was parked in his space on their drive. It was a dark green Citroen Saxo with a large 'Hacielo Spa' advertisement on the doors.

"Oh great" thought Scott.

"One of Ester's snobby fucking mates who works at the gym and spa, probably brown nosing one of the girls who dishes out the treatments, trying to get some freebies."

Well he was only grabbing his laptop so would not be required to engage in any small talk.

He pulled up a couple of houses down parking on the curb before walking to his house. As he passed he looked into the interior of the Citroen but it was spotlessly clean, no clues as to the owner. Pulling his keys from his pocket finding the long brass front door key he turned it in the lock as he entered. He was about to shout out a greeting but noticed Esters gym leggings strewn on the biscuit brown carpet, a gym top partially hanging from the stair handrail. He then heard a moan, a sound with which he was familiar, not recently but in times past. This was most definitely the sound of his wife having sex. He froze, his heart thudded in his chest announcing the unset of fear, emotion and anguish. It thumped hard in his rib cage and he felt a little sick. He was not actually too surprised but this was really happening and he grimaced at the very thought of it. He half considered sneaking back out and leaving, to go away and consider his options but knew he needed to be sure.

"She could be having a go on her favourite vibrator, the Purple Pulser I bought her from Anne Summers a couple of years ago. It could be she was having a lesbian fling with one of her posh mates, all posh birds were a bit dirty. Fuck, well, that wouldn't be so bad, could be even on for a three way. Need to check" he thought kidding himself knowing what he was about to witness and it was not going to be pretty.

He pulled out his phone pressing the camera button and switching to video. One thing that Stevie had taught him long ago was that photographic or video evidence is THE best form of evidence. Scott had tried to catch his boss Rhys out on more than one occasion by recording him but the sneaky fucker had never bit on the bait Scott had thrown at him. He crept up the stairs, stepping over another item of discarded clothing, Esters training bra. He thought it all a little stereotypical, a trail of clothes leading to the bedroom, where the husband or wife was playing away, ready to be caught.

"Doesn't just happen in the movies" Scott considered as he crept onto the landing towards the master bedroom. The noise from the bedroom grew louder as he crept closer.

"Ngggggh, nggggh, ngggggg, ohhhhhh, ohhhhhhhh"

The door to the bedroom was ajar by about ten centimetres and Scott stealthily moved ever closer finally peering through the gap.

His heart shattered into pieces as his eyes absorbed the goings on in his very own bedroom. The bedroom contained a king size double bed, Ester desperately wanted a super king; another black mark for Scott, plus some built-in wardrobes. Ester was on the floor between the bed and mirrored wardrobes bent over her backside high in the air, her head on the floor tilted to the side her cheek resting on the beige carpet. She was being vigorously fucked in the arse by an unknown assailant who had his back to Scott. He could tell he was young, brown all over without any whiteness or tan lines at all. His back smooth, hips free of sag and bulge, the glute muscles clearly visible as he pumped away. He was stood in a squatting position dunking his long penis into the stretched but well lubricated arse of his wife. Underneath, Ester was furiously rubbing her clit with her fingers.

He pulled his penis slowly out of her arsehole and stood to take a breather before reaching down placing both his hands on her backside pulling her bottom cheeks apart. Her anus gapped open as he pulled and stretched, a bright redness appearing from just below the rim before fading to black, like a well. The lad cleared his throat loudly and hacked up a ball of saliva from his throat and leant over let the thick dribble escape his mouth. It hung there for a few seconds before the weight released it from his lips and it fell into the waiting hole, it never touched the sides. The lad slapped her arse hard before resuming, ramming the full length of his penis deep into her making her gasp and moan once again.

"Ngggh, ngggggggh, oooh, ohhh"

Scott raised the phone videoing the action but this was no sleazy voyeur enjoying a hardcore peep show. Tears welled up in his eyes as he glanced across the bedroom to his bedside cabinet where a picture of his beautiful two girls sat on his lap as they celebrated his 36th birthday. He knew this was the end. The end of their family unit, this is what hurt the most of all. Not the betrayal, not the treatment this fucking cunt had dished out to him the past few years but the end of a compact family unit that would have otherwise served his little girls so well.

Ester had often called him names for not being decisive enough; gutless and spineless. Maybe she was right but now was the time to be decisive he thought as the anger began to bubble and boil up within him, building up into a crescendo as the young stud dunked, fucked, thrusted, poked, probed and plunged into his soon to be ex-wife's arsehole. Her moans and screams she was emitting together with his grunts and little comments about her being a slut, a dirty milf, seemed to propel him further towards a course of action. Ester was beginning to build into an orgasm as she clawed at her clit as the long hard cock thrust faster and deeper into her bum. Her lover began slapping her bum cheeks harder and harder, the red welts glowing ever fiercer with each contact. He stretched her arse cheeks even further apart as he rammed her hole deeper and deeper, grunting with the effort.

"Aargh yeah, arrgh" the lad began to wail as his orgasm edged ever nearer as he pumped his dick in and out of her quicker and quicker. He then let up the pace and pushed his cock slowly and deeply into her anus, all the way, balls deep for the big finish. The boy's ball bag squeezed against her bottom and Scott could clearly see the outline of his two testicles bulging in the stretched sack.

"Waaa, wooooh" Ester wailed.

Everything was building to a crescendo like a boiling whistling kettle. The blood pumped furiously in Scott's head, the rage building as he moved into the room.

Scott took one step and brought his right leg back before unleashing a kick towards his wife and her young lover. He tried to emulate one of his heroes, Jonny Wilkinson, the greatest rugby kicker ever, but this kick was not for glory, not for points, this was vengeance. Right on the laces.

The top of his foot connected with its intended targets; clit, cunt, arsehole, cock and bollocks all at the same time with a sickening force.

"Waaargh, aargh" came the combined cry.

Scott heard the bloke's dick make a cracking sound as he flew a foot into the air before standing stock still in shock before collapsing to his right onto the bed holding his groin, now a disgusting mess of blood, cum and shitty arse juice. Scott grabbed him by the hair dragging him off the bed and out of the bedroom, slamming the door shut and letting him make his escape. He did not really blame him; he probably knew Ester was married but just saw her as a randy old cougar he could bang while the poor dickless sap of a husband was at work. He probably was a gym instructor or something, probably had a few of his clients on the go at the same time. No, he blamed Ester and Ester only and so began his leaving speech.

"I knew you were having an affair long ago you stupid fucking bitch, don't you think I hadn't noticed your shaved fanny that clearly was not intended for my dick. Don't you think I hadn't noticed those little nights away with your so-called mates. This is how you fucking repay me and the girls, me working my fucking hands to the bone to try and meet your over inflated expectations of life. Well now is your opportunity to join the Chipping fucking Norton set for real, you are free to go and bag a real go-getter, a real rich guy made to measure for your needs. Sure you won't find it difficult. Not too convinced the baggage of two kids is too attractive, that plus your age, oh well you can find out. Before you start thinking of the divorce proceedings and trying to take me to the cleaners, I have full video evidence of your unreasonable behaviour and adultery right here on my phone."

She stared up at him from the floor, tears and mascara running down her face, maybe from the pain of being booted in the cunt, maybe from the realisation she had been caught out, maybe the realisation that life with Scott was actually okay, maybe not as extravagant as her friends but relatively safe and secure. Whatever it was, Scott was not interested in hearing what she had to say, he turned and left.

He walked past the Citroen still in the driveway smiling at the lad who was doubled over in pain in the driver seat, still naked. He decided to head back to Woodbridge firstly to see his mum and dad and secondly try and find his old mates Stevie and Craig, and repair some of the damage that had been done to their friendship. But first he had one other thing to attend to before he left. He started up the car, cranked the volume up on the pirate station and headed back towards his work.

CHAPTER 20

Horns of Plenty

They walked at a leisurely pace from Hampstead through Regent's Park after stopping for a couple of beers at a pub skirting Primrose Hill. Neither wanted to leave but the football and Craig awaited them with eerie expectation. Stevie thought about the potential outcomes of meeting him, the best he had the money, stashed somewhere in London or the south coast where he seemed to be holed up. If that was the case they could pay off DDK and see what happens. The worst-case scenario was that Craig did not have the money, none of it, just vague promises to pay it back. The middle ground was that he had some of the money.

Stevie had some stashed away both clean money in the bank and some dirty cash buried way out in the woods near Woodbridge, a place he used to walk the family dog, a glossy coated border collie, Sam. He died when Stevie was in Australia on holiday, following a massive heart attack just before he left. Stevie visited him at the vet the night before he flew knowing full well he would never see him again. The dog crawled out of his cage looking weak before settling into his lap, happy to see a friendly face amongst the sterile steel cages of the clinic. Stevie nailed a little wooden plaque to a tree in the woods with the words '*My Sammmy RIP*'. Unbeknown to anyone seeing this peculiar little commemoration 10 metres due north £80,000 was buried.

It would not be enough but he calculated he could keep the Hampstead house, maybe persuade Scott to sell the flat at Trentstone Towers. It would not be as painful as the fists, knifes and god knows what else DDK would administer if they did not pay. His mind wandered as he began to think about the ramifications, possibilities, trying to second guess what position, what danger Craig had put them in but it was incalculable. He would just have to wait to find out in amongst what have otherwise should be a decent reunion with his old crew from Woodbridge.

"Steven, is there anyone home" said Stacey waving her hand in front of his face.

"Sorry, I drifted off for a moment then."

"Something on your mind?" quizzed Stacey secretly hoping that it was her and only her that was occupying his thoughts.

"I have a few work issues to deal with, a couple of nasty deadlines to meet next week, that's all" he lied looking over at her as they passed near the entrance to London Zoo. A couple and their children came out, the two small girls jumping onto their scooters before whizzing past, their parents shouts to slow down and not to rush off falling on deaf ears as they laughed and raced each other down the tarmac path.

"What is it you actually do, you know your proper job in London?"

"Well basically, I am what many would call a management consultant. My area of expertise is that I help companies with all things to do with Europe. Errr, a simple example would be if one of our clients is thinking of introducing a new product into the European market then we would assist in appraising what needs to be done to meet European requirements such as labelling, safety and product conformance. We would also look at how much it costs. So, if like most companies they were manufacturing overseas, like China, then we would assess and maybe help reduce the landed costs of getting the product to and onto the European market. So we look at supply chains, terms of trade, import and export taxes, fiscal representatives, availability of free trade opportunities and licensing issues, that sort of thing."

Stevie had drifted into D&C mode, the mode that he needed to snap into whenever he walked through the glass atrium of the D&C campus, now nestled just behind Fleet Street in central London. The office on The Strand where he had originally started after blackmailing Tristram had long since been vacated, leaving the mice and rats to their own devices. The office move was just after Tristram was blown up on the bus, one of the last acts of terrorism by the IRA on the UK mainland. Tristram had remained on the books of D&C for a long time after the incident. During his recuperation the leaders of D&C assumed he would return but it soon became apparent that he would no longer be fit for a senior role in the company. They initially thought of getting rid of him on the cheap but he had a watertight partner contract, that and the potential bad publicity, meant he received a significant pay out. No one saw him again, suiting Stevie just fine. He felt no remorse, cold to it just like his drug dealing, blanking out the destruction he left in his wake. Market forces. Pure capitalism. If it was not him it would be someone else.

Stevie needed to leave drug dealing at the door to concentrate on the needs and demands of D&C. In the early days this was not possible. He was always out and about before, during and after work drumming up business in the city, forever jumping on the tube to go and have lunch or after work drinks with a potential new customer. When Ruby Edwards was at D&C they would be often found huddling in meeting rooms and coffee areas scheming away, most assumed they were busy working on client assignments but in reality they were either exchanging cash or drugs or discussing and targeting new customers. After Ruby took on most of the London distribution it became easier for Stevie to concentrate on normal work enabling him to knuckle down, it paid dividends during the crash and ensured his continued legitimate paid employment.

"Sounds interesting" replied Stacey trying not to sound as though she was lying.

"Sorry I will shut up."

"Ha ha don't apologise, better than the complete and utter bollocks that Craig used to spout. Himself, epic nights out, himself, big tunes, himself, straight twenty fours, himself and then a bit more about himself."

"He wasn't always like that" Stevie replied as he found himself reverting to type, defending his old mate, instantly hating himself and Craig for it.

The exchange made them feel uneasy both falling into an uncomfortable silence for the first time that day. As if to enforce the dark spectre of Craig that hung over them, a small thick black cloud crept towards the blazing sun in the otherwise bright blue sky, which slowly shrouded the Regents Park landscape in a gloomy darkness. A sharp cool wind whipped across the park, making Stacey cross her bare arms and shiver. Instinctively, Stevie reached around her shoulders giving her a cuddle and a small squeeze. She ducked her head into his chest and he put his head down so his chin and nose were millimetres away from her head, the odd whips of her long mousey blonde hair fluttering into his face. He breathed her in as they walked on looking like nothing more than a pair of lovers out on a romantic early evening stroll.

He willed the cloud to stay suspended in the sky to delay this first ever tender embrace, something he had been yearning for years. The sun reappeared quickly which instantly heated up the park and he released her from his light grip. He cleared his throat blushing a little at the physical contact between them both.

She giggled.

"You okay?"

"Yeah never better" he replied his smile getting wider as they looked at each other both confirming they both registered and consumed the moment. Similar to the moment outside his house an hour earlier, similar to that moment shared across the wedding table and in Stevie's case similar to the moment when he first clasped eyes on her down the C&C back in 2004. They left the park crossing over the busy Marylebone road, using the pedestrian lights, before turning right towards the pub on the opposite side of the road to the famous Madam Tussauds wax work museum.

"Never quite seen the attraction of that place, maybe to get a sense of what those that passed away looked and dressed like. But I could never get my head around why you would go and see famous people's waxworks who were still alive. Bit weird if you ask me"

"Oh I don't know" replied Stacey.

"Us little people don't often get the chance to mix with the A listers."

"Well, I think that's a good thing. Never meet your heroes that is what they say, you'll always be disappointed. My friend once met Robert De Niro he said his breath was as foul as your language when you get pissed up."

"You remember my nickname then?"

"Sewer mouth isn't it?"

"No you cheeky shit, it is actually muck mouth don't you know!" she giggled feigning a posh accent, laughing, landing a punch on his right arm.

"Okay well I will look forward to hearing you curse later."

"Hmm well I am not feeling in the mood for drinking to be fair, bit nervous about seeing Craig."

"I know what you mean."

The Globe came into view, the pavement outside full of football fans drinking enjoying the last slivers of sunshine and beer on offer before kick-off.

"Oi oi Stevie boy!!!!" came a cry from in amongst the crowd as they approached.

Stevie craned his neck as China emerged from the crowd draped in replica England football top, jeans and Adidas Beckenbauer trainers. Grinning from ear to ear, an obligatory pint of lager in hand.

"Hello fella, been a while. You well?" he yelped excitedly pumping his hand and cuddling him in greeting.

"Not bad China, not bad, you?"

"Alright Stace, what's happening?" he said kissing her on the cheek and giving her a squeeze.

"Hi China, your looking well, you been working out?" smiled Stacey squeezing his bicep in response.

"A little. Thank you for noticing, you know trying to keep the wolf from the door and all that" he replied slapping his belly vigorously.

"Who is here then?" enquired Stevie breathing in deeply keeping his nerves in check.

"Pretty much everyone, well everyone who is left in the area anyway. Baggins, Tanner, Shrub, Bedswell, Pukka, Pratty, Walker,

Allcock, Shaw, Ollie and Ellie, Allers, Silver Fox, Disco Stu, Wax, Elmo, Ewan, Bennie Wilcox, Chippie, Weak Bitch, Pollard, Derek Cheesemouse, Weldon....."

"Jon Weldon" thought Stevie darkly.

"Fucking Jon Weldon."

Stevie had never got on with him but knew Craig had in all probability ratcheted up the beef. Stevie imagined the conversation as they huddled over a bag of powder and rocks.

"Stevie is nothing but a cunt trying to push us out, he does not see Thames Valley as a priority, nothing compares to his snobby fucking London mates and thinks you lot are just a bunch of towny bumpkins. Don't trust him, watch him. He's a sneaky fucker..."

As they walked through the crowd his suspicions were confirmed as Jon raised his head spotting Stevie before looking down into his pint ignoring him. A subtle slight told Stevie all he needed to know.

"Look who I found loitering with intent" shouted China resulting in cheers and warm greetings from the other Woodbridge lads and girls.

"Alright Jon, how's tricks?" said Stevie with only the slightest hint of warmth in his voice.

"Not bad son, not bad. Keeping the head above the water, tough times though you know, tough times" replied Weldon holding his gaze.

"Where's Craig?" Stevie replied bluntly.

"No idea" Jon shrugged looking away sipping from his pint.

"Belled me yesterday said everyone was coming down here, so here I am" replied Stevie.

"Here you are indeed" stated Jon.

"You seen him lately?"

"Nope, was about to ask you the same question."

Stacey and the rest of the group standing nearby picked up the bad vibe between the two. All eager to see how this one would play out but keeping well out of it.

"You want a drink Steve?" interrupted Stacey.

"No it's okay, I will get them in. Pint?" he replied knowing full well that is what Stacey would go for, she was never a wine drinker, schooled in the art of drinking since her laddette days.

"Yeah cheers, but not Stella, Heineken if they have it."

"Alright anyone else?"

"No we have a whip going on if you fancy joining in the action."

"Nah it's okay, I don't think I will be able to keep up with you lot."

He turned to go to the bar as he was jeered for being a lightweight. Stevie actually saw it as a bit of an opportunity to keep closer to Stacey throughout the night.

They squeezed through to the bar, waving at a couple of Wood-bridge lads who were sat near the back of the pub protecting one of three large raised tables from the constant stream of drinkers asking if they could sit there. The rest of the Woodbridge group were outside but constantly checking to see if anyone was taking the piss trying to infiltrate the designated tables.

It was just under an hour until kick off with most discussing the impending match; who should or should not play, who would start. The main discussion points were around James Milner getting a start, most were unsure about the Aston Villa midfielder. The other topic was whether Steven Gerrard and Frank Lampard could play in the same team given their similar styles of play. The only unanimous agreements centred on Emile Heskey, all agreeing he should not be let anywhere near an England shirt but conceding there were not many other options. The volume in the pub was getting louder, the smell of stale sweat dotted around the room. Body odour; the only downsides to the smoking ban introduced back in 2008.

Cigarette smoke was always good at masking nasty smells in pubs and clubs but at least it was a lot healthier. Stevie had given up smoking on his 30th birthday and had never looked back although not having a cigarette with a pint in a pub always felt a little strange and he always felt that little urge creeping in the more he drank. That along with another familiar urge, a big fat rail of gear blasted up his nose and deep down into his lungs.

Supping their pints, they stayed for a few minutes propped up at the bar chatting, their bodies closer than would otherwise be normal, staying until new customers forced them on and out of the way. They went to the back table, chatting to his old friends from Woodbridge Pukka and Pratty sat on bar stools at the raised tables. There was a good view of the large fifty-inch plasma screen on the wall opposite. Next to them was a large group of younger drinkers, mostly black but a few white and Asians amongst them. As they were chatting one pulled out a plastic vuvuzela, the African horn all the rage at this year's World Cup and began blowing the horn loudly bouncing up and down as the group started singing.

"Engerrrland, engerrrland, engerrrland engerlllland"

"Fucking great, have to sit through the match listening to that" said Stevie as he noticed that several of the others also had horns stuffed down their belts and back pockets.

"Shut it, adds to the atmosphere, we are going to smash the US of fucking A" replied Pukka a ferocious football supporter who hated all other sports, especially Rugby. Egg chasing public school bumboys he would often state if anyone had the audacity to start talking rugger.

At that point Pratty stood up on the bottom rungs of his stool, peering outside.

"Ah Craig has turned up. Fuck me who is he with? Looks like a right bunch of fucking wrong-uns!"

Stevie's heart jumped in his chest as he stood looking outside. One thing he noticed was that Bedswell was not looking happy at the arrival of Craig, his arms crossed as a ragged looking Craig held out a hand for him to shake.

"Wonder what that is all about, probably fucked him over like he did me" thought Stevie as a shot of adrenaline rattled him, anticipating the reunion, the inevitable fight that was to come.

"Come on!" said Stevie to Stacey, who also wore a worried nervous look etched like granite on her face.

Craig was busy hugging his old comrades, particularly Jon Weldon and introducing them to a rag tag bunch of strange characters. One looked like a down and out Jesus Christ, long dirty reddish blonde hair and beard, a baggy linen long sleeved top and red hemp baggy trousers and a pair of leather sandals from which sprouted skinny uncut dirty toes.

"Yes bruv, this is Rod, Moon Monkey and Gully and this stinky dirty

ALL BACK TO YOURS

hippy is Skye, all the way from California. Been hanging with these fuckers down in Brighton for a while but the pull of the smoke was just pulling me back you know..... Wwwooooah yessssss" he yelled out at the top of his voice making the Woodbridge lads including Weldon nervous.

"Fucking yes, back with the Woodbridge crew, in the fucking hissooooose. Been too fucking long. Good to see you fuckers. Mr Weldon as I live and breathe, you alright son, what's been happening in the taxi business? Been much action in the back of the cab eh? You dirty fucking cunt, you fucking love it don't ya, picking up the pissed-up slags don't ya ha ha ha ha" laughed Craig manically.

Jon Weldon just smiled back, embarrassed as he was trying to cop off with Tanner's cousin, who was stood nearby wondering who the lunatic was that just turned up.

"Oh great, he is completely and utterly fucked!" thought Stevie as he and Stacey pushed through the crowd. They could hear him jabbering away a mile off.

"Anyone want any fucking nose bag?" Craig shouted. Weldon leant in close.

"Craig keep it down man, there is old bill over there" he whispered nodding his head towards the Marylebone Road where two Police stood leaning against the railings keeping an eye on the proceedings.

"Oh fuuuuuuck them, this is the World fucking Cup, they don't give a fuck about the boys being out partying" he roared in reply.

"Oi" he shouted at the Policewoman.

"You going to get some time off to come and watch the game officer?"

"We'll be keeping an eye on the score sir, rest assured" replied the male officer sternly.

"Excuse me CUNTstable, I was actually talking to your female colleague there, not you" he shouted back.

"We are both fine, sir now if you could keep your voice down that would be greatly appreciated."

As Craig turned around to the crowd muttering and chuckling inanely to himself he saw Stevie and Stacey.

"Well fuck me sideways, if it isn't the SAS, Stacey and Stevie, my two favourite peeps on the planet" he cried bounding towards them grabbing both in a group hug. He then roughly kissed Stacey on the lips.

"Hello babe, you alright darling."

Stevie's knuckles clenched white as he gripped his pint, furious at the state of him, no doubt fuelled by his fucking gear that he had fucking well nicked but the way he was acting with Stacey made him madder.

"How you doing mate" said Stevie in a way that sounded like he pitied him.

"I am doing just fine, abso-fucking-lutely topper mate" he blurted back, his eyes on stalks, the pupils dark pools.

"Craig, oi Craig" whispered Skye, the hippy, not caring he was interrupting the awkward reunion. He was making motions with his head towards the inside of the pub. Stevie could not bite his tongue.

"Looks like your mate is a little thirsty there, looks like he really wants to get in that pub for a drink eh?"

"Yeah I think you might be right, I am feeling a little parched myself, might have to go in there are get myself sorted. Tickle that itch. Quench that thirst eh? What about you fancy a ...... beverage?"

Stevie raised his glass.

"I am fine mate but you crack on."

Craig leaned in close, face to face, close enough for Stevie to see the full extent of the damage done; one of his red flecked eyes flickered side to side seemingly independent to the other, yellowing teeth, the drug addict look rounded off by the red blotches and cracked capillaries that littered his face.

"Permission to.....drink granted eh? Well fucking thank you for the royal fucking seal of approval."

Stevie moved his head so he could whisper into his ear rather than in his face, all of the Woodbridge brigade again fascinated but stood in silence pretending not to listen.

"When have you ever asked permission to do anything? As far as

I can tell you've done what the fuck you like ever since.....” Stevie stopped himself, mentioning the death of his mum was not on. He left the sentence hanging.

“Ever since what?” he questioned glaring back at him.

“Ever since fucking what?” he demanded

“Ever since we left school” replied Stevie coolly, not giving into temptation to score points or thrust the knife too deep.

“You're meant to be a mate not a fucking mentor, you know, why don't you start acting like it.”

“Fucking mate? You fucked me over. You.......” Stevie knew this wasn't the right time, he was angry, Craig was wasted. He stopped himself breathing out, calming himself.

“Alright, listen, me and you have much to talk about. Football is on in a tick so why don't we save that little pleasure until later, get things sorted and move on yeah?”

Stevie knew he would have to pander to him to try and salvage the situation.

Craig slapped him lightly on the cheek.

“Fucking right” he smiled as he turned away to stroll into the pub to search out the toilet facilities with his merry band of drug addicts in hot pursuit.

Stevie and Stacey looked at each other but neither had to say anything, this was going to be one long uncomfortable evening. They stayed outside catching up on the Woodbridge rumour mill, which still seemed to be full to the brim with tales of debauchery and mishaps. A cheer erupted from the pub as the teams came out of the tunnel prompting the pavement to empty as everyone rushed in to try and get a seat. All of Woodbridge including Craig and his south coast warriors were squashed in and around the tables. Some had barstools, the rest standing behind. China being the ever-present gentleman gave up his seat for Stacey who gave him a kiss on the cheek.

“Oiiii hands off my bird China, you perv” bellowed Craig putting him in a head lock. China and the rest of the Woodbridge boys and girls were giving each other nervous glances at his behaviour.

The pub cheered and clapped as the referee blew the whistle getting the game underway. The speakers in the pub were cranked up to the maximum volume so everyone could hear the commentary. The stadium in South Africa was full of colour, the local African spectators equalling the US and England fans. It looked hot, sounded noisy with the thousands of vuvuzela horns making the stadium sound like it was filled by an angry swarm of bees.

The lads at the table next to them began to blow their horns, sufficiently enough to start pissing Craig off. It was not so much the noise but because they were drowning out his expletive filled yet expert ongoing commentary. Anyone who did not play for Manchester United was either shit, dodgy, crap or wank.

"Oi lads pipe down with them trumpet things will ya!" Craig bellowed at them.

One of them reciprocated by blowing it back in his face, laughing, not giving a fuck.

"Give it a rest old man, we are just having a laugh, get into the African spirit."

"African spirit I'll leave that to you lot."

"Whatcha talking about bruv."

"Bruv? I ain't your bruv, you're the fucking brothers, you lot get into the African spirit. What the fuck is that thing anyway?"

"Have you not been watching the football mate?"

"Yeah course I fucking have, what is it?"

"It's a vuvuzela innit."

"Innit? Innit? Don't give me any of that fucking wog shit. Vuvu whatever, just keep it fucking down or I'll take it off ya and vu vu stick it up your arse."

A couple of Craig's new 'friends' were trying to look menacing in the background during this initial confrontation but failing miserably due to their skeletal emaciated junkie appearance. China made an attempt to talk to them but they were not interested in talking, he managed to get a few words out of the Skye bloke who mumbled at him.

"I am not sure what is colder over here, the weather or the women."

China did not linger, the smell emanating from him was truly horrendous and proved that British women still retained a degree of decency.

This little vuvuzela-blowing group from Willesden clearly did not give a shit about Craig or his mates. They were mob handed and knew it. To them the wild-eyed mouthy geezer Craig looked a bit tasty albeit out of shape but the accompanying space cadets would be wiped out in a couple of seconds. The rest of them, the Woodbridge contingent did not look too interested just happy to get pissed up, enjoy the football and swerve any aggro. So the Willesden boys kept up the horn blowing and mouthing off in Craig's direction, winding him up, turning the coil, ratcheting the spring.

Within minutes of the match kicking off the frosty mood at the back of The Globe lightened as captain Steven Gerrard latched onto a Heskey pass slotting a right footed shot into the bottom right hand corner past the US keeper, Everton's Tim Howard. As was standard practice the pub erupted, drink went flying and Craig cynically made sure a good amount of his pint went in the general direction of the Willesden lads which did not go unnoticed.

"Take that you fucking scouse torrets yank cunt!!" yelled Craig bouncing up and down.

Even though Craig was not much of a football fan, in those days he was a drug addict in denial, always looking for that 'special occasion' the slightest reason to get on it, in this case an England football match. The goal sent him off and the Willesden lads at the adjacent table were not going to ruin this special occasion. After strutting off to the toilet to celebrate, sniffing up a huge line, his sixth since being in the pub, he renewed his battle with the large group of youngsters. He continued mouthing off and berating them for their fashion, the usual mix of sportswear and casual. They did not seem to care giving back as good as they got.

Things took a turn for the worse when the US scored the equaliser on 40 minutes, Clint Dempsey, who played for Fulham, turned an English defender hitting a purely speculative effort from long range. It was fumbled by the England goalkeeper, Robert Green, who knelt down to collect the ball which unbelievably bounced over his down stretched arms and crept in over the line. Half time blew and the pub emptied out onto the street for a breather, smoke cigarettes and analyse the performance. By now dusk had descended and the pavement buzzed and hummed with the rowdy atmosphere. The Marylebone Road was now quiet, everyone had planned the evening's football well and the usual throng of traffic reduced to the odd taxi and bus.

Craig stayed inside with his rag tag hangers on and Stevie and Stacey escaped outside with the Woodbridge lads, all of whom avoided bringing up Craig's behaviour. Most of them still thought him and Stevie were best mates and did not want to slag him off in front of him.

"How's Scott? Seen him recently?" enquired China.

"Not seen him in nearly five years, got a couple of kids now, living up near Bristol I think. We are friends on that Facebook thing but not really spoke. Still think Ester restricts his movements in that regard. Think us lot are persona non gratis."

"Ha, ha think you may be right there. I saw him in Woodbridge last year, was down visiting his folks, he was actually in the C&C with his old man which was a bit of a surprise. Only stayed for a pint as the wives had a roast on the go back home."

The second half approached so everyone began to filter back into the pub, Stevie and Stacey held back, really not wanting to go back in. Stevie really had to speak to Craig but would have to leave it for now but he knew it was going to be an even more difficult discussion than what he anticipated. Craig was getting seriously smashed inside on gear, shots and Kronenbourg.

"You okay" said Stevie looking at Stacey who was putting on a brave face, a tight smile.

"Not really. He's a fucking mess, a fucking animal, what the fuck has happened to him. He has lost it. I have never seen him so aggressive. He is even worse than I remember" she replied holding back the tears.

Stevie considered what would happen after the match and it sent a shiver down his spine. Years ago, a club would have been on the menu but those days were long gone. Craig would want to get to a house, settle in for a lengthy coke binge. He wondered whether he had spilt the beans to his cohorts about the Trentstone Towers flat. He doubted it; it had been their secret for nearly 10 years and Stevie had been there enough recently to know no one else had been there. They rarely kept any drugs on hand, they normally had the operation so clockwork they would cut and distribute to their network within a matter of hours, not days. The obvious choice for the after-party would be Stevie's house in Hampstead.

"Oh fucking hell, fuck me" he thought darkly.

"Listen, I will get everyone back to mine afterwards, no worries. You can come back or grab a taxi with the lads from Woodbridge depends on who is doing what."

"Are you sure, you don't want him in your house, do you?"

It was an obvious statement not a question.

"Well after I speak to him he will either be a friend or an enemy. So we will see what happens."

Stacey put her hand on his arm squeezing him as she looked up into his eyes.

"Thanks Steven."

That look. That look. It was enough to make him break out in tears as the feelings for her bubbled up within, whatever those feelings were. Lust, friendship, admiration, love. Love. The thought of it both scared him and excited him with equal measures. This was your best mate's girlfriend, well ex-best friend and his ex-girlfriend. Did that make it right wrong? Indifferent? All other issues, Craig, the debt, the drugs, DDK, Skully, Kaiser disappeared. He swallowed hard as a cheer from within the pub interrupted them.

"Back in?" he said nodding towards the boozer. She nodded.

"Drink? My round I think."

"Yes, get me a JD and coke and make it a double, think I am going to need it."

The second half kicked off with Tottenham's Ledley King being substituted and replaced with Liverpool's Jamie Carragher. This was another chance for the pub to hear Craig's opinion on the matter.

"Fucking great. What fucking waste of a squad spot, some lame fucking black yid who cannot even fucking last 45 minutes of football. Only to be replaced with some workshy thieving scouse cunt."

A middle-aged man looked around at Craig who glared back in response, daring him to pipe up.

Stevie clocked that the Willesden crew were beginning to get a little tired of his antics, Craig was constantly mouthing off bouncing up and down on his toes banging into one of them, a tall black lad, whenever England got near the ball. Within minutes of the second half starting Heskey was sent through clear on goal by Aron Lennon with only the keeper to beat but shot right at Tim Howard who saved easily. Frank Lampard then had a decent left footed shot from outside the box saved and England began to press the advantage. The mood in the pub lifted. The US attacked down the left side of the pitch with Altidore flying past Carragher but Robert Green redeemed himself well by blocking a fierce close range shot that the cannoned off the cross bar.

"Scouse cunt!" yelled Craig again with gusto as the Woodbridge contingent shrunk inside and as the Willesden contingent plotted.

Wayne Rooney then hit a speculative long-range effort surprising everyone, which nearly crept in the right-hand side of the US goal but was just wide. From then on the minutes began to tick away, the US holding out in defence and flooding the midfield. England could not find a way through. England were sure fire favourites but the tension began to mount in the pub as a certain win looked like becoming a draw with only a point in the bag. Craig began to get more agitated as the football score, the drugs, the horns being blasted in his ear and alcohol took its toll. He was really beginning to lose his rag with the Willesden lot.

"I ain't gonna tell you lot again, stop blowing them things."

He stood staring them down who ignored him, smiling enjoying themselves.

As Craig turned his head back round to watch the television he muttered, just loud enough for them to hear.

"Black cunts"

It was then that the Willesden lads took their revenge. The main lad who had been taking most of the stick leant into his mates with a grin on his face.

"Oi, the cracker said he was gonna stick a vuvuzela up our arses. Tony, why don't you save him the bother wid your ting and we can give it him as a lickle gift, eh? Why don't you give him a taste of ya mothers special jerk dat you had last night eh?"

The boy Tony chuckled into his drink before slipping off the bar stool. Whilst being shielded by his friends he carefully pulled his Calvin Klein boxer shorts down and popped the mouthpiece of the horn between his arse cheeks.

"I ain't no batty but I am gonna have to take one for da team on this one" he giggled and grimaced, curling his nose as he managed to get the tip just up his bum. He turned around and faced Craig.

"Listen man, sorry me and de boys ruining ya footie game and that. These things can be pretty fuckin annoying yeah but they is a good laugh watching the footie and that. Here you can take dis one. Sorry."

Craig seemed quite pleased with the boys standing down, giving him the respect he deserved. He took the horn before looking round at both the Woodbridge lads and his crew slightly nodding his head, signalling that he had won this little battle.

He took the horn in his right hand bringing it up to his lips, the Willesden boys watching on trying not to look to obvious. He took a deep breath and gave the horn a good blast, surprised how easy it was to get a good loud sound out of it. He then started blowing hard on the vuvuzela bouncing from foot to foot, trying to get a chant going.

The piss taking started gradually from the Willesden gang who were all pissing themselves laughing as Craig bounced around showing off.

"Stop blowing that thing, your breath stinks!"

"Oi shit breath give it a rest!"

"Big up the man on the horn with crap breath!"

"Eeergh you been rimming your mate JC earlier mate?"

Stevie clocked what they had done quickly but Craig was still completely oblivious dancing around with his lips firmly attached to the shit encrusted mouthpiece. Stevie knew the consequences it would bring and a small spurt of adrenaline shot into his arms legs and chest in anticipation of the penny finally dropping, which it duly did.

Craig stopped bouncing as the registered the piss taking directed at him.

"Nah, nah man, keep up the tune shit breath!"

Craig looked at the horn in his hand taking a sniff. Then that it all royally kicked off.

Craig snapped the horn over his knee breaking it three quarters of the way up, leaving a sharp splinter of plastic from the remaining horn in his hand. Blinded by rage he launched at the tall black lad viciously stabbing it into his neck twice. It was so quick and so violent that no one had time to intervene. A fine mist of blood spurted out of his neck at a right angle. Stacey screamed as she caught sight of the blood pumping from his neck. Even Craig was a little shocked standing still breathing heavily, his chest rising and falling as he looked on at the lad crumble to the floor. What saved the boy's life was his friend who quickly ripped off his white t-shirt winding it around his neck before dragging him out of the pub screaming at the Police to get an ambulance.

Inside the pub it was bedlam as the rest of the Willesden boys piled into Craig and his crew. They left the rest of the Woodbridge boys alone having clocked they were as fucked off with Craig as they were. Skye instantly curled into a ball receiving a fair few digs, punches and kicks but most of their attention was on Craig who fought back well, the cocaine giving him a bit of an edge to start but the weight of numbers got him in the end and he took quite a pasting. The only Woodbridge member to get involved was Tanner who was so drunk by this time he did not know what was going on so steamed in regardless. He could barely stand and was quickly put down by a well-aimed punch by a stocky Asian lad. His nose squashed across his face, the fourth time he had his nose broken and as he laid there whilst getting showered in broken glass and half trampled on, he muttered.

"Oh for fucks sake, not again!"

The fight lasted all of two minutes until a squad of Police flew into the pub and arrested everyone who was in or near the melee.

CHAPTER 21

Perimeter Road

The origin of the name Woodbridge was simple enough although the old wooden bridge that once spanned the river, a tributary of the River Colne, was long gone, replaced in the 1960s with a functional cement and steel construction. A local association had been petitioning and lobbying the council to have a wooden pedestrian bridge built just downstream but to no avail.

Long before The Judge pulled up in his Vauxhall Cavalier the old aerodrome was their playground. The decrepit air raid shelters and pill boxes became their dens and secret bases. The long stretch of runway their racetrack, littered with grass and shrubs that had pushed up and through the old concrete. The woods that bordered the northern edge were riddled with well-trodden pathways and tracks perfect for off road BMXing.

During the Second World War the factories next to the airfield housed huge assembly lines, hundreds of workers putting together the final pieces of the now famous Spitfire and Hawker Hurricane fighter planes. Due to the shortage of pilots, caused by the numerous dogfights with the Germans over southern England, female pilots would put the planes through their final paces. They would test them out in the skies above Woodbridge before delivering to the operational Royal Air Force bases throughout the home counties. One of those pilots, Margot Langsley, became the most famous Woodbridge resident of all time after her heroics in World War Two. From her humble, nervy beginnings testing out the newly assembled fighter planes she became the only female pilot to see active service in the RAF during the Battle of Britain. After the war the factories finally closed moving to northern England where commercial planes were manufactured. The Woodbridge airfield was then left to rot.

The plans for the new housing development were announced during the school summer holidays in the 80's. The 14-year-old friends from Woodbridge knew all too well it would all soon be gone deciding to make the most of their playground during that long hot summer.

"Well suppose there will be more fanny with all the extra houses I guess" Craig sniffed as they discussed the news of the development whilst sat on top of one of the brick bunkers. Grass had been laid on the roof to provide natural camouflage from the eyes of the German spy planes. It was now just weeds and scrub but still provided a decent vantage point.

"Any fanny more like for you! Nah that's bad. Where are we going to play?" replied a concerned looking Stevie.

"Don't be a joey Stevie. Play? We are not going to be playing around like this, like kids forever. We are growing up, we'll be off out into town soon on our own, once we are allowed to get the bus and that. I've seen my brother change recently, started buying lots of clothes, even started smoking."

"Smoking is yuck, I am never going to do it. It stinks. My old man stopped last year thank god, remember? Gave up after getting that nasty bout of pneumonia. Real bad."

"Yeah that wasn't just down to the ciggies though was it? Besides smoking looks pretty cool."

"Yeah maybe it is quite cool. My dad's not cool though and he used to smoke like a chimney."

"He is pretty cool. A good laugh, not as cool as your mum though, she's great" smiled Craig as he looked across the large expanse of overgrown runway. His smile retreated as he began to think of his own mum. She was gone. Long gone. His recollections of her were beginning to fade over time. Each month, each year seemed to chip and erode his memories of her, diluting the images and experiences even further in his mind.

She died when he was 7 in the worst possible circumstances. No peaceful passing in her sleep. No quick merciful death. No time for long or short goodbyes. No will and testament. No opportunity for her to tell her kids that they will be okay, they should stay strong and look after one another. Instead she died in a car crash all alone one night out in the country lanes surrounding Woodbridge. She had visited her best friend in Brighton but decided to drive back so she could take her boys swimming the next day at the newly opened Coral Reef swimming pool. The slides, rapids and whirlpool baths the main attractions. She had a few drinks, not drunk but over the limit. After coming off the M25 she headed towards Woodbridge losing control at a notoriously dangerous corner before colliding head on with a tree. The force of the impact knocked her unconscious before waking up to find a branch of the tree deeply embedded in her neck. It had smashed through the front windscreen pinning her to the seat where she was unable to move, terrified and bleeding heavily. The blood poured from the wound congealing in her lap. The road was empty at 1am and she could do nothing but sit there and die. During her last moments she composed a short note to her boys and husband in her own blood on the driver side window. It read:

I'm so sorry boys, so sorry. I luv u all so much. M. X

As Craig looked out across the overgrown weed filled landscape that shimmered in the extreme heat of that summers day he began to cry. He tried to stop the tears but he could not and began to sob, quietly, his brown tanned shoulders which were started to develop sinewy muscle shook gently. Like a yawn often does, Stevie followed suit, the tears streamed as he looked on at his best friend suffering in near silence next to him. He shifted over next him placing his arm around him and they sat for a while holding each other, perfectly comfortable with their close proximity and embrace, nothing awkward, nothing remiss. Just two friends working their way through the early teenage years attempting to deal with what life had thrown at them.

As Stevie held his friend, neither saying a word between them, he decided to tell Craig his own secret tragedy. He had intended never to mention it to anyone but listening to his friends soft weeping he decided otherwise. At that time Stevie had only known for a few weeks but had guessed something was amiss ever since he asked his mum that unintended hurtful question in Dartmoor all those years before. He took a deep breath.

"You know I had a twin brother."

Craig lifted his head that had been resting on his arms that were being propped up by his knees.

"What? What do you mean you had a twin brother?"

"I had a twin brother but he died. His name was Jamie. Jamie Chambers."

Craig stopped crying, immediately turning from his own issues and grief to concentrate on what Stevie was saying.

"What do you mean? When? Where?"

"I only found out a couple of weeks ago. My mum and dad sat me down in the dining room, both scared witless they were, didn't want to tell me but probably thought I was old enough now. I thought someone had died. Ha, well, I was right, you know sort of. But I thought, you know, it was maybe one of my grandparents or a great aunt or something. It was terrible mate, state of my mum when she told me, could barely get her words out, my old man holding her hand as she explained what happened."

Stevie cleared his throat as his voice began to tremble.

"I never knew him mate. He died right there in the hospital when we were born. My mum nearly died too. Lost nearly 3 pints of blood. Err, not quite sure what it was all about, what like the technical term is. Something about us sharing the placenta and an atomic or something sac. I don't really know what it means but all I know is that I came out kicking and screaming and my brother Jamie didn't."

"Bloody hell mate I didn't know...." Craig stuttered and stalled not knowing what else to say. It was like his torment and pain had been flipped over to someone else in an instant.

"I keep having these dreams about running for the exit, trampling over people to get out. Keep thinking maybe it was me that killed him, me being selfish just trying to get out, kicking, elbowing for position. To hell wiv anyone else."

"No mate don't think like that. It was just fate, or luck or biology or whatever."

"I don't know, it is so weird thinking about it. Makes me feel all jittery and kind of guilty knowing there was another, well me, that was meant to be out here. Can you imagine though if he hadn't died? He might be sat here with us talking, playing, riding our treaders, you and him could have been best mates, you two might have bullied me, giving me a wedgie or a posting right over there on that tree ha ha."

"Ha, yeah, mad thinking about that. You would have still been my best mate though."'

"He apparently wasn't like an identical twin. I wonder what he would have looked like."

They both fell quiet thinking about Craig's dead mother and Stevie's dead brother.

Over the years Stevie thought about it a lot. How it affected his mum and dad and himself. He was sure those early years of being isolated in that house away from siblings was one of the reasons why he was who he was. He recalled going to school, at first being intimated and nervous by the big crowds of kids but over time the companionship, camaraderie, the cliques became addictive. He had learnt to keep himself entertained alone but that early period at school taught him how to interact with people, see from their perspectives, what worked when trying to make friends and what did not. Stevie knew deep down he was a selfish person, maybe not intentionally to close friends or family. He had tried hard in that regard but had still upset his family and friends like Scott over the years. He had royally fucked over many strangers and others like Tristram and hopefully soon to be Bainsey. The death of his unborn brother Jamie perhaps a reason why he was that way with little guilt or remorse for his actions and his lies. Born selfish? Possible. It was a notion he often used to justify his actions over the years.

They spotted the familiar figure of Scott riding up from town along Perimeter Road that skirted the old airfield. This shook them from their respective sombre reflective moods as they saw his grinning face as he jumped over two successive mounds on the track on his bike. He rode a Raleigh Grifter, Carole deciding it was more sensible than the BMX Burners the others had.

"Hi lads, blimey what's up with you two? I've bought my Panini swaps. You got yours?"

"Nothing's up mate, we are cool. No sorry forgot my stickers. Shall we head over to Ash Hill? And we can pop back to mine after and do it?'"

"Come on lets go. Last one there has Skills, African Bum Disease! Let's go."

CHAPTER 22

The Afters

Craig was dragged kicking and screaming into the back of the meat wagon as Stevie looked on, his emotions conflicted. On one hand off went any possibility of cash or drugs. Yet, and just like the rest of the Woodbridge lads, major relief in seeing the back of him. Tanner had been arrested after being scrapped off the pub floor. Weldon wisely disappeared just as it kicked off. All the south coast wasters were nicked except Skye the Jesus lookalike, maybe the Police did not fancy feeling the collar of the messiah. Everyone sort refuge in a bar down Little Portland Street.

Stevie now had no qualms about inviting everyone back to his house in Hampstead, everyone quickly summoning taxis as soon as they had the green light. Craig's demise breathed new life into the night as everyone relaxed. Fifteen or so ended up back at Stevie's, his booze collection taking a heathy beating. China was goggle-eyed at his drinks collection, quickly taking on the role of impromptu barman for the night, mixing mojitos which seemed to be all the craze after some of the lads had returned from a stag in Vegas. The drinks cabinet was further dented when Stevie retrieved half an ounce of coke from a tiny wall cavity upstairs, his private 'new customers' stash. Stevie knew that the next few months were going to be tough and he might as well enjoy himself. Standing in his kitchen he tilted his head back looking through the large Velux windows in the pitched roof briefly catching sight of a plane high up in the atmosphere, hundreds of faceless passengers with a thousand stories to tell on their way to destination unknown. He looked around and wondered whether he would be able to keep the house. DDK were no doubt sharpening their knives and loading their guns. The sinister looking bloke outside his flat earlier sure proof of that. He owed a lot of money, the only bit of gear was in his hand, thirty grams. He could probably sell it all to his mates right now and get over a grand, but it really was not worth it. Before he could surprise his guests with his bag of powder treats, China beat him to it, pulling out a small wrap winking at Stevie.

"The host is always first up on the ockee" he shouted.

"Very kind of you sir."

Others caught sight of the wrap and quickly disengaged from their respective conversations, all trying to act cool as they drifted over towards China, not wanting to look too desperate. Most had been drinking all day and fancied a light dusting of powder to keep them going.

"Oh Christ, here come the vultures" announced China, eyeing up those creeping unsubtly towards him.

"Alright you fucking gannets me and Steve are going first but I will rack up the rest for one, two, three, four, five... Oh fucking hell is no one else packing round here part from me?"

There were shrugs all around as China rolled his eyes. Stevie then flung his bag of coke onto the kitchen unit.

"Milky bars are on me."

"Fucking hell Stevie!"

"Go on my son."

"Look at the size of that stash!"

"You want some cash, mate?"

He looked over at Stacey leaning against the low-level wall separating the kitchen from the living room lightly swaying to *Vertigo* by Groove Armada playing on his new four speaker Sonos system. He was a little worried about her reaction; he could only guess the strife and horrors that Craig had subjected her to all because of the white powder.

She looked over seemingly regarding him with a warm albeit tight lipped smile, her eyes half shut. She was drunk but with that little smile his worries evaporated. He leant down snorting a long line deep down into his lungs, his first in nearly three years and it hit him like a steam train knocking him for six. He could not talk for a few minutes, stunned and gagging as the coke dripped down the back of his throat. He thought he was going to pull a whitey so he stepped backwards out of the fray. Everyone had their credit cards out, heads down, chopping and hovering up lines with gusto.

A wave of paranoia set in and he quickly went to the front door to check if it was shut. He vividly recalled a house party when he was 19, everyone was smoking weed and solid. Someone left the front door wide open. Two coppers simply walked in off the street and into the mix in the front room. Everyone froze, giving it the proper goldfish look until the reality of the situation finally dawned on them. A mad frantic hiatus followed as the entire party tried to leg it out of the back door. There was a crush as it was everyone for themselves as they tried to escape the clutches of the Police who were trying to grab and arrest everyone and anyone. The poor lad whose house it was had some explaining to do when his parents returned from a week-long break in Spain.

As he triple checked the door, he considered the man watching him earlier. He stood looking at the door, teeth grinding, trying to ignore the fact tomorrow would eventually come and he would have to deal with the mess Craig had left him in. He went to unlock the door and peer outside to see if there was anyone there but stopped himself placing both hands flat against the inside of the door.

"Forget about it, fuck it, enjoy tonight, have fun with Stace and deal with it in the morning. You're on your own now proper, your own destiny. Don't worry, don't worry, don't worry" he muttered to himself as his heart thumped a steady coke fuelled rhythm in his chest.

He rested his forehead up against the small glass window in the centre of the door. The glass was partly opaque but the centre was clear where he could just make out the dark street outside, partly illuminated by the orange glow of the streetlamps. He closed one eye peering through trying to make out the cars and whether there were any strangers lurking inside them. Suddenly a dark figure emerged from the street quickly bounding up the steps to the door. Stevie reeled backwards in panic expecting the door to be kicked in and his house ransacked by a swarm of DDK gangsters. He was nipped from the coke the shock made his heart thump even more. He looked up at the door, eyes wild and wired. A bloodied and bandaged face appeared through the glass window and for a split second he thought it was Craig before a wide grin then appeared amongst a mop of curly hair and blood streaked chin. It was Tanner. Stevie bent over breathing hard, laughing, trying to calm his nerves and the shock. He opened the door and shouted inside that the party had a visitor. Tanner emerged into the lounge to a hero's welcome, a large plaster over his newly flattened nose. He walked through to the kitchen area immediately clocking the rapidly shrinking pile of coke being snorted.

"Oh fluck, h-now de flackin ell can I do tha wid his" he mumbled nasally pointing to his nose.

Everyone creased up with laughter as Tanner went to the mini bar and sliced a lemon into quarters. He elbowed Bedswell aside, enjoying that all eyes were now on him. He racked a big line before sucking hard on a slice of lemon. With a grimace he a rolled up tenner between his lips and proceeded to inhale the line through his mouth. He staggered around the kitchen his face bright red, eyes watering, grabbing hold of China's can of beer and downed it in a desperate attempt not to cough. He finally settled down grinning holding his chest before announcing to great aplomb.

"Sniffing is for pussies...."

The party raged on, the music growing louder and cheesier as the drink and drugs were consumed. Everyone was taking it in turns to choose the music on the iPad, which was hooked up to the Napster streaming service, one song each which was either greeted with a cheer and dancing or booing resulting in the iPad being snatched away and the next song selected. Stevie had one more line but was content with that, unlike the rest of his Woodbridge friends who were on it like it was going out of fashion. He had not talked to Stacey much since they had been back, he was not sure why, maybe he had reverted to his previous type when she was with Craig which basically meant ignoring her. They were,

ALL BACK TO YOURS

however, exchanging quite a few glances and the thought of to-night's sleeping arrangements and the related possibilities began to creep into his mind. It was a three-bed house, super king size in his room, a double in the spare room and a pull-out futon in his study. There were two sofas downstairs, one in the lounge and one in the kitchen diner. He quickly began counting how many people were there, now 18 in total, some would get a taxi but nearly all those that still lived in or near Woodbridge would stay. Someone would be sharing his bed tonight and as he looked on at Tanner cackling away with Stacey he prayed it would be her not him.

He hit the spirits, bourbon and cokes and a little later gin with tonic and gradually a warm glow offset the frost of the cocaine. He was sat outside with Bedswell who was telling a story about when England thumped Germany 5-1 in the 2002 World Cup qualifiers. Stevie remembered it well, everyone forgoing the C&C in favour of the sports hall at Ash Hill Park sports centre where an enormous screen was erected in the sports hall. China had driven his Fiat Panda planning to either leave it over night or engage in a spot of drink driving, dependent on combined levels of alcohol, gear, bravado, stupidity and peer pressure. His clapped-out Fiat had a fabric sunroof, 'a convertible' he would often state with an amusing air of pomposity as he leant against his pride and joy. This meant it was the easiest car on the planet to break into. As they settled into watch the Huns take a pasting, Bedswell had craftily pocketed China's car keys before sneaking out. The en-trance to the park was dominated by a huge hill used for sledging in the winter and rolling down in the summer and that is where Bedswell decided to park the Fiat. A suitable beacon and symbol of automotive luxury for all to see upon entering the park.

Not long into the game two Policemen arrived asking for the sound to be turned down before shouting out they were looking for the owner of the stricken car. As China trudged off with the Police, confused as what had happened everyone was roaring with laughter and giving him wanker signs. Poor China missed 3 of the goals as Michael Owen and David Beckham tore the Ger-mans apart. Even worse, this became a favoured pastime in Wood-bridge, who could steal his car and put it in the weirdest spots possible. The middle of roundabouts, the disabled space at the local Police station. Even the bomb squad was called out one night after it was found parked up right under a huge electricity pylon near the M25.

Stevie was not listening, not because he had heard it a dozen time before, he loved the tales from Woodbridge like any other, but because the thoughts of Stacey were racing through his mind. He could not concentrate on anything else as she whirled in and out of his subconscious, teasing and courting him without her knowledge or active participation. He laughed when the others laughed and nodded along with only a vague semblance of the ebb and flow of the discussions and stories being told. She was behind him in the kitchen still dancing and he had to use all his will and powers of restraint to stop himself from looking round at her.

He eventually, inevitably lost the internal fight and twisting in his chair he looked over at her. She is was in full muck mouth mode, Shaw was filming her with his mobile phone encouraging her to bust some dance moves for the camera.

"Fuuuuuck off!" she bellowed in his face waving him away before continuing to bop away with China's girlfriend.

"Get that thing out of my face, you twat. Oi China pour us a Malibu and Milk will ya!"

"A what?"

"A Malibu and milk you bell end and make it a large one on the rocks."

"Large ones are my speciality."

"That's not what she said" she cackled pointing at his girlfriend as they both hugged and danced together, thrusting into each other in rhythm to the music.

"It's what you do with it that counts, they don't call me piston hips for nothing. I hope Stevie's spare bed is robust enough to take the punishment I will be giving it later."

She turned away laughing towards Stevie as he stepped into the kitchen from the garden.

"Where can I sleep then?" she enquired looking all serious and pouty with her arms folded.

"You can join China and his missus, sounds like it will be fun."

"Not really into three ways."

"Well there is a couple of sofas down here, there is futon in my study although Baggins is passed out up there already. Popped my head in earlier, he looks like Han Solo frozen in carbonite up there. Or you can crash in my room if you like?"

His heart began racing and he swallowed in anticipation of her response.

"Called" she replied.

"Fucking called! Even talks like one of the lads. She is fucking something else" he thought as she turned away to dance and as his heart nearly skipped a beat.

CHAPTER 23

Super Sunday Session

The flushing toilet woke Stevie up. The noisy groaning pipe work receded as the tank slowly filled now replaced by laughter and groans from downstairs as the other party casualties woke. He had his back to her but could tell Stacey was there, hearing her shallow breathing, her scent hanging deliciously in the air cutting through the musty alcohol and morning breath. He carefully and very slowly turned over but deliberately leaving his leg where they were, as he was enjoying the subtle contact; a bit of footsie yet the sensation was electric. She was still asleep. She looked incredible even without the makeup which she had somehow taken off the night before even though she was completely plastered.

After their discussion about the sleeping arrangement she had lasted another 40 minutes before disappearing quietly upstairs to his bedroom. She did not have any overnight clothes and riffled through Stevie's drawers to find some suitable pyjamas. She settled on a pair of baggy boxer shorts and an old stag weekend polo shirt, the type where boys had their most insulting nicknames printed. She squinted through her drunken eyes at the front which read in faded lettering *'Fishskins Stag Prague 2007'* turning it over and it read 'Red Sack'.

"Noted" she muttered before collapsing onto the huge bed. Within seconds of laying down her head began to spin, she hung on for dear life as the room flew around and around. She took two deep lungful's of breath in a vain attempt to try combat it but that familiar watery taste filled her mouth. She jumped out of bed, throwing open the bedroom and bathroom doors puking a steady stream of vile tasting liquid towards the toilet.

"Fucking Malibu and milk....twat!" she gagged before hurling up the rest of her stomach. She moaned resting her head against the cold porcelain, not worrying about its cleanliness. She breathed in and out deeply as her head began to return to normality and after 10 minutes of hugging the toilet she was back up on her feet. She ran the tap splashing her face, made an effort to take her make up off and washed her mouth out. She then thoroughly cleaned her teeth with Stevie's toothbrush before returning to his bed and falling into a deep alcohol induced sleep.

Downstairs Stevie had noted Stacey subtle departure and the nerves and excitement kicked in, anticipating sleeping next to her. He would never try it on with her, no chance, but the thought of sleeping in the same bed was enough. He then became worried, Craig mentioned she was a fire cat in bed, what if she was up there stark bollock naked waiting for him to fuck her brains out. His old schoolboy nerves kicked in.

He held out going upstairs until nearly 04:30, most of the Wood-bridge lads still going for it, somehow they were nearly out of nosebag. The 'select a tune' process was still going strong and after Stevie selected *Acid* by Ray Barretto a fantastic Latino jazz track from 1968, which was greeted well, he decided to call it a night. After a little dance he disappeared quietly up the stairs. His nerves and misgivings about her waiting lustily for him in his bed evaporated as he entered the bathroom. It was trashed, the toilet covered in sick, his toothbrush was in the bath and a flannel covered in black make up tossed to the floor. He tentatively picked up the toothbrush and closely inspected it, a few flecks of sick were in the bristles and a quick sniff confirmed it.

"Once a laddette always a laddette" he thought as he retrieved another toothbrush from an overnight toiletry case he used on business trips.

He crept into his bedroom; the curtains were not drawn so he shut them but not before peering out onto the dark quiet street trying to spot any DDK henchmen. Stacey was covered completely by the duvet only the top of her head poking out, the blonde hair splayed across his pillow. He looked on the floor. Jeans, socks, top, bra and a black lace thong all discarded.

"Fuck, she is stark bollock naked in there!"

He froze and automatically nudging at his penis through his jeans. Nothing, not a twinge.

"Not good. That fucking gear!"

He stripped off before carefully and quietly slipping under the sheets, breathing out slowly as he rested his head on the pillow. He did not sleep, the coke keeping his mind racing as it pinged and prodded his grey matter. His thoughts jumped from the gorgeous beautiful Stacey lying next to him to the horrors inflicted by DDK for the unpaid debt. He thought of the tall Willesden lad back in the pub, his neck cruelly opened up at the hands of his former best friend. His mind leapt towards Craig, banged up in a Police cell somewhere out there in London. He pictured Skully sharpening a huge sword on his lap Kaiser stood behind staring at him grinning from ear to ear.

On more than one occasion he tentatively reached out towards her only making the only briefest of contacts before nervously re-treating. The noise from downstairs did not help, the constant throb of the music, the kick, the bass mixed in with the bursts of laughter from his old beloved Woodbridge crew, all resisting sleep eager to keep the party going.

Yet it was okay. If he had his way he would stay in the bed forever, him and Stacey alone. He finally dozed off into quasi-consciousness until his bladder forced him awake. As he began to untangle his right leg from hers, she woke up.

"Morning red sack" she said in a deep sleep infused croaky voice.

Stevie blushed and laughed.

"Morning Muckmouth"

It was then he realised she was not naked at all but wearing an old stag t-shirt most likely with a pair of his boxers. He was stark naked under there.

"Oh great!"

He pulled his arms outside of the duvet and she noticed he was not wearing a top.

"Are you naked?"

"Err yeah I always sleep naked" he lied, his head throbbing with hangover and embarrassment.

"Ooh very bohemian and there I was thinking you were more on the conservative side."

His bladder was bursting and he had to go. Sleep had however helped with the earlier coke induced bout of impotency. His dick was rock solid, in a much better state than when he went to bed. He needed to piss but he could not stand up and revel a stonker; that would have been a bit much. So he swung his legs around and sat in the edge of the bed with his back to her.

"Right, avert your gaze please young lady" he laughed as he stood up and walked two steps to his underwear drawer where he pulled on a pair of boxer shorts and jogging bottoms. From the bed Stacey did not avert her gaze as she watched him. As he sat back down on the bed stretching his arms she looked at his long tanned back, lean rather than muscly. A deep red mottled scar ran down the length of his left side. She had heard the story of the summer of 1994 from Craig but the sight of it shocked her nevertheless. She wanted desperately to move in behind him and kiss his neck, wrap her arms around him and run her hands across his chest, breathe him in and fuck there and then. She wanted to ride him, push her nipples into his mouth and buck and grind him. She had been lonely for so long. But she restrained herself, not just because it was not the right time, she knew he wanted her, yesterday had confirmed it all but she could not. All because of the elephant in the room, a big one, in the form of Craig. Him and Stevie were best friends or at least used to be. They went back years, through some terrible times that she could only ever imagine.

There had been a lot of discussion about what would happen to Craig after the incident at The Globe and it seemed the most likely outcome was that he would be going down. Maybe for a long time. The very thought of it elated her. Maybe she and Stevie could finally be together. Many of the Woodbridge lads had been comforting her and asking her if she was okay, maybe they thought she still had feelings for Craig. She had wanted to put them straight on the matter. Scream and shout.

"I don't give a fuck what happens to the junky cunt. Let him fucking rot in jail with his junky mates. He is nothing to me. Scum bag fucking drug addict that does not care for anyone or anything other than himself. Fuck him."

But she did not, she kept quiet hanging onto the hope he could not negatively influence her life again or at least for a very long time.

Stevie left the bedroom smiling at her as he closed the door heading downstairs to check in on the troops and survey the damage. Stacey curled up under the duvet listening to the muffled laughing and jeering. Stevie returned jumping back under the duvet.

"We are all going down the pub down the road for hair of the dog in a bit. They do a cracking burger and chips if you model sorts are allowed that sort of stuff of course. You must be hungry after getting rid of yesterday's subsistence all over my toothbrush."

"Oh you noticed?"

"Yes I did, four out of ten for aim, the toilet is also caked in puke."

"Sorry didn't feel too great when I went to bed. I will clean it up in a bit."

"Don't worry the cleaner is in tomorrow she can do it. I will give her some puke payment on top."

"Come on then let's get ready. Oh by the way I happened to mention to the others down there that you were so hammered that I found you asleep on the floor rather than my bed. I had some rather quizzical eyebrows raised looks this morning. All perfectly innocent but you know what they are like."

"Hey no problem, I know all about the Woodbridge grapevine, anyway not too far from the truth, I was steaming" she groaned before leaning over placing a kiss on his cheek.

"Are you going to check up on what is happening to Craig?"

Stevie decided to put the record straight about him and Craig, he did not need to but he wanted to let her know that he was no longer a barrier between them, whether they continued as friends or otherwise. He sat up in the bed resting against the headboard.

"Listen me and Craig were done a long time ago. We maintained a business relationship for a couple of years but 5 weeks ago he stitched me up so fucking bad that I am in a lot of trouble. Big trouble. I was going to try and get it sorted this weekend, that's why I was partying hard last night. I never do gear anymore but I just wanted to enjoy myself. Actually having Craig out of the picture is kind of a weight off my shoulders. I am still fucked cause of what he done and I owe some nasty fucking fellas a lot of money but now I know it's all on me, no-one else. He is going down, what he did to that kid last night was brutal, that there was attempted murder. Doesn't matter if the fella stuck that horn up his arse or not. And you know what? I am fucking pleased about it, I am pleased for me and more importantly I am pleased for you, you deserve so much better than him. We were best friends since we started secondary school, me, him and Scott and later on The Judge. You could not separate us back in the day but Craig and me got into some heavy stuff and never really extracted ourselves."

He lifted his top to drive the point home. She did not say a word, letting him continue.

"You probably know this but Craig has two personalities that fight each other constantly. One is kind and gentle and good fun, the one you fell for and too be honest I don't blame you, I fell for him as well big time. The other is the selfish party animal, relentless in his determination to get fucked up. No brakes at all just an accelerator. Those two personalities hate each other and that is what makes him a very angry man. He had a tough upbringing with his mum dying and that when he was so young, I don't really know what that does to someone.

"And you know what I love him even now Stace, just like I love Scott and I love The Judge. I think of them always, the mad times we had when we were young, not giving a fuck, out there every night exploring, smoking dope, trying and mostly failing to get laid and my heart beats that little bit faster at the memories. I remember when we first met at school, within months Craig had smudged the purity of my school record; late attendance, truancy with many, many detentions. Later when we started drinking in pubs, what I used to love about Craig was he hated sad drinkers. If anyone was moping about, crying into their pints like half the old boys down the C&C he would harass and cajole them into smiling and having a good laugh. Kick start a sing song that only the old fuckers would know. Before you knew it he had most of the pub up on their feet doing an impromptu conga, snaking through the tables and chairs, out through the beer garden and back though the side door. Fuck me he was awesome, the energy he had, he used to brighten up a lot of peoples' days with his outlook and antics."

Stevie was getting misty eyed wearing those rose-tinted glasses but he knew better than anyone, nothing stays the same in life.

"Yeah well people and circumstances change. Friends move away, have other interests, sometimes your wives and girlfriends do not get along and you drift because of that. Sometimes you just grow apart. People grow up and usually for the better like Scott. But some people get worse like Craig maybe like me. And sometimes when people change you cannot do a thing about it, no matter how hard you try, no matter how hard you intervene, try to point them in the right direction. Alright, so becoming drug dealers wasn't the best idea to keep him on the straight and narrow but I thought that we could both have learnt from our previous mistakes and make some money out of it. For ten years I have tried with Craig, tried to steer him in the right direction and you know what I think I nearly succeeded. Remember we went to Scott and Ester's wedding? That was when I thought me or maybe you had cracked it. I thought that was him sorted. I thought you two were going to get married and it would all be good for him. But something happened and he lost it and I finally realised he was a lost cause and that is the worst feeling of all, feeling like I had failed my best friend but now I know it was not my fault. There are only so many times you can hit your head against a brick wall. I am done with him, just done with him."

Stevie realised he was crying whilst Stacey had shifted over to him sitting on the bed, waiting for him to finish unloading his feelings and thoughts.

"I am sorry" he blubbed wiping his eyes with the back of his hand and breathing deeply to control his emotions. Stacey put her arms around him and he reciprocated. He could feel her muscles in her back, toned and firm. She smelt good, she was warm and he wanted to stay there forever but she broke off knowing she had to say something.

"Craig is a drug addict Stevie and you're both drug dealers. What did you think was going to happen?"

"I am a drug addict Stace as well. Deep down I am a raging fiend just like Craig but I have controlled it. Most addicts are either in or out, no in-between but somehow I've managed it. A couple of blow-outs a year like last night, a few lines and I am done. Still get the urge, the shitty need for more but the hangovers and come downs are too bad now. Cannot function. Gear gives you ever diminishing returns over the years. Well for me anyway."

Stevie decided to say what he knew Stacey wanted to hear.

"I am going to give up all that nonsense anyway. Go straight. Pay back these fellas that Craig skanked and move on."

He did not like it but he was lying out of his back teeth and wanted to keep the lie as short and succinct as possible as though it were no big deal if and when he was caught out later. Stevie had accepted a long time ago that he did not like being told what to do, whether it was directly or inferred. Like now, as he knew Stacey expected him to cut out the drug business, quit and be done with it. So, as he had done a hundred times before he lied. He had lied in some shape or form to everyone he had ever known. He was one of the greatest liars; schooled in lying due to his raging drug addiction in years gone by. He never flushed, never blustered, the straightest honest delivery of a porky known to man. He had been doing it so long it was second nature. He did not particularly like doing it to Stacey, she was his dream, his intoxication that would ride rough shod over his addictions any day. He could see in his mind their future together but the cocaine business would have to endure a little longer. His reasoning was simple; if it was not him it would be someone else. Everyone would get their score with or without him being in the game, so why not. He was good at it so fuck it.

"Right come on let's not mope around crying over spilt milk. Come on, get in the shower, I am beginning to feel hungry."

"Oh god I don't, my mouth feels like Ghandi's flip flop."

"Your breath smells like it as well you dirty boy, go brush your teeth."

"What with my puke sodden toothbrush yeah?"

"Better out than in, I feel better for it now anyway."

Stevie showered taking his time letting the hot warm water

cascade over him. The wide bore head partly washing away his hangover that lurked in the shadows like a growling beast. Anticipating, hoping and praying for getting it on with Stacey he gave his pubes a quick trim after noticing he was looking a bit 70's in the nether regions.

He returned to the bedroom and Stacey was not there, he could hear her laughing at Tanner who had somehow fallen asleep for five hours sat upright in a wooden chair right next to an empty comfy sofa. He looked out of the window at the hazy sunshine, the leaves in the tress were not moving much so decided on chino shorts and a Ralph Lauren long sleeved shirt with cuffs rolled up. Some downstairs might comment that he looked like he was going to a job interview but fuck them, this is Hampstead! With his hangover idling in the background the thought of spending a few more hours with Stacey and his old Woodbridge pals was more than enough to motivate him. Skully and DDK would need to wait another day.

Everyone except China and his girlfriend, who had not emerged from the spare room, descended to the nearby Wells Tavern. Stevie and Stacey ordered pints of Fosters with a large lemonade top which did not go down well with those firing straight into pints of Stella straight off the bat.

"Couple of fannies."

"Is that how you Hampstead homo's roll? Jesus."

"You boys crack on, I am sure that you are enjoying your pints as much as I am enjoying this refreshing sugar infused beverage."

They managed to bag one of the few outside pub benches bathed in glorious June sunshine as they settled in for a long afternoon session. Stevie and Stacey sat opposite each other and within minutes their legs were touching and a lengthy clandestine game of footsie commenced. They were fully engaged in the discussions, banter, jokes and storytelling but there was another agenda to the day's activities of which only two participants knew about. Every now and again, such as when she was taking a sip of her drink, Stacey would look over at Stevie opposite with a look akin to pure burning desire in her eyes and she would push up harder against his calf with her legs. He would respond in kind, feeling like a teenager all over again. He was lusting after Stacey but it was now a bang on dead cert and it was a perfect opportunity, his house was no more than a hundred metres away. Most of the group sitting around drinking were making plans to get back to Woodbridge so sooner or later they would be alone.

China and his girlfriend arrived which added some much-needed spark to the afternoon's proceedings particularly as he was clutching a copy of the The Sun newspaper which had a one sentence reference to the incident in The Globe the night before.

A serious assault took place in a central London pub that required the victim to be raced to hospital where doctors describe his condition as serious but stable. A man has been arrested on suspicion of attempted murder.

Later on the group had been whittled down to half a dozen and as the next round of World Cup matches began to be shown inside the pub, Stevie and Stacey were left alone outside.

"Fancy going inside to watch Algeria take on that great football nation, Slovenia?"

"No thanks, had enough of the World Cup already."

"Leave it out, five weeks of relentless football matches all televised two or three games a day. It's pure footie overload, its ace. It's not going to be a productive month, that's all I know. You cold?" he said as noticed her shiver as the sun became obscured by the pub resulting in a distinct chill in the air.

"Yeah a little, shall we go?" she said nodding her head in the direction of his house.

"Yeah, I am a little peckish. Will knock you up a little something if you like."

"That would be nice but no more football!"

"Okay, deal" he replied before quickly necking his beer eager to get back without the others noticing.

CHAPTER 24

A Thai French Kiss

They explored Bangkok visiting a variety of different temples and booked on a river boat tour. The all agreed Wat Po temple was the highlight as they went late on in the day when it was quiet, very tranquil compared the hustle and bustle and chaos of the Bangkok streets outside.

In the evening they hit the world-famous Koh San Road where most travellers and backpackers stayed in Bangkok due to the cheap accommodation and huge number of stalls selling cheap fake clothes, music and trinkets. They entered Gulliver's Bar at the end of the street, Stevie ducking under the decorative Tuk Tuk, the Thai taxi suspended over the doorway on steel wires. The cool air conditioning made them shiver with pleasure as they escaped the oppressive tropical heat outside. They stayed for hours, trading war stories of the last few weeks with backpackers, most of whom looked on in amazement and laughter at the tales of paparazzi whores, road accidents and poor electrical wiring. Craig lost his temper with a typical public school crusty who sneered at the fact the Woodbridge lads were on holiday and not seasoned backpackers. He soon left after a very inebriated Craig had him round the neck threatening to burn his dreadlocks off.

They eventually left the bar venturing back into the humid night air that hung with an odd scented mix of gasoline, sewage and food. They walked up and down the Koh San Road perusing the various stalls but no-one bought anything as they were saving that for the last day. Craig spotted a fake ID counter and nudged Stevie. They were always on the lookout for ways to muddy the waters of their enterprise and the more fake identification the better. Next to this stall was a tall Sikh Indian in full colourful blue robes topped with a huge turban, a sight you did not see often in the predominantly Buddhist country.

He stopped Stevie as he passed by lightly putting a hand on his chest.

"Ah sir you have a veddy lucky nose."

Stevie thought himself relatively good looking but if there was an area that he was a little self-conscious about it was his nose. He reddened a little as Craig, China and Tanner roared with laughter. The fortune teller tried to persuade Stevie to have his palm read which he declined, he was quite superstitious and did not like the thought of someone predicting his good fortune or even worse, his demise.

They decided to visit one of the famous Bangkok red light districts. Instead of going to the most famous in Pat Pong they went to Nana Plaza, in the Sukhumvit district. Craig and China jumped in a Tuk Tuk, Stevie and Tanner in the other after negotiating a price. As they set off Craig yelled out.

"1000 bhart for the driver that gets there first!"

A hair-raising race through the busy streets of Bangkok followed. Midway through and after their driver pulled a wheelie Stevie had enough thrusting a bundle of notes to stop the driver acting like a complete lunatic. He looked a little annoyed but smiled the usual Thai smile and let off the relentless pressure on the accelerator.

The Nana Plaza was akin to a small shopping mall but only selling girls, flesh and titillation not clothes, cosmetics and electricals, there were TV's but transvestites not televisions. It was U shaped consisting of three levels. The lower floor housed typical bars with a few hostesses playing bar games to bridge the language gap between themselves and the farang. Tanner, China and Craig ran off giggling to explore leaving Stevie feeling like he did in Phuket. The underlying poverty and seediness outweighing the loud music, girls, cheap drinks and neon. He noticed a small bar on the ground floor that was different to the other go-go bars, it was called the French Kiss and was showing English premier league football, Chelsea versus Ipswich. The barmaid was a towering 6-foot ladyboy stalking the customers with an arrogant dismissive pout on her huge lips as she filled the drinks of the customers perched opposite on their bar stools. It was not just the height that was imposing it was her face, stunningly beautiful with sharp high cheekbones. Stevie had trouble drawing his eyes away before perusing the menu, mostly French but a few Thai dishes. He ordered Heineken beer, French bread, cheese selection and foie gras.

Next to Stevie was a giant of a man, like an American footballer with close cropped hair with a slight flat top, a strong jawline with huge biceps and a deep tan that gave away the fact he was not a tourist but most likely an expat. He was not however American as he was clearly a passionate Chelsea fan. They began to chat about the average start to Chelsea's season, the main highlight beating Tottenham 2-3 at White Hart Lane courtesy of a Jimmy Hasselbank brace. He was a little offish with Stevie but perked up immensely when the little Italian Gian Franco Zola stuck one past the flapping goalkeeper, Serini.

"Fucking get in there, yes the fucking Chels! Fucking love Zola, he will manage the boys one day. You want a beer?"

Stevie nodded in reply.

"Cheers, I will take another Heineken."

"Typical tourist eh? Don't like the local brews?" he stated holding up his bottle of Singha.

"Oh mate, I've been on it for about three weeks so trying to reacclimatise my liver to the European gear, and you know what, might just be me but I find that stuff gets a little warm quicker than our lager, do you not find that?"

"That is where you are making the mistake. I would never know mate as I never let it get to that point" he laughed deeply as he downed the bottle in one go.

"Anyway, how do you do my name is Stuart. What business are you in then fella?" he enquired curiously yet never taking his eye off the football match.

Stevie was glad he asked the question; he was intrigued by this huge bulk of a man but never liked to pry into other people's business and this gave him the opportunity to ask a few back without fear of repercussions. He had learnt a long time ago that no one likes a nosey parker.

"I am Steven and for my sins I am a management consultant and bit part property developer, too long in the office for my liking but pays the bills."

"Well the earth would fall off its axis without fucking management consultants wouldn't it, ha, ha. Only kidding son, sure it is very interesting. What's your niche?"

"Europe."

"Oh good god Europe, well if there is one thing I am looking forward to and that is the Euro, fucked off with having to change up each and every time you go abroad. When is it, next month it is being introduced?"

"First of Jan next year but you can start to change up next month in the banks. You're right though, it is going to amazing to have a single currency, can you imagine living somewhere like France and you have three countries maybe four on your doorstep, off you go and shop without all that messing about."

"Yeah it will be great for going over to Europe but I reckon us Brits are better off sticking with the pound mate, if one of them countries goes down the pan then all of them will. Best out of it or so my financial advisor reckons."

Stevie was about to respond about the European Central Banks guarantees but decided against it. He was however suitably impressed.

"Okay so he is a little right wing but he is a Chelsea fan" he thought before taking the plunge.

"What about you then, you do not look like you sit in an office all day."

"No I certainly do not fella, currently I work in Laos."

Stevie did not know much about the country, he knew it was landlocked, squashed between China, Burma, Vietnam and Thailand and was historically part of the French Indochina now run by a Communist government.

"What do you do there?"

"I run a bomb disposal company."

"You're kidding, piss off."

"Alright so I still have my arms and legs but not every bomb disposal specialist walks around with stumps for limbs. You want me to tell you about why I work in Laos?"

"Fucking right, that's mental! Want another beer?" Stevie replied excitedly.

"So you've obviously heard of the Vietnam War right? Well the origins of that ruck started right after the end of the Second World War. Not long after Imperial Japan surrendered Russia backed this geezer Ho Chi Minh, from the north of the country, who considered himself the rightful leader of Vietnam. He was a fucking red commie of course and he was supplied by the chinks and ruskies to fight the occupying French. All ended in tears in 1954 when Ho Chi turned up with his new army; the fucking NVA, the North Vietnamese Army, with a hatful of these Russian rocket launchers called 'katyushas' on the backs of trucks and wiped out a load of the frogs. After that the French, unsurprisingly the shitting cunts, were as good as done for and sent packing. The yanks should have taken notice a bit quicker because the French back home in Paris were still picking dried Nazi jizz off their Sunday best and didn't fancy another fight. Too right they were shit at it, ha, ha. Anyways there was a meeting to try and sort out the mess and just like Germany after World War Two it was separated or partitioned, South were pro-Western and allegedly democratic and the North was red, a communist socialist based state. The line between the two was called the 17th parallel, how fucking cold war can you get than that?"

Stevie was entranced by the conversation, he loved history but hearing from someone that lived and breathed it day in day out was intoxicating. Better than hanging around ropey looking whores who may or may not have a dick swinging between their legs upstairs.

"So, at this point the yanks feared, no scratch that. Shat themselves about the spread of communism and generally believed that if one country fell then all those around it would also eventually fall to the reds. The area of South East Asia had dozens of countries running from Burma down all the way to Indonesia and even Australia, meaning Vietnam was the first key battleground. The south of Vietnam however was in a fucking mess, the US backed this Catholic fella but he had particular dislike for the Buddhist majority. So he promptly started murdering them and ransacking pagodas and all that. That was never going to go down well especially after the Buddhist's started setting themselves on fire in the streets. The Central Intelligence Agency, the fucking CI fucking A then had him whacked and replaced. But it soon became clear no one was in charge in the south, so the north egged on by Russia started attacking. As the attacks on its navy boats and airstrips increased the US were brought slowly but surely into the war."

Stevie nodded and recalled the book he read all those years ago on that fateful train journey into London to meet Tristram.

"I read a book a few years back about the Tet offensive; the attack on US and South Vietnamese troops on the night of the lunar new year. From what I can remember it had effectively won the war for the North Vietnamese."

"That is right my learned friend, nice one, yep the Tet rumble set the record straight big time. The US used all the propaganda at its disposal to misinform the US population that it was winning the war but the Tet thing showed it was all a lie and the US were out of their depth and a long, long way from home. Okay so when you read that book you may remember that the NVA took a lot of casualties during the Tet offensive but it turned from a tactical loss for the NVA and Viet Kong, that would be the self-styled guerrillas, into an unprecedented strategic long term victory. That fuck-wad Richard Nixon became President of the US in 1968 and began pulling troops out but he upped the bombing to a whole new level and that my friend is why I am in Laos worrying about getting my Jacobs blown off."

He paused smiling.

"There had already been a systematic bombing programme in Vietnam called Operation Rolling fucking Thunder, sounds dramatic and it fucking was I tell ya. It ran between 1965 and 1968 but that sneaky cunt Nixon is one of the reasons I drive a fucking Porsche ha ha. Throughout there was a secret war going on which concerned the bombing of the Ho Chi Minh trial in Vietnam, Cambodia and Laos in the vain hope it would stem the tide of goods, weapons, clothes food and soldiers into strategically important areas in south and west Vietnam. I am a bit of a stats man and the stats from that war are un-fucking-believable. The US dropped over 2 million tonnes of ordnance on Laos in over 500,000 sorties. That equates to a planeload of bombs taking off every 8 minutes, 24 hours a day, 7 days a week for a whole 9 horrible years. They ranged from big 1,000 pounders to small cluster bombs no bigger than an orange, there are an estimated 80 yes, 80 fucking million of them things lying around out there. And mate I have seen first-hand the damage that they do, mostly kids, cause kids go and play in places that adults don't. So even although I am making serious coin I know I am actually doing something pretty fucking decent."

Stuart looked away from the television from the football being played in a far-off land where discarded bombs don't maim and kill thousands a year. He stares a 1000-yard stare at nothing in particular as he silently considers the information and his experiences. Stevie was in awe of the man thinking and knowing he would never see a fraction in his lifetime the things this man has. He then continued in a slow reflective melancholy filled tone.

"So all this, all this here is just really a legacy of war, here, Patong, Phuket where you've been fucking those whores...."

Stevie was about to interrupt and inform Stuart that he had never screwed anyone for money, screwed many people out of money for sure but never fucks whores however Stuart continued, still staring off into the distance.

"It's all just the detritus of war, the US marines would get some R&R and come and drink and fuck in Bangkok and Patong, the US Navy would anchor up and then let loose in Phuket. And it continues to this day, and the only reason was that shitty war. It's the only reason I am here if you think about it, just another squit, a fucking skid mark left over from the 60's."

Stuart eventually snaps out of his despondency by again chugging the rest of his beer down his throat in double quick time before pointing at Stevie's bottle. Stevie nods and Stuart in turn nods at the ladyboy pointing at the two empty drinks bottles. She is leant against the fridge feigning indifference and agitation at the request before eventually bending down to retrieve two beers from the chiller.

"So before all this I was in the British Army, served in Northern Island, then Iraq in 91 and then Bosnia. I am not bomb disposal by trade, I was part of the units in Iraq and Bosnia but I was team leader for overall security. Whilst the boys are on their hands and knees, deciding whether to cut the blue or the red wire we would be making sure they are covered from any hostile locals or spotting if someone was planning to set the things off remotely. A load of us were offered redundancies in the late 90's and I knew there was a tonne of work for us, so I set up a company and started touting our services to various governments. Laos has a big, big problem, the most bombed country in the history of this Earth. $2,000 for anything between 200 and a 1000 pounder, of which we do about three a day, and $500 for each cluster bomb. Anyone in Laos who locates one gets $30 a bomb, so you can imagine, there is a mini industry of getting out there and finding ordinance, bomb locating is now peoples day jobs. The sale of fucking metal detectors is through the roof in Laos ha, ha. I have a backlog of about six months, I have one fella that travels the country to where they have found a bomb and they rope it off put up a big sign that basically says don't let your kids jump on this."

"That's over two million quid" exclaimed Stevie.

"That's right, fucking good coin ah? but you imagine sitting there straddling a 30-year-old rusting 800 pound bomb in 35 degrees of heat and a 100% humidity. Knowing one false move could obliterate you and anyone else nearby in a milli second. It's brutal mate, and one of the reasons you come to a gaff like this to blow a bit of steam off."

"So what you defuse them?"

"No we blow the fuckers up, that's the best bit mate the blast wave of a 1,000 pounder is something everyone should feel, it is fucking intense."

"Anyway things are on the up with all that business over in New York. The third party security business is about to go through the roof, dangerous new world out there mate. Forget communism, the free world has a new enemy, Islamic nutcases. George Bush is a bonafide shit kicker from Tey-k-sas who is gonna kick some Arab arse and fuck the consequences and repercussions which is hopefully where I come in."

"I am flying back to the UK day after tomorrow to hook up with an old army pal, he has a security firm in the UK working in the more traditional space such as close protection, you know bodyguards and event security. He has a few ex-cops doing investigation work finding missing kids and catching husbands fucking their secretaries and all that. We are combining our two companies which will include my areas of specialism such as the bomb disposal stuff but also soldiers for hire. Some might call them mercenaries, proper armed security for whoever needs it, maybe ships sailing close to mad dog countries and that kind of thing. The company is called BlackView, pretty fucking cool name huh?" grinned Stuart as he handed Stevie a black glossy business card.

"Yeah that is cool, that's a mad business to be in that. Sounds a bit dodgy" replied Stevie knowing the contradiction he was making considering his drug dealing activities.

"Blokes with guns is always dodgy mate, doesn't matter if you are in the army or planning a post office job. It's always going to be a bit thingy."

"Fuuuuck" screamed Stuart suddenly making Stevie jump in fright.

"Fucking cunt, fucking diving cunt" he roared as Chelsea defender Melchiot clumsily tackled Marcus Stewart inside the box. The conversation stopped as the fallen English striker picked himself up off the floor and proceeded to drill the penalty shot past Bosnich, the cocaine sniffing Chelsea goalkeeper.

"Fucking wankers, that fucking Eye Tie fucking wank-stain manager, fucking knocked out of Europe last week and now drawing with these cousin fucking inbreeds, for fucks sake."

He shook his head draining the bottle and looked at Stevie his eyebrows raised in expectation. Stevie had barely touched his bottle but dug deep downing it and was just about to order when Craig, China and Tanner arrived.

"Just in time, I'll have a Singha please Mr Chambers. Yes fucking Chelsea cunts getting held at home, fucking love it" shouted

Craig, pleased as punch with the score line.

"You fucking what? I am a Chelsea cunt as you put it" dead-panned Stuart stepping off his stool going to his full height, all six foot seven inches of it.

Craig could take care of himself, a decent match for many but even he had the sense to bottle this one and start grovelling.

"Sorry mate, didn't realise you were Chels, just fucking about. I'll get the beers in, what you having fella, see you've met up with my good friend here" he whined placing an arm around Stevie.

"Yeah he seems pretty sound unlike some of his companions" replied Stuart eyeing up the trio. China and Tanner could barely stand both drenched in spilt beer, whisky and sweat.

"Yesssss have that cunt" he suddenly roared pointing a finger at Craig, digging him hard in the chest with his forefinger.

Sam Dalla Bona had fired in a rocket shot from twenty yards out past the Ipswich keeper deep in stoppage time to take three points at the bridge.

CHAPTER 25

Golden Virginia

T hey walked briskly back to his house hand in hand. As Stevie fumbled with the keys in the lock, Stacey pressed against him, he froze enjoying the sensation of close contact.

"Will you stop that? I am struggling to stick my key in the lock."

"As the bishop said to the actress" she giggled taking a step back, leaning against the brick work as he continued to fiddle around with his keys.

"Drink?"

"I think I have had enough and it's a school night for you remember. Let's go to bed" she replied lustily, a flinty look in her eyes.

"Okay you're the boss, you go up I need make a quick phone call."

He watched her bounce up the stairs and into the bathroom. He smiled as he heard the shower going and again a few nerves began popping into his stomach. The thought of getting into bed again filled him with excitement that was off-set by the fear of the phone call he needed to make but he dialled it anyway.

"Alright Howard Webb, this is Gary Barlow" came a voice on the end of the line.

They used a vast array of code names for people and places, time and dates. Names of famous band members was one. Starting out this was one of the more fun areas as they both vied for the best names. Similar to *Reservoir Dogs* no one wanted to be Mr Pink. As far as boy band *Take That* were concerned, Craig was Robbie Williams and Kaiser or other associates from DDK Gary Barlow.

For others Stevie was Sporty, Ringo, Keith Richards, Tinky Winky. Craig was Posh, Lennon, Jagger and Dipsy. DDK was Scary Spice (obviously), George, Ronnie and Laa-Laa.

"We've been waiting for you to call Mr Webb, trouble in the recording studio?"

"Yeah you could say that. One of the band members has left and took some of the masters with him. I am working on some new ones but might not be ready for a while."

"Best if we meet up then, next month (next week)?"

"Okay be appreciated if you could come around mine (central London) rather than yours (Tottenham)."

"Alright let's do early and how about we meet north of the border."

"Sounds good, see ya then."

North of the border was a specific spot near Smithfield's market and St Guys hospital next to a memorial plaque for William Wallace who was hung, drawn and quartered nearby in 1305 and subsequently made famous by Mel Gibson in *Braveheart*. It was a good location where they could walk, talk and thrash out the details of what was owed and how long to repay. It was also fairly public so Stevie was confident that he would not be on the receiving end of anything nasty.

He hung up hearing Stacey moving around in his bedroom upstairs. He followed suit by jumping in the shower washing away the sweat from a day in the sun drinking. He applied a liberal dusting of talcum powder whilst humming a Dr Dre tune replacing the line *"Smoke weed everyday"* with *"Talc your sack everyday"*.

He crept into the bedroom in case she had fallen asleep and was relieved that she was not. She was laying on the large bed in one of his t-shirts only just covering the smooth curve and rise of her hips. He initially thought she was not wearing any knickers but as he moved into the bedroom he noticed a few centimetres of a thin lace that disappeared from view between her cheeks. He instantly felt a twinge as he laid eyes on her, she was exquisite, simply one of the most beautiful things he had laid his eyes on. He swallowed hard, the sound seeming to reverberate around the room. She could tell he was nervous but if there was a situation where she did not feel nerves it was being partially naked clothed in the company of men. All those years of modelling in various stages of undress in front of the camera and an assortment of letchy leering males had made her confident in such situations.

"Hello!"

"Hi" replied Stevie nervously swaying a little as the situation and alcohol took its toll.

He laid down beside her with nothing but a towel around his waist and they immediately started kissing, slowly at first but as their hands began to explore each other it became more passionate, more heated. Their tongues probed one another, he put his hands around her, pushed up her back and felt her long slender frame, stroking up and down. She broke off attacking his neck with soft playful bites pushing him onto his back. The towel came loose from around his waist, it was still covering him but the bulge of his excitement was unmistakeable. She sucked and chewed his nipples, little bursts of pleasure rippled from head to groin like an electrical current and he pulsed and ached with the sensation.

She seized him through the towel with her left hand and softly rubbed it, the rough texture of the newly washed towel adding to the sensation.

"Must not buy cheap fabric conditioner again" he thought as he desperately fought to control himself.

She whisked the towel away and moved down the bed between his legs and took him in her mouth. She leant forward sucking him whilst firmly holding the base of his hard member, her blonde hair splayed across his stomach and he moved it back over her head so he could watch her. Their eyes locked as she worked her magic on him. After a few minutes he tried to get up to return the favour.

"Lay back down" she then commanded.

"Yes mam" he replied in a croaking American accent that made her laugh.

She straddled him easing the head of his hard dick into her, slowly moving up and down, not full penetration, teasing him.

She continued, her eyes closed biting her bottom lip as Stevie looked on in wonder at her. She leaned backwards off her knees placing both feet on the bed, cowgirl style facing him. Stevie continued to look on in sheer and utter amazement. She pivoted on him, turning slightly to the side before plunging down his length completely enclosing him.

A flood of sensation exploded, he groaned trying in vain to hold on but he could not. As he cried out she bucked up and down on him to ensure maximum pleasure from the abrupt ending.

She flopped down on him both breathing hard laughing and giggling lightly before eventually clambering off and going to the toilet to clean herself up. Stevie crawled under the bed sheets, his heart still beating fast in his chest, a smile on his face.

"Fuck. One pump and a squirt, great. Oh well, no one could have done much better being ridden like that" he giggled quietly to himself.

After she returned they held each other and she feel into a deep sleep in minutes. Stevie took a while to get off due to a mixture of apprehension for tomorrow's meeting with DDK and excitement of finally being with Stacey. He looked at her and hoped it was not a one-night stand thing. Girls were a different breed, she could leave tomorrow and that would be that, he did not think that would be the case but he was not 100% sure.

He did all the right things in the morning, creeping out of bed and quietly opened the front door to retrieve *The Independent* and the *Daily Mail* newspapers which he had delivered every day. He did not know why he got the Mail, maybe it was a routine thing. His mum and dad always read it. As he grew up him began to realise their right-wing bias and he bought it more for amusement purposes thinking about all the older generations getting in a flap as they devoured the lurid headlines of psychopathic illegal paedophile immigrants. He smiled as he read the headline on front page.

Legacy of the Laddette

Women's binge drinking is linked to alarming rise in teenage promiscuity and abortions, finds major UK study.

"Aaaaah perfect reading for the lady upstairs" he laughed as he turned to the back pages which were full of doom and gloom about England's chances in the remainder of the World Cup. He went through to the kitchen and was pleased that it was relatively clean, he had not noticed last night but China's girlfriend had cleaned up before going to the pub yesterday.

"If she is as kindhearted as that boy China then that is a match made in heaven."

He then left a secretary at D&C a voicemail informing her he was sick. His throat was hoarse and croaky from the weekends antics so he did not need to put it on too much.

He set about making breakfast, getting everything organised to ensure that it all came together at the right moment so nothing was left cold. First he put the bacon and tomatoes under the grill. He tended to alternate between back and streaky bacon whilst shopping. He stayed away from red meat as he had high cholesterol courtesy of his family genes but normally allowed himself a bacon sandwich at the weekend, normally after a run. He put the grill on half power as he preferred to cook long and slow ensuring the fat rendered and crisped up. From the bread bin he took out two muffins cutting them in half before placing them in his beige four rack toaster. He made two large mugs of tea, one from the Grasshopper coffee shop in Amsterdam and the other from Starbucks which he had nicked at some point, petty opportunistic theft was something he had never truly grown out of.

Next he pulled out two wooden serving trays placing them on the kitchen island, he squinted at the chopping board where there had previously been a large pile of coke, it was all gone, not a single crumb left. He put a large plate on each tray and squirted both Heinz tomato sauce on one side and HP brown sauce on the other. He was a red man but you could never tell with some people and getting it wrong was often sacrilegious.

The timer went off and he placed the eggs on the muffins and placed the bacon and tomatoes on the plates. He finished off with a healthy dose of seasoning via the salt and pepper grinders, also stolen, from the table at Scott and Esters wedding.

He took Stacey's tray and noisily stomped up the stairs with it.

"Breakfast fit for a princess" he announced loudly as he entered.

He wanted to make sure that there were no uncomfortable silences or awkwardness between them, so he played the host to its fullest.

"Blimey I could get use to this" she said jumping upright propping herself up with a pillow.

"Red and brown eh? Hedging your bets there Steven? Come on then what do you really think?"

"Red without a doubt."

"Correct in part, sausage sarnies are brown, all the rest is red but I will have a dip as you made the effort."

"Right I will be back in a minute. Will go and grab mine, oh and someone's been writing about you, hang on."

He returned with the paper folded up under his own breakfast tray.

"I think someone has been tailing you this weekend. He laughed as he threw the paper front page up."

"Oi you cheeky fecker, I gave up being a laddette in 2004. And as for being promiscuous you were the first person I have had intimate relations with for nearly six months."

"I thought you were quite enthusiastic, anyway enjoy your breakfast" he replied as he got into bed.

They ate their breakfast in near but not uncomfortable silence, the distant hum of Monday morning traffic and tweeting of birds from outside through the partially opened windows was enough.

"That was delicious thank you" she said leaning over to kiss him on the cheek.

"Blimey did you even chew it?" he said looking down at her empty plate, his still only half eaten.

She giggled and then slid a hand under the duvet and began massaging his penis making the tray on his lap bounce up and down. He stiffened under her grip as he tried to stop the cup of tea from spilling. She leant in close to him whispering in his ear.

"Hurry up!"

CHAPTER 26

Samaritan's Dilemma

Stevie had lost contact with Stefan Stockdale. After Craig was jailed he expected Stefan to contact him about supplying him gear but there was nothing. He put the word out, eventually tracking him down in Brighton, organised to meet him in a pub but he did not turn up. After another no-show he finally tracked down his home address. He nearly turned back when he saw the property, it was more or less a squat, the front door was wide open and as he approached a man was leaving clutching a Pioneer CDJ deck. Without knocking Stevie entered. The overpowering stench of cat shit hit him like a punch to the face as he entered made worse by the early summer heat. It nearly forced him back out the front door but he breathed through his mouth and stood in the front room. There was rubbish everywhere, a pair of long-haired men were passed out on the floor in a heap.

On the sofa sat Stefan, he still had his dark hair kept long but now could clearly see the receding grey flecked hairline. He was wearing purple Asian fisherman's trousers, naked from the waist up, his numerous tattoos clearly visible of varying degrees of age and quality, some which Stevie recognised from before. The detailed ornate sleeves on his arms still looked good, most likely inked in some of the best tattoo studios around the globe. But there were others; thick amateurish markings across his torso. Stefan eventually registered his presence in the room looking up taking a while to recognise who was stood before him.

"Stevie, is that you mate?" he half slurred, half groaned looking through one eye at him.

"Hello Stefan, yes mate it's me, how's it going?"

"Who me? Me? The washed up DJ? Ha, ha, haaaah. Yes mate I am all good, all good in the fucking hood" he croaked as he began to nod off again, his head falling forwards before it jerked upwards as he came back into the world of the living, kind of.

"Yes, yes all is well captain, all is well, hmmmm, good, good. Well, hmmmm I just sold my bloody decks which I'm obviously not happy about but needs must, needs must, indeed they do. Decided to give the gigging and that a rest for a bit, you know what I mean, wait until next summer and get back touring again. Still getting loads of calls to play out and that, just you know, man, cannot be bothered like."

Stefan glanced over to where his decks, records and CD's used to be, a few marks on the barren wall the only indication of his beloved equipment that had been there. He could not even see the empty shelves as he had sold them too.

Stevie kept fairly up to date with the dance music scene, he still loved it and thought 2010 was a decent time for house music. The US seemed to have finally woken up to the delights of electronic beats after years of being hooked on hip-hop and rap and it had exploded with a bang. Miami and Vegas were the new Ibiza and Berlin. House went through a weird phase a few years back going minimal, stripped down and soulless. Linked no doubt in part to rise in ketamine on the dance floors, the so-called k-holes aligned with the chugging monotony of the music.

Stefan peaked in popularity around 2002 and as the drugs took an ever tighter grip he became increasingly more unreliable and arrogant, demanding ridiculous riders and either turning up late or not at all and then refusing to repay any money paid up front. Bad news travels fast in that little sphere, so promoters began looking elsewhere, gradually gravitating towards the new breed of superstar DJs, not traditional DJs but producers and remixers like Milo, Layo & Bushwacka and more recently Calvin Harris and Hot Since 82. Stefan was spot on; he was washed-up alright. The old school DJs either had to diversify, like Sasha, who reinvented himself releasing the amazing *Revolver* album or Jon Digweed pumping out contemporary electronica and house under his *Bedrock* label both keeping in the limelight, up to date on the latest sounds and booked up behind the decks. Others had to make do with low paid old school reunion parties which begun to creep in amongst the regular club night circuit.

As Stevie looked on, he thought that Stefan looked incapable of mixing a vodka and orange let alone a couple of house music tracks. But worse was he was in no position physically or financially to start buying any gear. Fuck. That cow has been milked for all it is worth. He could have simply walked out and written him off, Stefan was so out of it he probably would not even realise or even remember his visitor. Stevie had disliked Stefan immensely over the years, half blamed him for bringing Craig down with him but they were actually just as bad as each other. But as he looked at him, surveying the wreckage of his home, he began to feel immensely sorry for him and as he had often done many times before a sting of guilt began to ripple through him. An often-temporary sting but a sting, nevertheless. So, he sat down and tried to talk to him.

"How are you feeling mate? You alright, do you want me to get you anything?"

"Eeeeargh? How is that, err, who is this?"

"Me Stevie. Woodbridge represents, remember."

"Aaaaargh Woodbridge in the area! Decent crew from Woodbridge, nice lads, cool little crew. Stevie you old cunt ha ha ha, hmmm. You got any powder mate, could do with a lil' pick me up, know what I mean."

Stevie had bought along half an ounce, on the off-chance Stefan was off and ready to go. He would have no trouble sniffing but paying him would be another matter entirely.

"Yes mate, here you go he said throwing the baggie on the table."

"Hmmm, nice one mate, nice one. Not done any powder for a while as it goes trying to lay of it, know what I mean? Fucking hell that's a nice bags worth, nice, nice, reminds me of the good old days eh? When Kings were Kings and people danced in the swaying fields until the sun rose eh?"

"I think people are still dancing till dawn mate."

"Yeah yeah, they are, yes they are, people are never gonna stop dancing well not until that sun in the sky has burned to its last ember and the world is no more. But the problem is though they are now dancing to someone else's tune, hmmm yes they are, someone else's tune, not mine."

He had his head over the table looking through one eye as he racked an enormous line. He took two attempts to get it up his nose. He kept missing. 'Air shots' they used to jokingly call it. Stevie and Stefan were not laughing now. Gradually the gear began to work its way through the numerous opiates, sparked his brain into a bit more life and like most folks high he began to talk. But this time it was different, Stefan was always a big head, full of shit and jam packed with ego and arrogance that was beyond compare. But now he was different and he talked in a way Stevie had never heard before. He began to talk lucidly about his life and like a cocaine lubricated zipper opened up. He did not look at Stevie once just stared at the wall opposite and talked and talked. And Stevie just listened and listened.

"I think about when I was growing up a lot these days, I don't know why, I just do. I cannot remember much. It's weird. They say that in the end when you finally meet your maker the only thing that you really have, no matter what you have done in your life, good bad or indifferent, is your memories. Ha, ha, ha well that's a joke I cannot remember fuck all about the last twenty years but my memories of being a kid are incredibly vivid, just like yesterday. You know I never knew I was different, I mean really different, until I was about ten which might sound odd, I thought everyone was like me, going to Bar Mitzvahs and all that thing. That was until I got my nose broken at school where this big lanky piece of piss fucking sucker punched me in the bogs. Nearly knocked me out but stayed lively just down on the deck like. Spat on me and called me a yid. I didn't really know what to make of it to be honest but from that day on I knew I was different; I don't look that Jewish only the lack of a foreskin really gives it away."

"So from then on between the years of twelve and sixteen I was like prey, fucking prey man. I had a shitty old time of it at school. I think one year I was coined every day for a whole year. They used to throw one and two pence pieces at me. Fucking yid cunt, Spurs scum, gas the cunt, Hitler had the right idea, fucking went on and on. Man I fucking hated it, I tried to persuade my parents to move me to a school in Golders Green where everyone was a kike but they wouldn't, could not afford the house prices there, which was bollocks, they had that Jew trait alright fucking tight arses ha ha. So had to ride it out at a comprehensive in Wembley. I tried to top myself one day, well not really tried, more like seriously considered it. Took myself up to Potters Bar train station, you know the one that all them people died when the train derailed and got lodged in the station. Was a few years back I think."

"2002" replied Stevie.

"Yeah, maybe, anyway was stood on that platform, you know in my school uniform, thinking about taking that one step when a fast train comes through the station. Fucking nearly did it mate, nearly did it...... Maybe I should have done, maybe I should have done."

He lit a cigarette and inhaled the smoke deeply into his lungs. Stevie was about to say something reassuring but Stefan continued.

"Acid house was what saved me, my salvation. Sounds cheesy I know but it's true and it all came about by accident. You know that I went to, what was probably, only the third ever true acid house party in the UK? My cousins' best mate was Nicky Holloway, I was depressed as fuck, about seventeen or so. My cousin fucking literally dragged my sorry arse down to this place that Nicky ran. It was at this place called the Project Club, this was before Ramblings Shoom even opened up south of the river. There was about forty of us in there, I turned up in my trench coat, I was a borderline goth to be honest trying to shake off the Jew thing I suppose. Anyway, I was skulking around in the corners of this little club eyeing up all these crazy looking fuckers wearing all this tie dye baggy shit and floppy hats. I remember how I felt sat there in my little corner chain smoking cigarettes seeing all these beaming smiles, best mates back slapping each other and hugging, it made me feel a hundred times worse. What are these cunts so fucking god damn happy about? I remember thinking I would never be like them. I was miserable, teenage anger and hormones destroying me from within. Plus, I felt persecuted, hated. Imagine being a Jew Stevie, knowing that half of the world's population wants to wipe you off the face of the earth and put you and any unlucky off-spring in the ground. Fucking sucks pal, fucking sucks and being seventeen, bullied, no girlfriend, a virgin with only a couple of mates who were not really mates! Fucking mates because they were Jewish and it was safer in a pack not because of some kindred connection."

"Well you know what happened but fuck me mate did it happen or what! IT happened. Oh fucking hell mate, IT happened all right. My cousin came bouncing over to my table where I was sat with a pint of flat cider and held out his hand. Through the darkness of this dingy club I could see this little white pill in his hand. Didn't have a brand or logo or nothing just a plain white pill. Didn't know it then but that little white pill was to be the trigger for my ascent, kabooom and catalyst for my descent, peeewoooooh. He was grinning at me like a village idiot, so I snapped at him. I shouted 'What? What the fucking hell is that?', he replied 'It's a pill fella and it's gonna make you feel good, feel reeeal good. Think you need cheering up cuzz, fed up of seeing your sorry slapped arse of a face.' As you can imagine I wasn't convinced."

"But it was probably enough of an argument for me so I necked it there and then. I remember thinking nothing could possibly make me happy so what is a poxy little pill going to do? So I continued to just sit there, face like thunder. Aaaah but fucking hell, it happened all right, you know, you've been through it Stevie. 20 minutes later it happened. I started to really feel the tunes, a little flutter in the guts as the bass-line dropped."

"Those were the days before proper four to the floor house music, it was late 87 and the music was pretty varied, a lot of different types of tracks playing, like old Balearic classics like *Jibaro* and that but I remember sat there as this track began to be played. It started off with the sounds of an audience cheering and this voice sang "Can you feeeel it" over and over and then the kick drum and this synth bass-line just dropped and then this warm, warm, warm synth pad just drifted in amongst the hi-hats fluttering into life and those little tingles began to happen, up my back in up behind my ears. You know the tingles Stevie lad, you've been there I've seen ya a hundred times out there on the floor having it but fuck me, fuck me, I sat there and it was like a revelation was happening right there in my soul, like watching your first ever proper sunrise with your first true love hand in hand. I remember every little detail of the moment, every little detail of the track. If I had listened to it in my bedroom the day before I would have probably hated it and turned off and listened to The Smiths or something but those synths got me tingling and the hi-hats got my leg going, juddering up and down as I sat there. The small crowd on the dance floor cheered and hollered as some more synth pads built and then a voice bellowed and let everyone know about Jacks House ha ha."

Stevie listened and looked on as suddenly Stefan eyes were once again ablaze with passion about the music and scene he so obviously loved.

"Oh man what a night, what a night. Before I knew it I was off and running, well dancing. I jumped off my stool and half danced, half ran over to the DJ who was raised slightly above the dance floor in the booth. I was buzzing and literally pleaded with him to tell me what the track was called.

"He was beaming from ear to ear his big mouth curling up at the corners. *'Can you feel it?'* mate by Mr Fingers, fucking top ain't it? he shouted at me. That DJ was Paul Oakenfold. Yep Mr Paul Okenfold playing in a dingy club near Charing Cross to 40 people. He became my instant hero and my role model, probably didn't realise it quite then but that was when I wanted to become a DJ. I locked that tune in my mind, my legs, my arms right there, locked it in the tune bank. I jumped back down onto the dance floor and that night, man, that night was the first time I felt accepted, I danced and danced and danced. I spoke, hugged and kissed probably every single person in that room, never experienced anything like it in my life man. No one gave a fuck about whether the next person was black, white, rich, poor, Christian, Arab or me being Jewish. It was mental and the person I hugged the most was my cousin. What a top bloke, can you imagine being at the start of the most exciting ground-breaking youth movement fucking thing that had hit London town, Manchester, the whole of the fucking UK for years and it was that joyous cunt that did it for me? The 60's was all about "Who You Were' the acid house scene was all about 'Whatever You Wanted To Be'. I wanted to be anything other than a fucking depressed goth Jew. My cousin dragged his freaky blood relative down with him to let him in on the secret. I remember later on that night he was stood at the side of the dance floor proper having it but at the same time I could feel his eyes on me. I could feel that he knew what he had done."

He took a breath as his eyes suddenly blazed with recollection.

"I dived head first into the scene. From the top board man. I am not talking about the drugs either, that all came later. The music, the culture. I tried to find out as much about it as possible. The US. Ron Hardy and his Music Box in Chicago together with Chip E, Larry Heard, Marshal Jefferson, Adonis, DJ Pierre. Frankie Knuckles moving from New York to Chicago to open The Warehouse, the reason why house music is called house music. The Detroit three from Belleville; Atkins, Saunderson and May creating techno out of the post-industrial wastelands of the motor city. The New Yorkers; David Mancuso in the lofts and Larry Levan DJ'ing for years at the Paradise Garage. The Europeans, basically Kraftwerk, riding the Trans-Europe Express laying the blueprint for modern day house and techno. But all that overseas history and knowledge was difficult to come by back in the late 80's, no fucking internet or Wikipedia back then. Just buying tunes, reading music magazines and hanging out in record shops. So I just got involved with the UK scene that was bubbling away like a pressure cooker ready to explode, which it did in 88. Trevor Fung, Tony Wilson, Rampling, Oakenfold, Holloway, Clink Street, Hacienda, The Trip, Shoom, Junior Boys Own, 808 State, Baby Ford, Sunrise, Genesis, KLF, LFO, A Guy Called Gerald, Spiral Trip, DiY, Orbital, fucking hell I could go on and on. You see it wasn't so much the drugs but the scene. You know, you were out and about back then. Young, dumb and full of doves. Set me free maybe, I don't know."

"Problem was from that first night I didn't stop for about eighteen years, fucking great times, travelled the world, seen some shit I have, had a laugh, met some heads man, like you and Craig, had a serious amount of sex but it has all lead to this place. Sat here, broken, full of skag, fucking skint as fuck, talking to fucking you. Brutal man, pure brutal. No offense, like."

He fell silent as those rose-tinted glasses fell off.

"And now look at me. Remember when you and Craig came over to

Miami that time. I was paid thirty-five grand for two DJ sets, thirty five grand plus expenses, of which there were many, to play some-one's else's fucking records."

Stevie tried to keep him positive but he could feel the mood darkening.

"Listen, me and you have never seen eye to eye but you are without doubt one of the best ever DJs I have ever seen play. I think back to some of those great nights, most of them involved you playing at some point. I would like to see the new generation mix two pieces of vinyl like you can."

Stefan did not respond. Stevie looked over and could see a tears welling up in his eyes.

"Do you need help mate? And I don't mean giving you anymore of that shit neither."

"I don't think I can, I am trapped, fucking pure trapped man. Wish I was banged up like Craig, could do with being forced into going straight but I don't reckon my body could take the withdrawal. Reckon I would fucking just die. Tried it a few times. It's like someone has an iron claw inside your body ripping ya to shreds. Trapped mate, cannot wiggle out of this one."

"No you're not trapped, you just need some help. Let's go now. Right now and I will get you booked in, today."

Stefan turned his head.

"You would do that? I don't have any money."

"I have so don't worry about it."

"You mean right now."

"Yep right now let's go."

Stefan's junkie brain started kicking in. The very thought of being in a car on a motorway without anything in him, scared the living daylights out of him.

"Errrr"

"Listen mate, go and get your works sorted, take a hit and we'll get you in the car. But listen I have a bit of money but not loads. Craig left me right in the shit and I am still paying for it. I will give you a shot at getting cleaned up and you can get back out there gig-ging again. But this is a one-time offer, alright, if you cannot hack it and give in that is it, I won't be back down here again with the same offer."

"I will try" Stefan weakly replied.

So Stevie had travelled to Brighton to try and reignite his faltering drug empire and ended up shelling out over £20,000 to put Stefan through a drug rehabilitation programme out in Wiltshire. Stefan had probably paid him and Craig over a million over the years and Stevie felt it was the least he could do.

CHAPTER 27

End Game

"**A**lright quieten down please, oi you at the back QUIET!"

"Thank you ladies and gentlemen."

The operations room on the fourth floor of the SO19 special Police unit at Shoreditch Police station was alive with noise and chatter as the anticipation of the forthcoming operation was discussed in huddled groups around the room.

Superintendent Alex Jarvis walked into the large room to give the final briefing after being given the formal green light. The SO19 armed response unit had been working closely with the team from Operation Trident for the last two years and had been involved in several joint-ops. Some of these had gone off without a hitch, arrests were made and criminals successfully prosecuted, all round good jobs. Others had not, some gang members had come out shooting or wielding a variety of weapons, knifes, swords, CS gas and all manner of other things. In some cases they had opened fire, injuring and in some cases killing the criminals. Irrespective of the different outcomes this is what these officers lived, trained and prepared for. These events did not come around often, one maybe two a month and most were an anticlimax in the greater scheme of things. Some officers had been in some legendary shoot outs and were well respected, seemed to walk with a slightly more arrogant gait, chests puffed out a little more. In their heart of hearts these were who SO19 all looked up to, who they aspired to be whether it was a sniper from distance or the first through the door with a flash bang and a Heckler and

Koch at the ready.

Jarvis surveyed the room casting his eyes across his team, mostly men but with a small compliment of women. He was old enough to have witnessed a huge change in the Police force. Twenty or thirty years ago this room would have been thick with cigarette smoke, full of overweight, semi alcoholic coppers. He regarded this new breed with a great deal of pride; young, clean cut, fit and athletic. They looked more like a SWAT team from a Hollywood blockbuster. He was in no doubt that many had a corrupt streak in them, just like his good self but he had not deemed it necessary to find out. He had been wise in his younger days in the drug squad and had put more than enough back for his retirement and he was not going to risk his gold-plated retirement package. In addition, he received a regular payment from Lord Lawton every month as a retainer and if Cee Bugg was killed today he was in for at least £10k.

He confidently looked around the room, there was a vibe, a vibe that this one was going to go off and a good chance their firearms would be discharged. In anger, in retaliation or for protection. Whatever. During 2010 there had been open warfare between the predominantly black gangs on the streets and housing estates all over London. There was no real reason for it as some seemed unrelated and localised whilst others, such as the current Dam Dem Kings and Burchess Street Crew beef, seemed inextricably linked. Maybe it was the remnants of the recession, people becoming more and more desperate given the governments drive for austerity. The violence spilling out onto the streets as the gangs of London tried to expand their drug dealing operations and territory, grab market share, get whatever slim pickings were available. Maybe it was sheer boredom and lack of opportunity for inner city youth. Whatever it was, the disagreement between of DDK from Tottenham and BSC from Tower Hamlets was flaring up and revenge was due to be served up on the streets today.

Intelligence strongly indicated that Cee Bugg of DDK was going to kill a member of BSC and it was the SO19's job to stop that happening and take him off the streets. It was of course Jarvis's secret task to have him killed, on specific orders from Lord Lawton. Given the situation, the intel and Cee Bugg's propensity for aggression and violence Jarvis thought it could be done. Difficult but doable. All he had to do was get this little speech right. He had to get their fingers just itchy enough for one of them to pull the trigger when the time came but he could not of course give them a direct order, which would be tantamount to an assassination. He remembered the rumours about what Margaret Thatcher had allegedly told the head of the SAS before they stormed the Iranian embassy siege in 1980. Six armed gunmen entered the building taking 26 hostage for six days. The SAS in full view of the media stormed the embassy killing all but one of the terrorists who slipped out with the fleeing hostages.

The Iron Lady "did not want any ongoing problems!"

If it was true, the commander would have been in no doubt what that meant and maybe that was the reason why the SAS team went in so hard, firing dozens of rounds. As he thought about Maggie clutching her handbag, giving her murderous orders, he slowly walked to the front of the room taking a deep breath before addressing the SO19 team.

"Okay listen up. I know that you have all read the operational brief and you all know what is expected of you, where and at what time you are due to be and who is accountable for what. But let me summarise."

"Mark Buggan aka Cee Bugg of the so-called Dam Dem Kings or the DDK gang hailing from Tottenham is currently at home, probably asleep. We have two lots of surveillance at the address, one out front and one out back. As you know we could get the call at any moment but we had a tail on him last night. He attended the Glass Club in Hackney until approximately 03:30 am and went home with a nice young lady which means we do not expect lover boy to be up and about until at least 2pm. That is two hours away but let's not drop the ball, from here on in we are on official stand by and we need to be ready to go at a minute's notice. Okay?"

"Yes boss" came the united reply. A ripple of adrenaline and pride tingled and prickled Jarvis making the hairs on his arms stand on end.

"Chris are the cars ready down in the pool?"

"Yes sir all ready, all fuelled."

"Everyone been to and checked out at the armoury?"

"Yes boss!" came another reply in unison.

"Anyone missing anything?"

"Tony has gone to get a ram jam just in case he gets into a property."

"Good idea. Okay so let me continue. So Cee Bugg is not particularly happy with the murder of his cousin Faxman which as you know happened 2 weeks ago at a club in Poplar. He was hacked up whilst taking a piss by a rival gang from Tower Hamlets, the Burgess Street Crew or the BSC as they are commonly called. They have been subtly probing into DDK territories in and around Tottenham and Hackney since Christmas. DDK look to be going on the offensive and Cee Bugg has been given the thumbs up to take out all of the BSC perpetrators starting with the suspected knifeman who lives in one of the main housing blocks in Tower Hamlets. He generally uses taxis to get around, he lost his license a couple of years ago and was fed up of being caught behind the wheel. From what we understand he will travel down by cab, probably pick up a firearm on route, we are not sure where and from whom. From there it is likely that he will wait around until dusk, go to the rival targets flat and carry out the hit."

"So, as per the brief we will take him on route. It is likely that he will travel down from Tottenham on the A10 and then onto Amherst Road, a cut through to the A107, the Upper Clapton Road."

Jarvis pointed to the large satellite image printout on the operations room wall.

"Tom's team, B Unit, will be parked up here, on Ellingfort Road. If it's a go, and it will be unless he takes a detour, Tom's two vehicles will block the road, here, forcing the cars to a stop, all blue lights and sirens going to make sure there is no misunderstanding it is the Police and not a rival. Unit A, led by Collins, will pull up back and sides in usual box-in formation."

Jarvis then prepared for the final most important part of the speech.

"Okay now I want to get serious. Cee Bugg is not one of these plastic gangsters that we come across more often than not. You have all seen his rap sheet. I would have been scared shitless of him when he was 14 yet alone 23. Now he is going to be armed, we are 99% sure of it and he will not be afraid to use it either. He is suspected of involvement in at least 6 murders in the last 3 years, so I do not want anyone taking any undue risks that could cause harm to either you or the public. Keep low behind the vehicles, blues and twos will be going, he will be in no doubt that it is the Police and if he sees good sense he will drop his firearm and go to nick quietly. However, if he has a firearm he knows he is going away for a long stretch so, and let me make this crystal clear, if you see a gun and he looks like he is going to use it against you or your fellow officers, then you have just cause. I and the Chief will back you all the way, just remember that. I don't want any misplaced sense of restraint if there is just cause and a clear and present danger."

Jarvis scanned the room, making eye contact with everyone, locking the serious grimace on his face, making sure every single one of the officers had registered what he had just said and that it had sunk in. This was serious, do not fuck about.

"All right, please keep reading the brief, keep studying the maps. Dave here is on the radio constantly with the surveillance teams, he will give you the nod when we are set. I will be travelling with Unit C just behind A. Any questions?"

Jarvis scanned the room again.

"No? Okay good, all right good luck and see you on the other side."

Jarvis purposefully strode out of the room and began playing back his speech in his mind, he thought he had done a good job. He did however have a little bit of insurance though; hedged his bets a little. One of his officers, Collins, was a little loose, a bit more cavalier and gun-ho than the others. Jarvis had made sure that he would be leading A Unit in the front passenger seat of the first car that pulls up behind and on the left of the vehicle. Cee Bugg was likely to be sat in the back-left passenger seat of the taxi and would likely exit the vehicle on the left. Collins would be closest to him from the get-go and if he saw Cee Bugg had a gun he would in all probability shoot him.

Jarvis had taken him to the side the day before and given him a pep talk, a little franker than the speech he had just given in the operations room, again he was careful to choose his words carefully but he was sure to land the message. He massaged Collins ego like a good football manager sometimes would with an under-performing striker. He said that he trusted Collins most in terms of decision making and being calm 'under-fire'. He visibly saw Collins chest swell with pride and Jarvis was sure that he would not want to let him down. He had sewn the seed beautifully.

Hours passed, the early buzz being gradually replaced with boredom as the house in Tottenham remained still and quiet. The newspapers were read back to front and numerous litres of coffees consumed. Then finally at 16:30 the communications operator raised his hand in the air, signalling an incoming update. He hunched over the radio unit with his large headphones scribbling notes, the team surrounding him hungry for news, eager for action. In nine times out of ten, there would be a 'stand-down' the operation cancelled for one reason or another.

Over in Tottenham, the two surveillance officers in the back of the white Ford transit van were peering through the blacked-out privacy glass as the front door to Cee Bugg's house opened. Out came a young girl wearing a glittering dress clearly worn the night before. Cee Bugg half appeared around the door wearing jogging bottoms, no top, a thick chunky gold chain hanging long and low between his huge, bulging, pectoral muscles.

"She looks a bit dishevelled" grinned one of the surveillance team.

"What's the betting she walks off like Jon Wayne? Put the call in" chuckled the other.

"Unit Zebra this is Unit Delta, suspect is active, repeat suspect is active. Unit Alpha, Bravo and Charlie please deploy to your holding areas over."

"Roger that, over" replied the comms operator before standing up to address the room.

"Mark Buggan is up and out of bed, all units deploy to holding locations, all units deploy" he stated firmly enough so all the room could hear him.

The operations room sprang back into life as everyone started rushing around gathering kit, gulping down the last dregs of water and coffee, putting on Police caps and flak jackets. Most ran down the stairs rather than using the lifts as the adrenaline and expectation began to bubble up. Jarvis was calm as he walked to the lift hearing the echoed chatter from his team that emanated up from the concrete stairwell. Down in the carpool he sat in the front passenger seat of the 3 litre Vauxhall Omega unmarked Police car. In the boot housed an impressive armoury of weapons, three Heckler and Kock fully automatic MP5SF's, two pump action twelve bore shotguns, a Heckler and Kock G3 sniper rifle and four Gloch 26 pistols. For many years the UK Police force did not carry weapons but times had changed. Jarvis recalled interviewing a Jamaican Yardi several years previously who whilst in custody grinned at him, telling him the yard love the UK because they can do what they want with no repercussions. He sang him the song.

"The cops don't bang and the law don't hang."

Previously hardcore violent criminals did not fear for their lives during bank robbery, heists, high jacking or whatever. Just a stretch at her Majesty's leisure but on the street it had changed and the Police had to follow suit. Jarvis heading up SO19 saw it more than most. There was on average 1,000 firearms offences in the 1970s which had risen to over 11,000 by 2006. SO19 was created in its wake in 2004 under Scotland Yard working closely with Operation Trident designed to tackle black on black gun crime.

As they left the Police compound Jarvis fiddled with the radio, the commentary from filling the car, there would now be constant updates every minute regardless of whether Cee Bugg had gone back to bed or not. A succession of Police vehicles left Shoreditch proceeding at a steady speed the short distance to the north.

The teams arrived at their holding location, a rundown industrial estate close to Tottenham Hale train station, and began another wait. It was a run-down area with most industrial units unoccupied so the three cars would not warrant too much attention. They parked and waited. After 30 minutes Jarvis stepped out to take a piss. As he was halfway through Collins shouted to him from his car.

"Boss we've got movement, hurry up!"

"Fucks sake" muttered Jarvis as he tried to empty his bladder in double quick time, there was no question of stopping. He tucked himself back into his trousers too quick and as he jogged back to his car, he felt the cold wet sensation down his leg, making him shiver.

"Fucking hell" he muttered as he cocked his leg and tried to dry off the crouch of his trousers.

"Come on boss let's go!!!!" shouted a hyped Collins urgently.

In spite of the piss stain Jarvis grinned to himself as he plopped down in the seat telling the driver to go. Collins was seriously fired up.

"*Fucking ace*" he thought excitedly as they screeched out of the industrial estate.

They drove in convoy towards the A10 at a steady pace. There was no panic as the surveillance team were tailing the taxi which had picked up Cee Bugg from his Tottenham house 10 minutes earlier. They were providing a second by second running commentary on location and position. There were three surveillance vehicles following him, all of them alternating the tail to ensure that he was not suspicious about anyone following.

Jarvis's car was quiet letting Unit A, the car in front, do the liaising on the radio. Jarvis would step in to provide direction if needed but he was confident that everyone knew their job, role and position.

"Suspect on A10 passing your junction on left in mark dot 30 seconds. Reminder suspects' vehicle is Mercedes silver C class. Suspect in rear, back left."

Jarvis grinned again as the three Police cars slowed so not to be in full view of the busy A10 ahead.

"*Perfect. All is going to plan.*"

Jarvis saw a flash of silver on the road ahead before Collins's car gunned towards the junction at speed. The front surveillance car directly behind Cee Bugg slowed up to let all three unmarked Police cars out as he indicated left. A perfect switch had been made. Collins car was an older battered pool car and Jarvis had purposefully chosen a black officer to drive, he was not pursuit trained but with his beeny hat he would not arouse suspicion if Cee Bugg glanced back at them. They had already planned to try and get a member of the public in between them at some point as they knew he would be picking up a gun during the journey and they needed a natural buffer to give them a bit of distance and time to react. Jarvis hoped it would be a quick handover. If Cee Bugg got out of the taxi the original surveillance team would go after him and the three cars would hold up somewhere and continue on the A10 towards the A107. If not, then the Police could be far enough back to continue after the firearm was passed directly into the taxi from the street.

The opportunity for a buffer arrived as a blue Renault Clio appeared with a young teenage driver at the wheel from a road on the left and Collins's car let him out giving them the desired barrier. If it was an old boy or a woman he would never have let him out as there would have been too much of a risk getting stuck behind them.

They turned into the one-way section heading through Stock Newington Common. A few hundred metres ahead they approached a pedestrian crossing next to a pub. A skinny Rastafarian, complete with a huge Rasta cap in a wheelchair started to cross. Halfway across he slowed up, one of his wheels had stuck and he held his hand up in apology to the traffic. Cee Bugg's taxi was three back in the queue. Jarvis strained his neck to see what was happening, the nerves kicking in with the unscheduled delay. From the right he saw a young black man dart out from the pub crossing the road quickly. As he passed the Mercedes he reached into his Adidas tracksuit and pulled out a brown paper bag. He put his hand through the small gap in the window that had been quickly wound down. The exchange took place. Unit A was keeping up a running commentary of what had just happened.

"IC3 male wearing dark blue Adidas tracksuit passed a package through the taxi window, now proceeding south on foot down Rectory Road away from A10."

Jarvis got on the net.

"Unit D do not turn onto A10, continue on down to Rectory Road and apprehend the suspect please, make sure you go in fast and make sure he does not get a call or a text off please."

"All units, all units. Suspect is now considered armed and dangerous. I repeat suspect is now considered armed and dangerous."

Jarvis was absolutely fucking buzzing.

The convoy moved slowly back onto the two-way section of the A10. A few minutes later, Collins voice broke through on the radio.

"We are approaching the turning to Amhurst Road, Unit B please be prepared to move on my mark if suspect does not take this route."

"Roger that, over!"

As they approached the turning the taxi did not indicate left and the officers in all cars froze, nervously waiting to see if the taxi would continue and send their plan into disarray. Jarvis would then need to take control and think on his feet. The routes ahead and implications rattled through his head as he stretched his neck to try and see what was happening.

At the last moment and to everyone's relief the taxi turned left onto Amhurst Road which was the cut through from Hackney to Tower Hamlets. As it turned Cee Bugg, always careful, leant forward in his seat and looked back at the cars following. The civilian car between the taxi and the unmarked Police vehicles did not turn left and carried on leaving Unit A, Collins car, pulled in directly behind them. They had been anticipating this, Collins had a cigarette between the grinning lips of his mouth and the black officer at the wheel was belly laughing at a joke.

Cee Bugg eyed the up but was unconcerned so tried to relax back into his seat. He had had a terrible hangover but two blasts of coke had swept it aside providing the necessary focus for what he was about to do. The anger and thirst for revenge for his cousins killing was bubbling away and he could not wait to put the gun into the guy's face and blow him away. He gripped the handgun, a well-oiled Sig 226 in his palm, turning it over in his hand feeling the weight, guessing how it would jolt and recoil as he fired, knew that he would need to get in close. The taxi driver knew what was going on but kept his eyes firmly on the road. DDK often used the taxi company and their drivers just drove, wherever they wanted. It was as simple as that, never looked into the back or in the rearview mirror, never asked questions, never engaged in any conversation unless prompted. Rape, drug dealing, violence, threats, insults, blackmail, robbery everything had happened at one time or another in the back of their cabs but they just kept quiet and drove. For this they always received a hefty tip on top of the fare.

Cee Bugg leant his head back and looked at the different types of shops and buildings and tried to calm himself down. He saw a Turkish grill bistro and a tiny knot of hunger appeared in his stomach rearing its head above the adrenaline, cocaine and residual alcohol from the night before.

He was brought back to his senses as the taxi driver jabbed his brakes sending him reeling forward in his seat. All of a sudden blue lights and sirens filled the air as two unmarked Police cars bolted out of a side street. For a moment Cee Bugg thought they would continue up the road in pursuit of someone else but the noses of the car bonnets were aimed directly at his taxi. Immediately he knew he was in a corner. The thought of vengeance disappeared from his thoughts and escape was his only objective now. That or 7 years inside for the gun. Before the taxi had even come to a proper stop his door was open, the sounds of sirens, men shouting and tyres screeching flooding his ears. He jumped out just as another Police car came flying up the street, he turned on his heels and ran back the other way, legs pumping, gun in hand. To his left was a small grass area with a couple of banks of phone boxes, a single tree and a bench with a path leading up to a small office block. Ahead of him appeared Collins, gun raised in two hands screaming at him to drop the gun. Cee Bugg skidded to a stop, involuntarily raising his right arm to counteract the sudden brake in speed and accommodate a change in direction. Collins saw the gun rise. He fired.

Cee Bugg felt the impact of the bullet hitting his right shoulder before he heard the guns recoil. It span him back around a full 180 degrees before being shot again by another Police marksman who was covering him from behind the door of his car. It hit him square in the chest, two inches above the heart ripping through and shredding his aorta and part of his pulmonary artery. He staggered a few feet towards the grass, managed to fire off a single round before collapsing and taking his last breath. His final moment, like a parting insult, was the sensation of another bullet hitting him in the lower torso. There was no pain, the noise, the blue lights faded into nothing and the bullet felt like a small nudge in the ribs like a tickle. And then he was gone.

CHAPTER 28

Works of Art

T he Police, the government and the local authorities could not have expected the aftermath following the fatal shooting of Cee Bugg. Within hours the rumours began to spread like wildfire among the housing estates and streets of Tottenham. The Police had assassinated him, whacked him, shot him down like a dog in the street. The Filth. The 5-Oh. The Feds. The Rozzers. They had done him. As soon as Skully got word he exploded with grief, rage and anger. He had been tight with Cee Bugg since year dot. They had more or less set up DDK together. He phoned Lord Lawton.

"Hello" answered The Lord in his distinctive clipped tone.

"It's me what the fuck is going on, I need to meet you right now, ya hear me?" spat Skully.

"I am afraid I am a little indisposed at the moment old chap. I will tell you what the expletive is going on though, but all in good time. Today is awfully busy. However, I can meet you at this time tomorrow in the usual place."

"Alright laters and don't be late."

"I will try and remember those orders. Cheerio!" said Lord Lawton who immediately turned to his bodyguard, ex-SAS six foot seven of pure muscle.

"The natives from the north side of the river seems a little agitated, better bring me a vest and bring some protection. You never quite know what these fellows might do."

Twenty four hours later they met in an antique shop near Regents

Park. Skully on his own, Kaiser waiting outside in the car whilst the Lord was accompanied by his bodyguard standing a few metres behind and to the side.

"As I said on the phone, what the fuck is going on?"

"It would be very much appreciated if you did not use that kind of language with me dear boy, it may be suitable around your band of merry men but it certainly is not around me. Now, please calm down and tell me what has irked you so much on this fine August day."

"You fucking know what's up, your fucking crew whacked my boy, dats fucking what's up. I pay, you keep my squad protected. Protected! You ere me, protected. Tune into da local news man and check it. One dead, man fucking down, a 187 on my fucking block, dat was my fuckin boy right dere innit. Shot down like a fuckin animal. Shot by your crew, de real criminals, de real racist scum in Landon Town ya ere?"

"Listen old boy, I am not familiar with this street slang that you so eloquently speak but I do not have a "crew" as you put it. I heard about the fatal shooting yesterday but I would suggest to you that the Police do not drive around London shooting people on nothing more than a whim."

The Lord paused before chuckling to himself.

"By god I wish they would to be quite honest with you but alas they do not. If your boy, as you so put it, was shot by the Metropolitan Police Department then there would have had to have been a jolly good reason for it. If you cannot control your little gang of hooligans then there is not much I can do about it no matter what our arrangement is."

"Yeah our arrangement, dats a fuckin laugh an all. You stick me up to a twenty per cent commission this year and what have I got out of it. Fuck all! Dat's what. You don't do shit, ya just sit up in ya ivory tower racking in de coin, the dollar, when everybody else out dere hustlin, tryin to make dere P's."

"Listen, I am simply a middleman that put people I know on one side with people I know, like you, on the other. However, if you do want to take advantage of my services then you need to abide by certain protocols, particularly regarding communications and ensuring I have a high-level view of the people and geographies involved."

"But this is not a monopoly to speak of, if you do not like the arrangement then you can simply walk away and carry on with someone else. It's a free country. Off you trot and I will find someone else that does appreciate the arrangement."

The Lord paused before hitting him with the big reveal.

"Someone like Steven Chambers for example."

Skully's eyes blazed wide with shock, before desperately trying to reign it in, feign ignorance, poker face the rich white cunt but it was too late. He had showed his hand. The Lord spotting it with ease.

"Never heard of him."

"Oh really, well he came to see me the other day and we had a rather lively discussion about YOUR current business arrangements. You talk about 20% not being particularly palatable, well he in unison is not too enamoured with your strong-arm tactics and rather repugnant interest rates on a debt that he had little to do with in the first place. A little pot calling the kettle black, don't you think? No pun intended of course."

Skully twitched at both the racist dig and the unveiling of his connection with Stevie. Furious he moved towards The Lord but was instantly stopped by the bodyguard who simply shook his head before pushing him back with the palm of his gigantic hand. Skully had no choice but to comply taking a deep breath to calm himself.

"Yes, Mr Chambers is most aggrieved with you using pricing measures and tactics simply designed to remove him from the picture. Arrangements which by the way you did not obtain my prior approval for. You have also been making valiant attempts at finding out who Mr Chambers' main network is. Now if you recall how this works, I approve everything in this operation, prices and the network of key distributors. It is true I do not need to know all the details but I require a certain level of information to establish if the balance is correct in London and indeed elsewhere in the country. North, East, South and West."

"Exactly mate, I was conducting some research into his little outfit and was going to bring it to you for approval."

"Okay, well, let me make myself clear, it is not approved. You stay away from Mr Chambers, do you understand me. I do not mean to be rude or offend your race but I do need good white drug dealers as well as black."

Skully's eyes were nearly popping out of their sockets with rage. His mind ticking over trying to make sense of what he had just heard.

"How the fuck did that little cunt find out about The Lord, impossible, not only impossible to find but to fuckin meet up with im. Sneaky backstabbing motherfucker. Dat boy is pure dead, pure fuckin dead."

His brain whirled with questions, rage and paranoia.

"Yes, no problem" he mumbled in reply.

"Sorry I did not quite catch that. Would you mind repeating yourself?"

"Yes no problem."

"Right good glad to hear it. Now, about your other issue. As just discussed, if you would like to make significant moves against anyone in London which also includes shooting some poor bastard then you need to come to me. You do what you want in the street, mugging, ripping people off, knifes and all that poppycock. Those sorts of shenanigans do not interest me. However, if a turf war that includes this little outfit from Tower Hamlets gets out of control then you inform me. I will not have gangs wandering around the streets killing people with guns in plain sight. It is not on; my bosses and the public do not like it one little bit. Anyway, surely someone like yourself should not be worrying about those BSC kids. Hmmm maybe you have not got things as under control as I thought. A BIG man like yourself?"

The Lord raised his blonde grey flecked eyebrows in question but no answer came from Skully who looked nothing more than a little petulant, albeit chastised, schoolboy being told off by the Headmaster.

"My reading of the situation is that some of your organisation are simply underperforming, getting a little too complacent. I think you may have been watching too many music videos, all that rap and grime nonsense with all those references to bling or whatever vulgar trash you call it, waving around notes and guns. Sounds like you and your boys are letting your guard down, getting trapped and sliced up in some nightclub toilet? Sounds a bit amateur hour to me."

Skully could not believe his ears.

"This old cracker cunt knows fuckin everything!"

"So what I would recommend is this. You worry about core business objectives first and personal vendettas second. I assume these little skirmishes are not going to pull down the numbers this month?"

"No."

"Good okay well you should be getting off. I think I might stay a while and peruse some of these fine antiquities on offer. Goodbye."

The Lord did not offer his hand simply turning his back on Skully. Meeting over. The bodyguard moved towards him, an additional hint to leave. Skully retreated out of the door before bounding down the steps to street level to where Kaiser was waiting, car running. As he sat down in the back seat, the rage filled his ears like red toxic mist.

"Find Stevie, find him and fuckin whack im. Dat fuckin boy is a dead man."

Kaiser turned in his seat.

"I know where to find him."

"What already? How certain?"

"Been digging around and it's 100%."

"How long for?"

"He will be there for time."

"Good. Alright leave it for today, we need to mass the troops for tonight. Drive up to yard I have got some calls ta make seen? Fuckin hell man, dat old codger in dere he is gonna see something else. There is a storm brewing, a fucking revolution. Fuck dat white piece of shit."

Lord Lawton looked down at the street from the window of the shop watching Skully shouting at the weaselly looking white man in the driver's seat before furiously punching a number into his phone.

"Hmmm, I have sneaking suspicion that that fellow is not going to heed my advice."

The Lord reached into his pocket and dialled a number.

Stevie answered.

"Hello there young man. I thought I would let you know that a certain someone is not a very happy bunny, I would lay low for a while if I were you. Please do not go completely off the radar though, remember what we talked about before, okay?"

CHAPTER 29

No smoke without....

T he protests and demonstrations regarding Cee Bugg's death started the night before with family members and close friends gathering outside Tottenham Hale Police station to have their say on what had happened. It went off relatively peacefully but all it changed the following night. Skully had issued an order to DDK to invade the streets and protest, focus primarily on Tottenham. Instigate and encourage trouble but make sure to not get arrested themselves. He was going up against The Lord but he could deny it without evidence. The growing crowds became more noisy, restless and aggressive as DDK infiltrated, spreading rumours and dissent. As with every other self-respecting gangster in London DDK were now using Blackberry phones, the free messenger service tailor made for nefarious gang activities. This coupled with Facebook and Twitter meant DDK was getting the blood up of every young angry black youth in London and beyond.

Rather than stay focused and potentially penned in at Tottenham Hale, Skully persuaded Cee Bugg's family to organise a protest march to the main Police station. Get more mobile and difficult to contain. The crowd amassed to over 3,000 people and moved off down the High Street toward Tottenham Police station. A low-ranking officer greeted the jeering crowd before trying to talk to the family. The shouts started with a few plastic bottles thrown towards the station. The Policeman nervously retreated inside only to return mob handed in protective clothing. As the noise levels grew they were joined by a squad in a riot van.

One of the DDK had been steadily plying a notorious young wannabee gangster girl with vodka. As the chanting and abuse grew, egged on by DDK gang members, she broke through the front of the crowd hurling a glass bottle at the Police line in front of the station.

Four Police officers reacted, immediately grabbing her and pinning her to the floor. She was only small and the overzealous actions played right into DDK's hands. It all kicked off, the crowd surged forward and the London riots started in earnest. This initial disturbance in the heart of Tottenham lasted for several hours as the mob ran amok. Cee Bugg's family looked on in vain and despair. The Police were caught on the back foot unable to contain the trouble with running battles all night long. There was widespread looting particularly in the nearby large retail units where several large electrical shops were relieved of their goods.

Dawn broke the following day with the riots making headline news. The scenes of the carnage and the inability of the Police to contain the trouble seemed to encourage other poor neighbourhoods and estates, the excitement growing during the day, everyone glued to their Blackberry's eagerly anticipating nightfall. Not many cared about Cee Bugg, most wanted a new pair of trainers or a flat screen television plus the opportunity to stick it to the man, get one back on the Police. Much of the black youth of London had enough of the treatment handed out by the Met, racial stereotyping resulted in regular stop and searches on the streets, and all allowed under the 1994 Criminal Justice and Public Order Act. Tonight, their pent-up frustration would boil over into the streets and they were planning to take them back and show the authorities who was really in charge and control.

As dusk began to fall over the capital residents battened down the hatches, making plans to stay off the streets. Several, particularly those in areas near to large council housing estates, decided to leave until it had all blown over, hoping their properties would be intact upon their return. In west London, Kaiser was following up on his second task assigned to him by Skully. Behind him in a white transit van were four of DDK's gangsters, all tooled up and not happy about missing out on the action happening outside. They pulled up around the corner from Trentstone Towers, Kaiser jumping out of his Mercedes and into the back of the van and went over the plan one last time.

Stevie received the call from Lord Lawton, he was alone at Stacey's house in Buckinghamshire.

"a certain someone is not a very happy bunny, I would lay low for a while if I were you......"

Well he did not have to be a genius to work that out, he thought back to the meeting with Skully a few weeks back. At the meet near Smithfield's Market, Kaiser pulled up in a Range Rover, Skully hopped out the back and they walked slowly up the road. Skully was cutting him off, offering him two deals one of which was the only option.

Option 1: Stevie paid him back all the money he owed within a week which would now include a 38% interest charge due to late payment. Do that and they would continue business as usual but with a lot more scrutiny and 'micro-management' as Skully termed it.

Option 2: Stevie to give up all the names, addresses and telephone numbers of their main distributors. Do that and Stevie would only have to pay two thirds of the debt and he could walk away. No punishment, no retribution, nothing. This was the only option. Stevie knew it and Skully knew it.

"I'll let you know" Stevie had replied. He walked away with the eyes of Kaiser and Skully burning in his back as he departed.

Stevie had already figured out this would happen so had already made his move. Never one for appreciating others telling him what to do, he went for a third option. Fuck Skully, fuck DDK, cut them out. Do a Bainsey, swerve them and go straight to the top. And then carry on.

"a certain someone is not a very happy bunny"

The Lord's words rang in Stevie's ears as he nervously debated his decision as he stood in Stacey's house enveloped with paranoia as he stared out of the windows into the deep green forest that surrounded the property. Could he stay here? Did DDK know about the house? He knew they were well connected and informed by the likes of The Lord via numerous Police informers plus crooked cops.

Luckily Stacey was out of town away for a few days for one of her last ever modelling assignments. One of the lads mags was doing a special *"Where are they now?"* feature on ten of the most famous glamour models from the 90s. The majority had long since bagged themselves rich husbands or low tier league footballers or bankers. Stacey being one of the exceptions through her successful interior design company. This was one of the main reasons for wanting to do the shoot, show some of her bitchier peers what she had done rather than snaring a sugar daddy in a trap. The shoot was up in Manchester and as soon as Stevie got the call from The Lord he phoned her telling her to stay up there. She was worried but did not pry instead organising to stay with one of her friends in Chester.

He left the house the following day twitchy with fear as he slowly opened the front door, the 30 metres to the car seemingly a huge distance. As he crossed the driveway the cracking sound of a branch snapping out in the woods echoed around. He sprinted to the car in panic putting his foot down, driving fast through the wooded lanes expecting to see a gaggle of pursuing thugs in his rear-view mirrors. None appeared. He calmed down thinking of his options. One year ago he may well have simply disappeared, used a fake passport if necessary with some hidden cash, lay low for a couple of years but now there was Stacey and he could not leave her, never.

As he drove, to where he did not know, he considered his options, staying at the house in the woods or with friends in Woodbridge was out, he could hold up somewhere in the west country but then he thought about what Lord Lawton had said.

"Do not go completely off the radar."

Three nights before Stevie watched the local news on TV, mouth agape, as the story broke regarding a fatal shooting by the Police in north London. The news presenter described the victim as a senior member of a Tottenham street gang and a picture of Cee Bugg in typical gangster pose, gold chain, not smiling, fingers hooked throwing up a gang sign flashed up on the screen. His mind played back to that day back in 2005 when Connor was relieved of his duties in the most brutal fashion. Cee Bugg answered the door, stood behind him and Craig, guarding them, to ensure they watched as Connor was persuaded never to re-enter the drug business in London or consider retaliation. As he drove his mind raced trying to piece together everything.

"Was all this a coincidence? Was it all connected? Did The Lord have something to do with any of it? Was this the end of DDK? The end of Skully? What plans has The Lord got in store?"

"He seemed to like me, I think through that oh so British hard yet ever so polite exterior there was there a connection. I think he might have my back in this one."

He suddenly found himself laughing and shouting as he drove.

"Yeeeeeah, yeeeeeah fuck DDK. It's me and The Lord now boys, your time is fucking over!"

As his confidence and bravado grew he decided to head to and sit tight at Trentstone Towers, sure in the knowledge only three people on the planet still knew about it; himself, Scott and Craig. No one else. Fair play to Craig that even through the most horrendous phases of his addiction he had never taken anyone anywhere near the place. Stevie was sure about this. Since him and Craig split the business he employed both old and new techniques. The first a simple strand of human hair across the gap of the utility cupboard door, held there by a very small piece of Sellotape near the base. Then there was a web cam that recorded and streamed video twenty-four hours a day to an encrypted website. Any movements would trigger an alert which was emailed to him. Stevie continued to watch and review the stream and recorded video but it was always just the mail coming through the door. Trentstone remained a safe house.

He would need to go sick for a few days from work at D&C but it would be okay as he had a bullet proof sick leave record over the years. He had a stockpile of films to watch, he would order takeaways in the name of the long-time rent paying resident, Nicholas James Bush and wait it out for whatever happened out on the streets. Leave it to others to do the dirty work so he could resume business, at a higher level together with The Lord.

As he drove up Portobello Road he noticed it was quieter than usual, lunchtime was always busy as people descended on the market to sample the wide variety of food on offer by the stalls and cafes. However, there was a vibe now, no doubt about it. The discussions on the radio channels were focussed on the events of the last two nights. All Police leave had been cancelled and everyone in the Met and large cities across the UK began preparing for what everyone was anticipating being one of the worst nights of violence and destruction the country had seen for a long time.

He was careful as he drove making sure he was not being followed, taking shortcuts, cutting back on himself and once he eventually arrived he parked his car in the darkest recesses of the vast car park underneath the building.

Kaiser saw him drive up over the huge steel bridge that crossed the railway line and phoned his crew in the van.

"That was him, follow him up to the 31st floor, flat 3149. Go to work on him and give me a call when he is softened up."

Stevie stepped out of the lift on the 31st floor, his heart beating fast as he stepped out of the lift before waiting near the stairwell listening out for any signs of anyone coming up. Again, there was nothing just the cool summer breeze drifting through the structure from the south. It cooled him calming his nerves a little. He walked slowly along the long passageway towards his front door. As he put his key in the lock, he looked back down the corridor surprised to see a young black lad maybe 16 or 17 appear from the lift area walking towards him, his head down, hoody up, hands buried in pockets.

Stevie looked at him, key in hand. He did not know any of the neighbours but assumed a fair proportion were black and again calmed himself as the key slid into the lock of the door. Suddenly when the lad was within 20 metres he looked up at Stevie and started running at him, fast. Behind him he caught a glimpse of two other men also charging down the narrow corridor. The shock shuddered through his body to his hands as he scrambled to unlock the main lock, he span the key, the two mortice bolts clicked open and then stabbed the other key into the second door lock, a standard Yale. He turned it quickly anti-clockwise pushing the door open with his shoulder falling into the small hallway. The black lad was almost there as Stevie slammed the door shut, however, his assailant managed to get his elbow between the door and doorframe preventing Stevie from fully shutting it. He put all his weight against it but realised quickly that the other two men who were thundering down the corridor would now easily force the door open. He let go and sprang back into his living room as the gangster fell into the room before jumping quickly up a long shining blade in hand.

In the corner of the room by the kitchen doorway was an antique umbrella holder, containing a large umbrella and a couple of old golf clubs. Stevie jumped to the side pulling out an old Slazenger seven iron golf club. Without thinking he instinctively swung it at the advancing knife wielding intruder. The club head hit him hard on the side of the head knocking him sideward, the sound reminded him of when he did Kurt all those years back in Somerset. This was different as this lad would not be getting up again, his eyes rolled shut as his skull caved in just above his left ear.

His accomplices came flying through the front door just as their stricken colleague crashed to the floor hard with a loud thud. Stevie involuntary yelped out loud with fright before bolting into the kitchen barricading himself in with the large American fridge. He did not have time to ponder how they found him. But found him they had.

That was it. That was that. He was trapped.

Fucked.

CHAPTER 30

Itchycoo Park

S tevie made the call to Stuart CEO at BlackView. After a painful and prolonged explanation Stuart finally remembered him from years ago back in Bangkok. Stevie was sure that if he had not decent understanding of the Vietnam War he would have drifted into the outer reaches of the Stuarts sub conscious never to be recalled again, just another ghost from the sweaty, seedy underbelly of Thailand. Curious, Stuart agreed to meet at his office in Devizes in Wiltshire, Stevie headed down on a Great Western Railways train out of Paddington. A familiar barely noticeable smirk appeared on his lips as the eight-carriage train slowly picked up speed and the Trentstone Tower loomed into view above the west London suburbs before disappearing in the gloom.

After an awkward start Stevie fished out the business card Stuart had given to him all those years before in the sweltering heat of Bangkok. The BlackView logo had since been updated and replaced but Stuart seemed to regard it fondly as he looked at it in his huge hand.

Stevie gradually opened up stating he was in a cash business mostly off the books and was being taken for a ride by a supplier. He went on to explain he wanted to find out who was up in the chain so he could attempt to sever the link and work directly with them. He mentioned black market goods and an organisation in Tottenham. Stuart did not take long to figure out it was most likely drug related but kept this insight to himself.

"I can find anyone on the planet, so it should not be a problem. However it costs both time, manpower and money. Sounds like the business you are in is one where people cover their tracks well. And that means that the fee is likely to be not insignificant."

Stevie loved a double negative to drive a point home and he smiled inwardly at the comment before appraising Stuart sat across the desk. He had aged well in the intervening years. BlackView was obviously doing well. He still retained the muscle, maybe a little looser around the hips probably still hitting the gym, that much was guaranteed. His mind wandered back to Skully. This was a one off make or break deal, money could not be an issue even though he was running seriously dry. If he did not find out who Skully worked for he was fucked, he was out of the game. Stevie did not want to just give money away so breathed in and went into negotiation.

"How much?"

"Well I don't know, if you can tell me where this fella will be at a certain point in time well that would be a start."

"This I can tell you. I am meeting him tomorrow at Smithfield's market in London. But listen I know you guys are no doubt professionals but you need to make sure they are not spotted. I've seen these lot in action before, any sign of bother and they will clam up and slam the door shut for a couple of weeks maybe months and we might have to wait ages for another opportunity."

"No bother, we will be sweet. Trust me I have a big crew of specialists expert in the arts of surveillance, investigation, staking out, computer nerds to track money, all sorts. We will find out who they are but this is going to cost you £65,000."

"65k? I just want to find out who he or she is, I don't want their family tree!"

"Plus VAT by the way."

"With all due respect, fuck that and fuck VAT, this is cash only, I am not going on any books on this one."

Stuart swivelled from side to side in his large leather office chair rubbing his bottom lip. All an act. Deep in thought, considering and thinking what could be done for this young man.

"Alright 75 grand, cash and you don't get a report, you get a slip of paper with a name, address or phone number that's it. Plus that is for one month's effort, if we still haven't got anywhere you'll need to pay me more but you never know this fella or lady as you quite rightly point out, you libertarian you, might well be deep and does not want to be found. No contract written up, just a bag of money. Deal?" he replied, his face set in stone.

Stevie's instinct was to go in lower, bring him down but he backed off with a sigh.

"Alright deal" stated Stevie extending his hand to Stuart.

"Your boys Chelsea have certainly had a change in fortune since we last met, still following them?"

"Yeah it's all pretty decent but not sure we are going to get much out of this season, started well but think we blew it over Christmas and the new boy Torres seems to be lost at our gaff. Fifty million fucking quid well spent there I think not. Kind of miss the old days though to be fair, atmosphere down the bridge is shite these days, too many plastic fans and corporate bell-ends hanging around the gaff. Still cannot complain too much about the Russian pumping all his illicit cash into the club. See you later mate, be well son."

As soon as Stevie left Stuart called Lord Lawton.

"Hello Stuart, you keeping well? Get back from the continent okay?"

"Yes fine thank you sir, I will fill you in about that when we next meet. We couldn't bring it forward could we as I have something I need you to be aware of. I don't think it's anything too serious but most definitely intriguing."

"Hmm that sounds frightfully interesting, yes that should not present a problem, when were you thinking."

"Anytime this week is good for me, as always cleared the decks after the little jaunt overseas."

"Yes can be exhausting work I imagine. Well I am okay for tomorrow at about 3pm if that suits, can only manage an hour tops, so no lunch I am afraid. Shall I meet in the usual spot. Weather is okay it would appear."

"Sounds good, see you then."

"Goodbye."

Stuart clicked off the mobile phone. He hated the way The Lord always said goodbye in a harsh abrupt tone. Always had a ring of menace and finality about it and he half expected a hitman to appear from the shadows to stick a round in his skull. He involuntarily shivered at the prospect before considering the lad Stevie who had appeared from nowhere. He was right to inform The Lord of the developments. He may already know, he was like a spider with a huge web cast not only across the UK but also the globe, ready for someone to be entangled and caught before he slowly scuttles towards his prey.

He thought back to the first time he had met The Lord and the subsequent first operation that he was involved in. He was invited to the MOD, the Ministry of Defence to provide an overview of BlackView services including capabilities, experience, number of personnel, equipment, global contacts, sub-contracts and the like. The initial outline was the MOD were looking for third parties to provide security services in Iraq and Afghanistan once the respective 'wars on terror' were over. It was the type of gig that Stuart had been waiting for since setting up BlackView.

He had been lobbying the MOD hard after securing enough UK based security contracts to give them the asset base and structure that could meet their stringent requirements. It had seemed to have paid off and as the meeting progressed Stuart began to get a good feeling about his pitch and more importantly what it could mean for the future. A lucrative MOD agreement and possibly, in future, a foot in the door when it comes to the motherload, introductions to the US Army. Mouth watering.

At the end of the meeting he was asked to stay behind in the room on his own. It was odd and Stuart began to feel uneasy. He was left for around 15 minutes before The Lord entered the room accompanied by one of the MOD officials from the earlier meeting. Stuart could immediately tell he was ex-military, ex-public school, probably Harrow. He knew the sort having worked for several during his stint in the Army.

"Stuart this is Lord Lawton, one of our regular consultants."

"Lord Lawton this is Stuart Bradley, head of BlackView Security Services. Right oh I think I will leave you both to it. Lord would you be so kind as to see Mr Bradley out when you are done?"

"No problem, thank you so much."

The Lord took a seat opposite Stuart. Silence followed as The Lord appraised him from top to toe, soaking in those first impressions. Stuart began to sweat, a trickle running down his back. This guy made him seriously uncomfortable.

The Lord then broke off the silence as he went on to explain he needed personnel for a military operation the following year. He was a little vague on the details just sounding Stuart out but letting it be known quite clearly that if he did not wish to participate then BlackView would have zero chance of securing any contracts with the MOD in future, ever. Stuart knew that he could do nothing except accept the proposal.

The operation turned out to be a complete disaster from start to finish. The Lord and god knows who else were sponsoring a coup, overthrow the government of Equatorial Guinea securing the oil and precious metals that lay underneath her soil and seas. A team of fifteen BlackView snuck across the border, the right-hand element of a pincer movement on the capital, Malabo. Unbeknown to them the main force numbering nearly 100 mercenaries were all arrested on a Zimbabwean airstrip who alerted the Equatorial Guinea Army to the possible presence of mercenaries within its borders. On the ground the left-hand pincer team comprising of nearly 20 South African ex-special forces were captured but crucially managed to get a radio message off to the BlackView team just in the nick of time. The group including Stuart tabbed hard through the night managing to evade capture before finally staggering across the border to the relative safety of Cameron. There they were nimbly assisted by the British Embassy staff who sneaked them out of the country unnoticed. Not a great start but nothing Stuart could have done to alter the outcome. However, The Lord kept his promise. BlackView were on the MOD 'approved' list resulting in numerous contracts in the Middle East providing anti-piracy services to shipping in and around the Arabian Peninsula.

Stuart had heard rumours, tales and whispers of how The Lord's overseas operations were funded and that is how he knew the man Stevie was looking for could well be him. Stuart liked Stevie, quite intense, knows what he wants, a little arrogant but a straight talker with little bullshit or bravado. Stuart may well have just put a death warrant on him but it was better to let The Lord know than keep it to himself, he was not stupid.

The following day they met on a park bench in St James Park, central London, a traditional favourite location amongst spy networks across the globe. By coincidence it was the same day Stevie was meeting Skully at Smithfield's market.

"Tell me about our friend down in Angola."

"Yes that is all cleared up, there will not be any more issues with that regard."

"Okay, take long?"

"No just a bit of a chinwag and he seemed convinced."

"Hmmm"

"Sent him a little present later on in the evening that no doubt solidified his decision making."

"Good, good, I did hear about those little details through another channel, very original. Well done. I will organise the fund transfer in the usual way, probably next week."

"Okay."

"I need to have one or two of your guys in India next month or so, border fighting season is starting up, need some training and exercises for some of the guerrilla groups up there. Need to get some supplies in as well. Our Indian friends are all on board but cannot be seen to be getting their hands too dirty so they will do some facilitation in the usual way so should not be any bother. Probably need to go out on some initial foot patrols show them or remind them how it should be done, usual rules apply."

"Don't get fucking caught!"

"Indeed" replied The Lord with a faint smirk on his lips before Stuart tentatively began to explain his meeting with Stevie.

"Alright so there was that other thing I wanted to talk to you about. I had a visit from this fella. Completely out of the blue, not one of your usual visits it has to be said."

"Sounds interesting please proceed old boy" said The Lord as he shifted his position towards Stuart, his interest piqued.

"So several years ago I ended up having a few beers with this young lad in a bar in the Far East."

"Where many business arrangement and relationships flourish!" stated The Lord enjoying or perhaps reminiscing about the notion of exotic clandestine encounters in the tropics.

"Yes but he literally was a kid back then not even 30 at the time. Anyway I had a few beers, bit of a chin-wag, gave him my card, but that was about it."

The Lord seemed to lose interest in the story as looked at his watch, a plain white-faced Raymond Weil with a simple black leather strap, a clear signal to hurry the story along.

"Anyway, nearly 9 years later this fella rocks up at my offices down in Wiltshire, willing to pay 75 big ones to find someone."

"Oh really, who?"

"You."

This reengaged The Lord's attention as he sat a little straighter and rotated further on the bench to face Stuart.

"Go on."

"Alright so this fella is obviously knee deep in the black market, drugs specifically. He did not divulge of course but he mentioned that he needed to find the main man so he could bypass his current supplier. He said he works for, under duress it would appear, for a street gang called DDK out of North London, Tottenham to be a little more precise. Basically I think they are putting the squeeze on him or he thinks he is going to get double crossed, killed whatever. So he wants to continue in his given trade but not working for these ....."

"Jungle bunnies" interrupted The Lord darkly.

"Well what has that got to do with me?" The Lord challenged as he stared Stuart in the eye holding his gaze waiting for an answer.

A cold wind whipped suddenly through the park making the trees sway as Stuart shifted nervously in his seat thinking he may have played this one wrong. Maybe The Lord had nothing to do with the drug trade, maybe the grapevine was wrong maybe he had deeply offended his paymaster with the suggestion. He could not wiggle out of this one, so he kept going regardless.

"Errr well I may have this wrong but from what I have heard, you or someone you may know is the taxman for the Turks for smack, a couple of black street outfits, one of which being this DDK outfit, for cocaine and the Russians for vice. Just rumours like but you know how they talk. So I didn't do anything thought I should get your counsel on the matter, much easier."

"You've been a busy little boy haven't you, sticking your nose in some rather unpleasant places hmm."

"No, no just rumours like. You know how 'they' like to talk. Not been digging at all, I errr just, errrr, just thought I would test the water with you, you know I like to tell you everything that I think you might be interested in" stuttered Stuart who was now seriously squirming as The Lord held his gaze with a stern look etched like concrete on his face.

"Forget it I....I ...." stammered Stuart.

"You took the 75,000 though I take it?"

"Err yes."

"Hmmmm."

The Lord crossed his legs before stroking his chin his gaze now dead ahead watching the comings and goings around the park.

"What was this fellows name?"

"Steven Chambers" replied Stuart noticing a spark of recognition in The Lords eyes, a slight subtle twitch that proved he had been right.

"Okay, I will take £35,000 and you can give him my details, just my name and mobile number. Agreed?" he ordered raising an eyebrow at Stuart daring him to make a counteroffer.

"Agreed, just chip it off the next payment."

"Jolly good idea. Right thank you for the meeting and I look forward to seeing what this Mr Chambers wants to see me about. He didn't look too unhinged did he?"

"Nope pretty calm, cool and collected, you'll probably quite like him."

"We'll see" The Lord replied as he left without offering a hand or a farewell.

Stuart breathed out slowly as The Lord departed walking slowly through the park, out of the gate and into a waiting Rolls Royce.

CHAPTER 31

Lording it up..

S tevie was sat at work, high up in the offices of D&C drafting new internal training material for the new intake following a big recent recruitment drive. A sure sign of economic recovery if there ever was one.

His desk phone chirped loudly, the display indicating it was the reception calling from the lobby downstairs. He checked his diary, it was clear so racked his brains to recall if he was expecting someone but came up blank. He picked up the phone and reception informed him he had a visitor, he asked for a name but none was forthcoming, a friend was all she said. Ever since the blackmail of Tristram, Stevie was nervous regarding unexpected guests turning up at the front doors of the D&C offices, keeping the illicit side of his life very separate to that of the corporate world. He was careful, he never talked or hinted at anything, never handed out D&C business cards to friends, never told anyone where he worked only occasionally talking to close friends about his work and places he visited on client assignments.

He nervously strolled towards the clear glass lifts located bang in the centre of the building. As he descended he watched the D&C machine working in all its glory, seven floors of open plan office space housing hundreds of consultants all beavering away on a multitude of client projects and proposals. He was proud to work for them and this feeling pinched at his nerve endings, the niggling dread that it could be all over in an instant. A bullet or blade from DDK, Police raiding the D&C offices busting open his locker that currently contained eighty-four grams of pure cocaine.

He exited the lifts and slowly walked towards the reception eyeing up the visitors that lurked and lounged in the large sofas. Any sign of DDK he would walk away before fielding any subsequent calls by telling them he was busy in client meetings all afternoon and take his chances later on. He had already sussed out an alternative exit via the estate security team in the lower floor which he checked could be used by employees although was clearly not protocol. He peeked around one of the large structural columns that rose from the floor and up through the giant atrium. There was no one that appeared to cause concern. He kept scanning. Then he saw him, someone not immediately apparent, seemed to bend into the background which was why he initially missed him. He was a shade under six-foot-tall wearing a baseball cap, sunglasses, a grey lightweight jacket and light brown khaki trousers with white trainers As he looked him up and down, one word screamed at him; 'BlackView' and his heart raced. He knew the man was watching him through his sunglasses even though his head was cocked to the side as he nonchalantly read his newspaper.

"He it comes, the fucking Post-It note that I paid seventy five big ones for!" he considered as he breathed in deep and made himself known even though he knew full well this man knew exactly who Stevie was, height, weight, a detailed description.

"Hello there, I am Steven Chambers."

"Hello, here this is for you" the man replied in a detached manner handing over a single yellow post-it note.

He did not care if he played it cool or not as he quickly scanned the details written in bold letters in thick marker pen. It simply read 'Lord Lawton' together with a mobile phone number. Before he could say thanks the man had turned on his heels and walked out of the revolving door. Stevie watched him as he left, noting his professionalism which radiated from his gait and manner. A simple glance at his watch before looking up at the sky as if to confirm the time with the sun before slipping away into the crowd of suits milling around the D&C campus.

"No time like the present" murmured Stevie to himself as he flicked the edge of the note with his finger before pulling out one of the two mobile phones he had in his pocket and punched in the number.

A voice answered that was simultaneously deep yet slightly high pitched at the same time.

"Hello."

"Hello is that Lord Lawton?"

"Yes it jolly well is and whom do I have the pleasure of conversing with on my private number? It would not happen to be one Steven Chambers, aged thirty-seven, the one and only child of Richard and Barbara Chambers originating out of Woodbridge, Buckinghamshire would it?"

"Err yes it would, errm, I would quite like to have a quick chat with you if you do not mind."

"Not at all, you sound like an interesting chap. There is a lovely little antique shop in Regents Park, it would be ideal if you could meet me there tomorrow? How about half twelve? I understand you work just off Fleet Street so should not be too much bother for you."

Stevie was a little stunned by the response but quickly checked his diary and confirmed the meeting, taking the address and began punching the details into a search engine on his phone to find the location.

"Cheerio look forward to seeing you then."

"Err yes, thank you, goodbye."

The following day and after a sleepless night where he acted out the meeting in his mind over and over again, Stevie arrived at the little antique shop squeezed between two huge terraced town mansions. He walked up the steps and as soon as he entered a man appeared from behind a curtain and drew a blind down over the door and turned the sign from 'open' to 'closed'. Without saying a word he produced a small purple velvet bag.

"Everything in there son, phone, wallet, jewellery, glasses, coins, travel cards even your contact lens, not that you wear them of course."

Stevie did as he was told, he was half expecting such a reception, he felt like he was at airport security as he double checked his pockets were clear.

"That's it."

The bodyguard proceeded to expertly pat him down, not caring about offending or violating his human rights by groping his dick, arse and nut-sack before pulling out a mini metal detector similar to what you found on the doors of many London nightclubs. He then very carefully checked each and every button on his shirt, unbuttoning each one and checking behind in an attempt to establish if he was either wired or filming him.

Maybe they knew exactly what he was like thought Stevie as he raised his arms in anticipation of another thorough rub down this time the upper torso. Satisfied he was not carrying either weapons of surveillance equipment, the bodyguard who looked remarkably like the BlackView operative he met briefly the previous day, walked to the large wooden desk striking a bell twice as though he were in a hotel reception. He then walked backwards towards the large window fronting the street and stood stock still his hands clasped in front of him, positioned to cover the front door. Stevie heard footsteps on wooden stairs and seconds later a curtain the size of a standard doorway was pushed aside and there was The Lord, dressed in a smart three piece pin striped suit, red tie and off white cream shirt.

"Good afternoon Mr Chambers, find us okay?"

"Yes thank you, err do I call you Lord?" he enquired confused about etiquette.

"Yes that is the done thing as I understand it."

"Okay right, err, so yes Lord I jumped on a Boris bike, seemed quicker than faffing around on the tube" said Stevie nervously realising that the Lord was about as likely to use a Boris bike as Stevie was to pilot a 747.

"Errm so thanks for taking the time to see me, errr, so I have a little problem that I would like to explain to you and then perhaps if you agree with the rather unfair predicament that I find myself in then I have a proposal that I would like to put to you."

"That sounds most interesting, I have to say when I became aware of you seeking me out I had a little think about what on earth it would entail, especially considering me being a Lord and what have you. Without any disrespect I move in somewhat different social circles to both you and your motley crew of associates. You know I am often approached by individuals and organisations, companies, charities, unions, special interest groups and the like and in each and every case I always set aside some time, in advance, to try and figure out what it is that would like from me and what it is in return they can offer me. I expect that you try and do exactly the same thing in your job Mr Chambers down at Dawber & Cooke? In fact, I know Mr Jonathan Bland, your ultimate boss quite well, we are Harrow alumni as it goes. I am a little older than him but we have met on numerous occasions and had the pleasure of doing a little bit of business together."

Stevie gulped as the extent of this man's knowledge and network which became more and more evident as he talked. This was a carefully planned and executed speech which The Lord had no doubt used on many occasions. It was quite unnerving. He was still a little unsure how this was going to go as he glanced at the bodyguard.

Stevie attempted to speak but was silenced with a hand gesture from The Lord.

"There I was enjoying my breakfast, scanning The Financial Times whilst contemplating your little visit today and trying to second guess your agenda and objectives. Before you commence with your, no doubt, well-rehearsed oration shall I tell you what I think?"

Without waiting for an answer, The Lord continued.

"So first off, you employed the services of BlackView on a cash only basis and paying them well over the odds to track me down. £75,000 in cash, of which by the way, £35,000 has been given to me in exchange for granting you this audience. BlackView is one of several organisations that I use regularly for various pieces of work.

Stevie smiled at the thought of trying to spot the BlackView operatives when he met Skully a couple of weeks before when it was all probably organised with a simple phone call.

"Forty large for a phone call, fuck, easiest piece of business that Stuart fella has probably ever done" thought Stevie.

"Anyway I did not need BlackView to tell me you were a cash rich, well relatively speaking, individual wanting to remain off radar for certain services that would indicate you are involved in what would have been known during and after World War Two as the black market. You see I have several associates, business partners and contacts that are that way inclined and I see to it that the majority of this sort of nefarious activity is, errm, how can I put it, contributing to the good of the Union."

"You mean, you tax it."

"Hmmm well yes in a manner of speaking, I understand that the street employs a variant of taxing, if I understand it correctly."

"I would not know much about that as I am not from the street but yes I have heard about taxing."

"Hmmm yes not from the street indeed. Woodbridge, yes a very nice little village from what I recall, went there once for some reason or another. Anyway onwards with my supposition and please do stop me dear boy if I get this completely arse about face. Back in 1996 a low-level street dealer called Christopher Baines was arrested, after an anonymous tip off, walking down the high street in Woodbridge fully laden with class A contraband, namely cocaine, ecstasy and a small amount of amphetamine. He was promptly arrested and his house searched where they found two underage girls whom the aforementioned Mr Baines was having sex with. The arresting officer applied the usual tactics upon questioning and he squealed like a little piggy giving up or grassing, as it is so lovingly referred to, his supplier an Irish chap called Ian, real name Connor or sometimes known as Carffie for some reason or another."

Stevie sat in the red leather chesterfield chair quite enjoying the show, never knew Connor as Carffie though, maybe a DDK alias. The shock of how much The Lord knew had faded and now he fully expected him to reveal he knows Stevie has a small birthmark that looks like South America on his hip.

"This was where of course I got to hear about things. The reason being is that this Connor chap was what the American Mafia might call connected. Connected to DDK, the North London gang who are in turn loosely connected to a quasi-state sponsored organisation headed up by.....ME" stated The Lord letting this information hang in the air.

"I then received the call from one of my numerous Police contacts. I suggested that they do not look too hard for this Ian/Connor chap but due to the rather heinous crimes perpetuated by one Mr Christopher Baines I recommended the full force of the law was brought to bear on the individual. The presiding Judge opting, with some encouragement from me, to give him the full term, seven and a half years if I recall correctly. We cannot have people like that walking around our fair land, now can we?"

"We certainly cannot" smiled Stevie trying not to give away The Lord was accurate in absolutely every regard and detail.

"Okay, so you, Steven Chambers, and your best friend Craig Winters take over the narcotics enterprise from Mr Baines by somehow connecting with Connor even though he went underground and did not venture into Woodbridge after the Baines arrest. How did you do that by the way?"

"A bit if planning and a large slice of luck, we staked out Kilburn for weeks hanging around in the pubs and clubs hoping to bump into him! We were nearly about to give up when we spotted him in a cinema."

"Ha, very fortunate! I am surprised you didn't get your knee caps bashed in by the IRA sympathisers down there. I suspect Craig might well have pulled out the Irish heritage card if it had come down to it eh?"

"Yeah maybe" replied Stevie now grinning and shaking his head in disbelief at the mine of information The Lord had on them.

"So things went very well as far as I understand it, you boys built up the business and distribution channels throughout the remainder of the 90's, kept your noses clean, well sort of, Craig is a little more of a live wire than you it would appear with a few arrests but never for holding contraband, until recently of course."

"So, you and your partner in crime are doing well you have a few companies where you wash your money, beauty salons and a couple of property companies. Very wise by the way, making your hard-earned cash disappear and crop up a bit later all clean, fresh and taxed. And the good life continues but you do so well in your given enterprise a certain someone became lazy, that would be Connor. His suppliers, namely via the head of DDK, the chap they call Skully became aware that Connor only ever sold to you two gentlemen. This is all well and good but it is business and when you figure out such information you act on it and you cut out the middleman. This can be done in this endeavour of course but only with Executive Board approval of course" stated The Lord grandiosely pointing at himself.

The Lord was slowly but surely getting to his point but was not quite giving it up just yet. He continued.

"Listen young man I generally deplore violence but sometimes it's necessary and I understand that you witnessed DDK giving Connor his P45. I do apologise old chap as I believe blood and bruises are not your thing either, good show but we do need to make sure that ex-employees stay away and don't get any delusions of revenge or grandeur. Anyway, on with the story."

"Skully and his little crew of homies or whatever ridiculous names they call themselves, let it be known that Connor is out and you have stepped up a level which means more cash for you and a better price to your network whom it would seem were also very careful, no doubt coached in the dark arts by your good self Mr Chambers aye?"

Stevie nodded in confirmation.

"All is going rosey with the DDK thugs but things start to unravel, particularly with regards to Mr Winters who I can gather started to dip into the merchandise. I suspect that you did all you could to stop him but then the recession hit and everything went completely tits up not just for you or course but for the whole country. You and everyone else did what they had to during this time, tightening the belts and what have you. I suspect our boys in Tottenham did not give you too much of a hard time over purchases and sales?"

"Surprisingly so, yes."

"Well that's because I told them to batten down the hatches keep things ticking over until the good times roll again, which pray to god are just around the corner. My philosophy during these times is you cannot get blood out of a stone so what's the point in trying. I notice that you both wound up the companies in 2008 as a result but you obviously decided to keep going with regards to selling drugs, which perhaps in hindsight, was not a good decision. So as the economic downturn bit and your partner's descent into drug addiction deepened, your relationship with Mr Winters never improved. So it all accumulated in Craig being arrested for attempted murder in a pub quite near here during the recent World Cup. He tried to cut a deal by the way, gave up you and Skully actually but he was not really being done for drugs, he had a fair amount of personal on him but it was in one big lump and he could not have been prosecuted for dealing. Not much honour amongst thieves these days eh? Something else happened in amongst all of these goings-on as well which resulted in you being late paying Skully. What was it?"

"A few weeks before the World Cup Craig did a disappearing act with five kilo's and I was left holding the proverbial baby" sighed Stevie, wincing at the situation.

"Ahh that makes sense. And to top it off one of your key customers and distributors Christiano Pittelli was pinched carrying half a kilo. He gave your name to the Police by the way, which I managed to sort out, you can thank me later. This was no doubt a real kick in the teeth as these combined events significantly impacted your business. Looking at Mr Pittelli's background he probably supplied most of the Notting Hill elite, a fair amount of your business went his way I can imagine."

The Lord raised his eyebrows and placed his hands palms down on the large antique desk before he continued.

"The end result is Skully spotted an opportunity to remove you, snatch your suppliers and take you out of the picture, just like they did with Connor."

"I can I just..." interrupted Stevie before being hushed down by another simple gesture of The Lords hand.

"You need to understand my young friend that there are others matters at play here and it's all building up to something, I am not sure what exactly but I may have to put back together the puzzle over the next couple of weeks and months. What I suggest you do, IF and that is a key question here my good friend, if you want to be a piece in that puzzle then I strongly suggest to keep your head down. I have your number."

The Lord stood up, smoothed down his suit and adjusted his tie before switching off the table light, a green glass and brass model with a price tag which Steve noticed had a £250 price tag. He held out his hand.

"Goodbye Mr Chambers."

"Goodbye Lord Lawton" replied Stevie as he firmly shook his hand before turning to leave the shop skipping down the steps to street level. As he walked away forgetting the Boris bike his head span with The Lord's information and statements as he desperately tried to interpret them and read between the lines.

CHAPTER 32

Clink Street

*A*s per usual and as regular as clockwork I am jarred awake from my delightful slumber by the loud buzzing of the electro-mechanical security doors being opened by someone out there in the control room of this fucking prison. This is followed predictably by shouting and hollering from the fucking scum inmates, sometimes the guards, all of which echo off these white coloured gloss walls. I stretch out, the tips of my toes just touching the metal bars at the end of the bunk bed.

There is no sign of movement from above, the whiny fucking little cunt they put in here a few weeks ago. He's only a kid but he had obviously been given some half-baked advice about prison, too predictable; show no fear, don't back down and all that shite. I saw him out there when he first came in, trying to look tough and imposing in the yard and communal areas but as soon as he got into the cell with me that all changed. As soon as the fucking cell doors locked shut he seemed to deflate, out goes the air that puffed up his chest as he strutted around like a peacock out in the population. But as the doors closed he thanked fuck he had got away with it yet again. Yes success! Another day without a kicking or a chiving out there in amongst the lags. Yep as soon as the doors slammed their inevitable slam he started; fucking whinging and whining about the injustice of it all, how he was caught and his so-called mates got off scot free. How it wasn't fucking fair that a previous conviction for fucks knows what went against him but also alluding to the fact his mates grassed him up. He started to really nip at my fucking head and the clunk of the door would signal the start. What am I a fucking counsellor, sent here *to psycho-analyse the prick and make sure he is going to be alright? Fucking fuck that.*

So in the end I did him a favour and got it all out of the way for him, stopped the suspense of when and where he was going to get done. Would it be the shower room, in the gym or in the yard? Probably didn't think it would be in the cell which is where I battered him as soon as he piped up the last time. Felt good as well, nice release of the tension that I could feel building up in my shoulders and in my chest ever since I got out of that nice hospital ward. Wish I could go back really, at least they kept you levelled out with all those lovely drugs they made you ingest. Less time to think, less time to ponder, less time to think about those on the outside and, my now, peers, colleagues and enemies on the inside. I needed that hospital bed at the time though to be fair. Fuck me I was a fucking mess, delirious and crazy and dangerous to everyone around even me. I needed to be kept away from the everyday haunting by that spooky relentless white ghost, those pearly white incandescent gorgeous rocks of coke and crack. Even now the thought of it makes my fucking mouth water and my lungs crave. Mmmmmm the deliciousness of it all, breathing those fumes deep, deep into your chest and feel the cleansing of your soul, the lift that you want, that lift and release you neeeed. Aaah Casper you little white translucent cunt you are the only thing that can scratch that particular itch deep, deep down inside of me.

Ohh yeah. No hang on mate, stop fucking thinking about it. You're a fucking realist, be true to yourself. Okay, got it? Yeah? Good. I just did a bit too much that's all, need to medicate my usage when I get out that's all. No need to knock it on the head, one of life's pleasures isn't it? Shit I did go a bit fucking off the rails though, all that business down in Brighton. Fuck. That was fucking Stefan's fault. God knows what's up with that prick, too much into the brown that's his problem, fucking junky. That shit just makes you lazy, plain lazy, should have stuck with the white. Oi Casper I can see you peaking over my shoulder you little sneaky cunt. Teasing me. Torturing me with the thought and desire of sniffing, burning and sucking that shit into the depths and into the blood. At least you shoo'ed away the skin ants, horrible, pure and simple those were but Casper has been haunting me ever since for sure, just like now.

Shoo Casper, fuck off, stop it. No, think about Stefan instead, he's alright, a good mate but then again he's fucked it up as well. Should have concentrated on the studio work and less on the white and then the opiates. I don't think that old bird helped matters, fucking living off the state for years, lazy hippy slob, not worked a day in her life unless you can call selling friendship bands at some manky flea markets work. Nah, if Stefan had been properly at my side it would have been alright but that skanky old wench dragged him down to her level. I suddenly think of The Judge, another who was led down the wrong path by the love of his life. Before I get too deep into those thoughts, I get another twinge.

Fuck off Casper, I still feel you not far away lurking over near my shoulder blades. I squeeze my fists into balls with the effort of ignoring him and his whispered overtures. Push him to the back of my mind.

Oh that girl! That poor girl in Brighton. The image of her pops up in my mind, brutal.

Still think about her, the one who carked it, still remember her skin when I poked her when I woke up, fucking horrible it was, like creepily cold. Cannot blame me at all for what happened, I don't really remember fuck all from that weekend. What could I do though? I wasn't in control, that's what happens when you've got 5 kilo's of stolen cocaine as percy. You're gonna go a bit fucking coo-coo aren't ya? I didn't care about it at the time, stitching up Stevie. Hmm wonder what happened there? Sold his Hampstead gaff probably, never went there but heard it was alright. The cunt can afford the debt, no problem and he can usually talk himself out of a kicking. No sure about them DDK fuckers though, bit tasty when it comes to dishing it out. Anyway, back to that Brighton busines, I wasn't the instigator, no, no chance of that. All the Brighton lot are fucking deviants; they are doing the same old shit week in, week out, I was just unlucky. Nothing but an unlucky bystander, don't recall fucking her either although I probably did. That's what happens in Brighton, throw your biases out the window and just let animal instinct take over, fuck and get fucked.

I am deviating. I am now thinking about arseholes. That is what happens with Brighton, sooner or later the topic of bumholes arises. Guaranteed. If you live in Brighton your gonna have something stuck up your arse at some point, doesn't matter who you are or what your *supposed sexual preferences are.*

Fuck it I am not going to deny myself a bit of pleasure just cause English convention and etiquette suggest otherwise. If some fucking bird fancies sticking a finger up my arse and tweak my gee spot and bring me off, just like fucking god intended, well actually invented, well crack on love and good on ya! The cunt gave me a button up my arsehole that needs pressing, it's as simple as. If a bird doesn't fancy playing by the laws of nature then that is cool, some will, some won't. Personal preference.

I won't deny it, I have had a fella slip me a length a couple of times, it's not so bad, bite ya lip, keep your head down and arse in the air and think of Britain. When you're on the session and have the horn, fuck it who cares. It fucking saddens me to think of all those men with that golden button up their shitters that haven't had it pushed. Because it's gay? What the fuck! If it's so fucking gay why the fuck is it up your arsehole in the first place! It's not gay, that is pure mechanics at play whether it was defined by gods will or Darwin's theory on the whole matter.

What else happened that weekend down in Brighton? I do vaguely re- call trying to punch some cunt but I was just wind milling, forgetting what the old man and brother tried to teach me when I was a wee lad, elbows tucked in, hands up. Took a few slaps, think the fella was from Birmingham and I just fired into him calling him a thick cunt with his divvy fucking accent and shit drugs. He tried to leather me, sure of it, but didn't feel a thing, head too buzzed of gear and that GHB shite. I just stood there laughing at him as he laid into me, that was until he caught me with a decent one on the side of the head and I went steam- ing in still laughing my head off as I pounded his swede in. His fucking face looked well fucking shocked. Well that's it son, don't fuck with me. I fucking love a swedge as the jocks would say, built for it and will laugh gayly in your face as I cave it in. A girl that lived at the gaff was screaming her head off as we crashed around the front room, wrecking the TV and coffee table. Don't know what she was going on about, the place was a fucking hovel anyway. That was a different place to where the orgy was though and not sure how I went from one place to the other. The thought of walking through Brighton town centre in that state is not a good image and memory, so I tuck it away.

And then there was all that nonsense that bought me to this very cell. That night for the World Cup, that shitty tourist pub up town, what was it called? No, no idea, the one on Baker Street. Anyway, I do remember sticking that coon with the trumpet thing, the vuvuzela thingy. Shouldn't have got fucking wide should he? Cunt. Giving me shitty lips, not as shitty as his brown fucking boat race that all of a sudden went a crimson red as I done him in the neck. Attempted murder, fuck off! If I had wanted the cunt dead he would have been dead, simple as that. Talking of a decent ruck, after I done the boy, it went off big style just like a wild west movie even that hippy wanker from San Francisco got stuck in and a few of the Woodbridge boys but not many. Not happy about that. What the fuck was that about? We've all been tight for years but that night they didn't want to know. Saw Tanner get involved though, top lad, a bit precious, you know, bit of a fence sitter. Cannot fucking please everyone in this world you know mate, sometimes you need to take a side, even be a bit selfish and look after number one. Anyway, I was grappling with this black lad who was in a rage at me for doing his mate, just holding him at arm's length round the neck, popped him a couple of decent shots but he fucking chibbed me with something, knife probably. That I did feel, cunt, sharp pain just above my right hip. Stupid place to do someone though, fuck all there mate, should have done me the other side and up a bit, spleen there, normally stops anyone. Wasn't bothered though kept going and that was when I saw Tanner getting sparked. Never could take a punch that boy, quite a big fucker as well but a chin like wafer thin glass.

Yeah a good old punch up, which had it not been for getting sent down by the musty old cunt in the wig, would have been laughed about down the boozer that night but some people just want to make mountains out of molehills.

Yeah funny that, disappointed with the Woodbridge chaps. Saw Weldon swerve getting involved, also that shitting cunt Bedswell took a large hearty step backwards as the wogs piled into me, still probably got the hump about that piccy of him and that whore in Thailand. Serves him right. Any cunt that is going to pose for a picture with some disease ridden prozzy is fucking well asking for a blackmailing in my opinion. The prick was grinning at me as I was carted off into the meat wagon, he'll fucking get his when I get out, cunt. But it was not his mush that I remember most clearly through, the red haze as the *filth scrapped, punched and kicked me into the van. It was Stevie, my old mate Stevie together with Stace. Only caught a glimpse though as a blast of pepper spray robbed me of my vision and breath. That was a mistake by the pigs, only reinvigorated me and I managed to get a hand free and smash a coppers face in. I was as surprised as the pork was, fucking amazed I managed to get a couple of decent shots in on his piggy fucking snout even though his head was encased in a riot helmet. Bullseye! Think I bust it which I was rather pleased about, even after they tazered me in the van out of sight of the fucking liberals but fuck that, they are forgetting who they are fucking dealing with. Craig fucking Winters, fucking NICEIC registered, taken more electric shocks in my time than that cunt in The Green Mile.*

Anyway, yes, I caught a glimpse alright and it has stayed with me ever since. On one face was pity and the other relief. The pitying look was from Stevie as though he were stood on top a pillar of self-righteousness and smugness, cunt. My old mate, my old business partner, we had the world in our hands and look what happened. But I had it right not him. I enjoyed and celebrated our successes with gusto. That cunt should smell the roses a bit more. Fine I nodded at the right times, took his counsel when needed but after that debacle in 2007 and 2008 I was only ever going to take a wee pinch of Stevie's nose in the air advice. He was the one that fucked it up not me, pumping all our money into fuck knows where. Taking advice and direction from that fucking smarmy fuck Nathaniel Gray, the city hammer. Never liked him, low life slime sucking sleaze ball persuading Stevie to part with our fucking dosh. The City Hammer? Pah! I gave him a hammer alright, right round the fucking mush the cunt. Stevie never did find out about the hiding I gave him, ha, ha, I REALLY enjoyed that.

As soon as it started to go tits up with the cash from the old financial crisis malarkey I was around Gray's gaff sharpish, lurked in amongst the dark shadows of his apartment block, waiting. Nice gaff overlooking the Thames just down the river from Craven Cottage, cracking little ground but a shit team is that Fulham all right. Needed some patience that night, three fucking hours I waited and as every second ticked by and as every snort of coke off a key the anger just bubbled up in me. If that cunt had been another thirty minutes I would have killed him as soon as he turned up, for sure. As he walked up oblivious to the impending danger he swiped in through the front doors with his key card. I steamed right in behind him just as the door was closing, I clamped my hand over his that was still holding the key card and I squeezed hard and felt the satisfying feeling; a small bit of give as the card cut deeply into his palm. The blood flowed quickly but I didn't let go and I forced him into the lift and up to the top floor. I remember his face, looked a little bit like a Mexican, tache and goatee, and pitted skin and long thick eyebrows. Not tanned like a Mexican though that day was he? The financial meltdown that was occurring all over the place had obviously hit him hard or maybe it was the sight of me, the colour drained from his face with deep black rings around his eyes accentuated by those smart LED down lights in the brushed chrome of the mirrored lift. That wasn't the only thing that was going to hit him hard as I snarled into his face.

"Where's my fucking money cunt, Where's my fucking money cunt..."

He seemed to shrink into his suit as I continued to berate him before the lift doors pinged open giving him a small period of respite, which wasn't going to last. I dragged him to his door still squeezing his hand and the key card against the sensor lock like one of those in a hotel, very fucking smart. The green light flicked on with an audible click of the door lock and I booted it open throwing him into his penthouse flat. He ran around the coffee table in a feeble attempt to escape but there was no way he was getting away unless he jumped off his balcony but I didn't reckon he had the guts. Later the cunt proved me wrong on that front but not that night as I steamed towards him smashing my fist into his face knocking his two teeth out in one go. Boom! Blood pissed from his mouth as I screamed at him.

"Doing you a favour you buck tooth cunt, go get some fucking veneers if you can afford it after paying me back."

He spluttered something whilst trying to get to his feet but I wasn't interested in listening to him so I booted him in the ribs hearing a satisfying crack as his body leapt two foot in the air. He already started to sag after just two fucking smacks and he gave in, not putting up any sort of resistance or defence. I pulled him to his feet and threw him into a dark leather armchair.

I then recalled one of his stupid fucking nick names, Stunt Dick, Stevie reckons he was a stand in when actors are too shy or have too smaller dicks to get it out on film or TV. I had to take a gander didn't

I? Not sure he could possibly have the length and girth to outgun me, so better have a fucking gander I thought. I whipped down his cacks and you should have seen the cunts face, thought I was gonna fucking bum him, he wishes, the cunt! Any way I have look at his chap and yeah, give him his dues, he was packing but fuck me, the state of his bell-end. Obviously a snide Jew, which figured, the skanking, robbing cunt, as the foreskin was off but the state of his helmet! It was battered, looked like a old bit of fucking leather. Fucking horrible and highly unlikely Tom Cruise was gonna want that manky, disease riddled chopper standing in for him. So I fucking boot him in the cock and balls and he really begins to wilt as he collapses onto the floor

"Not having you pass out on me so soon son, you little shitting weasel."

And I pulled out my trusty glass pipe and a big, a very big bag of crack. Lovely. I thrust a rock into the funnel grabbed his hair and shoved the pipe between his lips, the absence of his front teeth meaning this was much easier than anticipated, like a cock in a well lubed fucking fanny. Like the fucking seasoned pro that I am I fired up the rock with a lighter in the same hand as that holding the pipe.

"Suck like you suck on rent boys' diseased cocks you cunt." I screamed.

He started spluttering and gagging as the gorgeous stinking smoke goes down his throat. This is pure Woodbridge vintage crack this stuff, should be fucking paying me and here I am giving it away and the fuck is not wolfing it down. Half of it is escaping! How fucking dare he, I thought.

I removed the pipe, ignoring the blood and spittle, and I showed him how it should be done. Someone somewhere gave me a good set of lungs. I sucked hard. The rock shrank under the intense flame enveloping it, the glistening ball of hard snow reduced down to nothing. Beautiful it was. The white ghost filled my chest and I high fived and hugged my old mate Casper as I held it in, not daring to breath out as explosions pinged off in my head and I felt those muscles in my back and neck ripple.

I frantically delved into my little bag of tricks pulling out a smaller rock making sure he smoked the lot. He turned purple, the white pasty face slowly filling up, his eyes turned a blood red and began heavy breathing. What the fuck? This cunt was meant to be a city highflier he should be on the nose and rocks every night, it was like he never done the shit before. The cunt was fucking scoobied but mission accomplished, he was fucking wired to fuck so I could continue to give him the bad news as I laid into him again. The gear worked a treat as he scrambled around the flat like a rabbit trying to escape a fox, desperately trying to evade my clutches but to no avail. I just started winging furniture out the way and simply kicking all the doors in. It was a pity though, the guy had good taste, a huge plasma screen got a vase thrown through it and an expensive looking glass dining table shattered into pieces.

These high specification flats have decent sound proofing so I took my time, not worrying about any nosey neighbours. After a while he started to beg, fearing for his life as I beat him with my fists and boots. He started babbling about the Turks and money or something.

"Fuck the Turks, you need to be more worried about me, this is merely the start. You're gonna be hacked up in a minute and thrown in the river unless you give me my FUCKING money!" I remember screaming at him.

After what seemed like five minutes but was probably nearer half an hour he is properly whimpering, proper broken. With a resigned look on his bloody face he pointed a broken crooked finger at a painting of a Spanish dancer. I turned and stood looking at it, satisfied with the job I had done. I would have preferred to have taken a bit longer but that Casper had stopped whizzing around my head and was looking a little up tight tapping his watch.

"Yes mate another rock, fucking good idea."

I looked at the painting. I hadn't noticed it up until that point. Even through my rage I gasped at the beauty of it. The dark background emphasised the dancers flowing red dress, a take on one of those flamenco numbers but sexy as fuck. The full breasts, the slim ankles and high heels so perfectly painted they almost looked real, like a photo. Amazing it was. There was a moment of calm in my mind and for a few seconds the wheels stop spinning as I regarded the artwork with a smile on my lips. I fell in love with it. I carefully lifted it from its hook before gently placing it on the floor. The beauty of the painting in stark contrast to the ruins of the smashed up apartment. There was a black safe in the wall, looked like a Burton Torino, very difficult to break unless you have a cooperative owner of course.

I screamed at him to open it but he looked at me pleadingly, like a fucking puppy dog before spluttering out some shit trying to get me to leave him alone.

"Please, please it was a sound investment plan, no one knew what was going to happen don't, please. Everyone has lost, everyone, the whole frigging city, the whole friggin planet not just you" the cunt spluttered through bloodied, cracked lips.

He was simply forgetting who was dealing with. Not fucking Stevie that's for sure, who seemed to simply shrug his shoulders and mutter something about high risks equal high rewards, accepting it, being shafted by the little cunt. Well I am not Stevie, I don't give a flying fuck about the small print, the get out clauses that state the value of investments can go down as well as up. Well fuck that, I am more in the old school brigade where a deal is a deal and a gentlemen's handshake is an agreement full stop. That cunt promised the earth and delivered nothing except a few acres of sand in fuck knows where, worth fuck all. Some cunt lined his pockets and one of them was that wretched ball of snot, piss and blood at my feet. So I pulled him up ignoring him and he finally opened the safe after I twisted his left arm up behind his back nearly snapping it. The contents were disappointing but better than nothing, about £40k in cash, a few other documents which looking back now I wish I had taken. My job there was done. I stood there, feet wide apart still breathing heavily looking down at him. I wanted to throw him out the window but hearing about them Turks I thought I would be nice and let them have their fun, let's not be greedy. So I nutted him across the bridge of his nose letting go of his collar at the same time. He hit the deck out cold, just a bad fucking dream this Mr Gray but maybe something to think about next time before you fuck someone over.

I was going to tell Stevie about the £40k, really I was, I was going to cut him in on half but I thought I would be better off on my toes for a bit just in case and skipped over to Amsterdam using my trusty Nicholas James Bush passport. Stayed for a few weeks and blazed through that cash a bit too quick. Started off in the five-star Grand Hotel but ended up at a hostel in the red light district but that was fine. I can rough it when I need to, never forget my roots. Unlike Stevie, that pitying look, the fucker.

After I had done all the cash on gear and eastern European whores I managed to get away with mugging this big fucking black geezer who was walking home after plying his drugs to all the gullible tourists. Cannot believe I got away with that as well although he didn't see it coming, straight forward iron bar over the head from behind, riffled his pockets and cacks like a pro then off-ski. Had some iffy gear that was barely worth snorting but a fair old amount of Euros which helped for a few more days.

Jesus fucking Christ, that look from Stevie as I was hauled away by the five oh. And then there was Stace, my beautiful Stacey with that look on her face that made her look ugly as fuck. Like sneering at me, together with a look of pure glee on her face. Christ, she might as well have been popping champagne it was that obvious. Thinking back on my behaviour I can hardly blame her, she wasn't interested in all of that stuff, staying up days getting on it, she had done all that in her twenties but she knew what I was like so not entirely my fault. The problem was you cannot explain to anyone that hasn't scaled the heights and plumbed the depths, they think you can just stop. But you cannot stop, you need to slow down first. Difficult to explain. It's like a woman trying to explain to a man the concept, the feeling, of carrying a baby for nine months and the subsequent pain and joy of childbirth. You cannot grasp it. That is what it is like when you're in deep. It's like trying to explain colours and landscapes to a blind person. Try to explain to someone who is white what it is like to be black. Not happening dude! Try all you like, they just will not get it.

It was like that with Stace but I reckon I can sort it, make a big effort with her when I get out. You never know we could get married, not sure I love her, I think so. I definitely love the thought of her no doubt about that but if I'm honest I love myself more. Too selfish that is my problem but she is a cracking bird, decent ride and not a bad laugh. Maybe me and Stevie could get ESG Property Ltd up and running again and employ her as our chief designer, working with the architects, all the trade, she would be brilliant. She loved that when we were doing our gaff up. Sure I can get back in her good books. Should not have had her pay me off for the house, that was pretty stupid of me but I needed the cash real bad then. The haunting was crippling back then and the cash was needed to fend off Casper and them other ghosties and skin insects. I knew her old man would stump up the cash as well, fucking super loaded that fella, another reason to make *a bit of a go of it with her when I get out. I just need to keep a handle on the gear, need to ignore that white spook that nags me constantly and so incessantly.*

It's with me even now as I lay here in this little cell with cuntybollocks up there lightly snoozing. The apparition swirling around in my mind, body and soul instigating that constant craving for the powder and or the rock. The devils dandruff, yayo, Shirley Bassey, flake, powder, charlie, snow, gear, rails, lines, bumps, toots whatever you called it I fucking crave it every single second of the day. Those initial detoxing days in the hospital were murder but the super strength opiates and pain killers counterbalanced the desire. Here alone, well to all intents and purposes alone, in this bland plain whitewashed cell I could murder a hit. But a hit I am not going to get, one of my defence arguments was that I was a hopeless junky and needed help. It helped a little bit when the sentencing happened as long as I could stay clean inside and out. This means regular piss tests and although the cannabis traces would be staying in my blood for a few months any increase or anything new and that was it, another two years on the sentence. Cunts. Going have to suck it up, could sort me out though, got to get rid of this fucking horrible gut. Never quite sure how I got it, never ate in the last year, just sniffed and smoked. Weird.

Going clean and sober isn't gonna stop this rage in me though. I've always had it since Mum left me and Shaun. It bubbles, boils and simmers. I just fucking lose it, I cannot control it, and I just fucking explode sometimes over the slightest little thing. Like that whistling noise I can hear coming from that fucker's nose up there on the top bunk. I can feel the heckles rising in me as I am sat here thinking about it. It's like a claustrophobic kind of feeling but instead of suddenly panicking, flaying arms running about and hyperventilating, I just simply smack people, hard.

I kick him. Up through the slats making him yelp as I shout at him to shut the fuck up. I tell him he'll be whistling for the rest of his life after I snap his fucking beak.

I head down to brekkie and get in the line where I go for the porridge. Started eating a bit better now, none of that fried shit, need some fuel for when I go down the gym and do some weights, maybe a run. Yeah get the horrible gut shrunk, get that six pack back again.

It has been an interesting week, loads of rumours flying around about what was happening out there on the streets. We've all been huddled around the televisions trying to find out what has been going on. Looks like all the coons had kicked off in London, specifically up in Tottenham after some black lad, who I thought I recognised, got whacked by the old bill. All the aggro going on, riots and shit has those DDK cunts names written all over it. Not surprised and glad one of them fucking got it. A few of us chat about the riots but I keep my connections with DDK under wraps, keep it well shtum.

Surprisingly I get a visitation notification in my cell for the 14:00 visiting time. It reads Charles Willoughby. I look at the name and seek out a connection, scanning my damaged brain of all those people I have met over the years. Car smokes, house parties, raves, music festivals, short breaks, long holidays, traveller raves, illegal warehouse parties, squat parties, brothels, pubs, clubs, crack dens, restaurants and shooting galleries but no one comes to mind. Charles Willoughby? Sounds posh maybe one of that twat Christiano's contacts. Whoever he is, it's worth going along, keeps me away from this snivelling prick up top.

As I walk through into the visiting room I see him. Kaiser. Skully's right hand man. That rage that festers within me begins to rise into my neck and I begin to tense up. My natural reaction which I am struggling to suppress is to run at him, maybe hop onto the nearby table and jump heroically from table to table dodging the outstretched hands of the prison guards until I get to him and boot him full in the face before jumping down and pummel the fuck out of him. But I do not, I just breathe deeply through my nose just like the prison physiatrist told me to do. Count to ten, think about the consequences. Smacking the fuck out of the cunt sounds like a top consequence you cunt. I hate Kaiser and all his crew, despise everything that they are, fucking street niggers the lot of them, they don't just make their estates look untidy but make the residents, the good people that live there, feel unsafe and vulnerable. The pasting they gave Connor and his mate was out of order, didn't let it show though. Stood there didn't I, not flinching as they panelled the mick in that front room. Didn't even blink when you heard that grotesque yet lovely sound as knuckles meet flesh at speed and with power. I showed them I am cut from the same cloth, I don't give a fuck, I dish that shit out if I need to but normally I don't, I'm above all that.

He is dressed like he always is, like a fucking wrong un. White vest, gold chain, black leather jacket, skinny jeans which I have seen are beginning to come back into fashion, not that this rogue knows anything about that. He has bypassed all fashion for years and just dressed the same way no matter what. As I walk slowly I duck ever so slightly to get a glimpse of his footwear. There you go you fucking fuckwad, black leather slip-ons and white terry towelling socks, what a fucking.....well I cannot even think of a name to describe him. I think back to all the names we used to call kids at school and then over the years. I think of them all but still nothing can describe him, he is beyond fucking description.

I sit down and stare into his cold ferret eyes, he still looks the same, a few more wrinkles but this is a guy that has always looked old. His pointed shnoz making his face even more rodent like than I remember and then it comes to me. A name for this man, a rat. Vermin, sneaky, makes your skin crawl. So I let him have it.

What do you want fucking ratboy? I say glaring at him. There is no response from him, no reaction to my childish name calling. The old playground rhyme rattles around my head making me feel foolish.

Sticks and stones may break my bones, but names with never hurt me.

I do not let on though as I continue to stare, the rage and the crack ghosts churning in my chest. And then the rat speaks, slowly.

"I thought I would come down and say hello, you must get ever so lonely in here. Thought a visit from an ex-business partner might cheer you up."

He said the word ex with venom letting me know there was no going back, which of course I fucking know anyway.

I reply, keeping cool.

"I didn't know your name was Charles, shall I call you Charlie from now on rather than Kaiser. Quite an apt name considering your line of business."

Even now the word Charlie makes me quiver a little inside as I imagine snorting down a gigantic line, with Casper nodding his approval at my antics. Kaiser replies grinning at me.

"Talking of ex-business partners, Stevie been into to see you? We would like a word with him."

Here it is, the segway into what he is really after. He's after Stevie. Maybe he didn't pay. Doubt it, too shit scared. I wonder what the score is with him. I play him along a bit.

"Heard he is in Scotland" I say smiling with my arms folded. "Or was it Peak District?"

"Or was it Southend oh I don't know, me and my memory." "What's he done then?" I ask.

"Must be something serious to have you come all this way for a visit. Did you get a nosebleed when you went past Watford?"

"He's been a very naughty boy Craig, very naughty and you know we don't like naughty boys don't cha?"

"Good. Glad he's been naughty, he use to pander to you fucking lot, I tried to tell him otherwise but wouldn't listen. Anyway good luck finding him cause you aren't getting shit out of me."

I fold my arms again and look over towards a really fit looking wife or girlfriend chatting to her lag. She is definitely getting a bit on the outside and by the look on his mug he knows it as well.

Kaiser reaches into his inside jacket pocket and he pulls out a photo, he holds it up looking at it. He smiles and looks at me knowing he has now has my interest. He turns it around and slips it onto the desk so it is facing up at me. As the image begins to register in my brain I feel that familiar uncontrollable white noise build up in my skull up fizzing to a crescendo and that anger, the brutal intractable rage erupts up into my chest. I reach out and grip the table, my scarred knuckles going white with the effort. His sly smile curls up in the rats face and he speaks.

"He was fucking her behind your back for years" he says making a hissing sound as he expels air through his lips.

As I look at the picture of Stevie holding hands with my Stacey, sat in a bar, pub or restaurant, her laughing at him, I can barely think as I am incandescent with rage and betrayal and before I know it I have blurted it out.

"Flat 3149, Trentstone Tower, Westbourne fucking Grove."

CHAPTER 33

Pudding Lane

The sun was setting as Scott joined the A40 during the short journey from Woodbridge into London, the fiery ball still visible in his rear-view mirror. He turned left trying to recall the exact route to Westbourne Grove. He had only been once, enough to put him off visiting since, until now. It was during Notting Hill Carnival in 1998, a huge contingent from Woodbridge had attended and had spent most of the day at the Sancho Panza then Good Times sound systems, with DJ Norman Jay playing a mixed set of funk, hip hop and soulful house. Scott, Craig and Stevie snuck off 30 minutes before the end. Scott was keen to see where 'his' newly acquired property was located. He did not particularly like the area, a huge crew of dodgy looking blokes hanging around outside made him nervous but Stevie tried to reassure him this was all to do with the Carnival.

Scott however nodded in appreciation as he entered the flat admiring the decor but mostly the amazing views of the urban sprawl below and beyond. To Scott the whole tower seemed to be humming with activity, vibrating from the thud of music reverberating throughout the structure as people shouted and screamed out of the windows and on from the balconies. Craig attempted to carry on the party pulling out some of their stash from one of the bedrooms. Scott remained passively silent as Stevie bollocked him before turning to him shrugging his shoulders attempting to show him that he had grown up even if Craig had not. The tower block made him feel uneasy.

Nerves jangled through him as he drove through the outer suburbs of London listening intently to the radio at the events unfolding in London and other inner-city areas around the country. He knew that Westbourne Grove would be effected. He double checked the car doors were locked.

"What the fuck am I actually doing?" he muttered as he grimly drove on trying not to think of Ester, that fucking cuntbag, or his beautiful daughters, no doubt sat at home wondering where their dad was and why mum was walking funny. The only slim positive thought was recalling how good it felt punching that litle cunt Rhys in the face at work in Bristol.

He skirted Notting Hill remembering that Craig's girlfriend Stacey once lived nearby. Scott liked her, admiring how she had somehow once nearly tamed Craig, not an easy job, one that him and Stevie had failed at. He had heard that they split up and briefly wondered what she was doing now.

As Scott turned into Golbourne Road the huge tower emerged from behind the rooftops. The top half of the tower baked in late evening summer sunshine, the bottom shrouded in a foreboding dark shadow. The streets were quiet, just a few small groups huddled in and around shop doorways all now looking in the direction of the large red pink railway bridge as his car approached. Further ahead Scott clocked a huge mass of people, mostly black teenagers, milling around under a smaller block of flats opposite the Trentstone Tower. He eased up on the accelerator as he approached the bridge as another bought of doubt about trying to find Stevie enveloped him. He hunched forward in his seat as he looked up at the tower, squinting his eyes as he searched the upper floors to try and identify the flat. Many people were out in their balconies looking down and out across London trying to spot any disturbances kicking off in the immediate area. Someone had hung a huge banner from their balcony *'RIP Cee Bugg - Justice!'*

Scott looked to the top right-hand corner of the building searching out the windows, the dying sun still reflecting off the glass of the upper floors. He thought he saw some movement in one of the flats.

"Was that Stevie he could see?"

He reached into the door well of the car retrieving his glasses. His eyesight had been getting worse over the years but rarely used the prescription glasses for driving or otherwise. He cracked open the case pulling on the frames before looking up at the tower which now appeared in his vision in crystal clear high definition. He briefly wondered again why he did not use the glasses more often before slamming on his brakes in shock. He stopped the car dead in its tracks bringing it to a standstill halfway across the railway bridge. His mouth dropped open as he could clearly see Stevie half hanging out of one of the top floor windows.

He panicked and even though the car windows were nearly all the way up he screamed.

"STEVVVIE!!!!"

"Jesus he's going to fucking jump."

Scott scrambled out of the car. He stood in the middle of the road staring upwards. The large group of teenagers to his left also noticed the drama unfolding up high on the 31st floor.

Kaiser, sat in his Mercedes just out of sight of Scott, noticed the nearby crowd of youths looking up. Previously with a wide smile on his face he had been listening to BBC radio as the news reports rolled in from several of the London boroughs. It was kicking off everywhere.

"What a beautiful thing" he thought as he emerged from his car curious as to what the youths were looking at. Maybe young Stevie was being dangled out of the flat window by his crew. Now that would be a great sight to behold.

As he slowly strolled towards the tower, he heard a soft banging and thudding coming from the boot of his car. He stopped turning around clicking the key fob. The boot clicked before springing upward. He looked down at the figure inside cocking his head to the side.

"I hear you knocking again, I will fucking gut you like a pig. I don't know if you've heard but no one is around to save you, so lay back, close your eyes and shut the fuck up."

He slammed the boot shut. Reaching behind his back he readjusted the handgun wedged in the small of his back held in place by his belt. As he walked away he sang loudly.

"London's burning, London's burning. Fetch the engines, fetch the engines. Fire fire, Fire Fire! Pour on water, pour on water.

London's burning, London's burning. Fetch the engines, fetch the engines.
 Fire fire, Fire Fire!"

"Stevvie!!!!" screamed Scott looking up wondering what the hell was going on.

"Jump cracker!" shouted someone from the crowd who had now moved nearer Scott to get a better view. A sharp crack that sounded like a gunshot vibrated around the estate from above.

Scott and the crowd gasped before falling silent as they attempting to register exactly what they were seeing.

And then Stevie jumped.

"Nooooo!!" yelled Scott as he saw Stevie fling himself off the window ledge as a shower of sparks and fire jumped around and out of the open window.

"What the f......." Was all he could say as Stevie's right hand flung out a small package above him before Scott realised it was...... a.......fucking parachute!

The crowd gasped again before cheering as they finally realised what this maniac was doing. Suddenly and unexpectedly the corner section of the flats exploded, the windows blowing outwards in a brilliant shower of flame, light and glass. The percussive rumble sounded deep in and around the nearby housing estate, the echo and reverb throbbed off the cement buildings and narrow compacted streets.

Stevie fell fast as the small canopy took time to catch the air but by the 18th floor it wrenched open the main parachute canopy slowing him down enough to enable him to steer away from the main building. The crowd whooped, hollered and clapped most assuming it was a stunt for a film or TV show, many craning their necks up and down the road to see where the camera crews were.

"Stevie, Stevie" screamed Scott waving his hands above his head as he descended fast towards the road.

Stevie heard his old mate and they caught eye contact. Stevie would have normally greeted his old friend in a broad smile but he was struck down with a peculiar mix of outright fear and adrenaline. All he could do was to pull down hard on the steering toggle as he fought the parachute from heading towards the huge crowd, most of which he assumed, incorrectly, were DDK. He swooped to the left before noticing from his elevated position the deep cut of the railway line. He pulled down right for fear of being struck by a train or electrocuted on the adjacent underground line. He shot back up into the air as he swung hard back to the right, his body now nearly above the main canopy, in danger of losing air and crashing down onto the hard cement below. Again, he pulled downward now swinging back and forth frantically fighting to regain control, Scott suddenly and very quickly came into view.

He hurtled into him instinctively grabbing hold of Scott in a bear hug for fear of being pulled up into the air again by the parachute. Scott was knocked backwards, hitting his head hard enough on the concrete road to make him see stars but not quite enough to knock him out. He shrieked as his world suddenly turned red before quickly realising it was the parachute that had landed on them both. Stevie now sat astride him quickly tugged at the clips of the harness, after freeing himself he looked down at Scott grinning as the relief of being back on terra-firma flooded through him.

"Don't fucking tell me, one hundred per cent pure adrenaline" deadpanned Scott quoting Patrick Swayze from the film *Point Break*, one of their favourite childhood films.

Stevie was rushing with adrenaline as he jumped up pulling the parachute off them both before reaching down and locking hands yanking Scott to his feet. He nodded towards his car that was idling away on the bridge.

"Is that your c....."

'Craaaack'

A gun shot echoed out. A bullet went zinging past Stevie's head, the second time in ten minutes he had been shot at. It hit Scott's car bonnet ricocheting off, hitting the curve of the metal railway bridge. The large crowd hit the floor in unison as Kaiser, now a mere 50 metres away, took aim again. Both ran to the car diving in as he fired the bullet which embedded itself in the car door, a splinter of metal slicing through the interior panelling hitting Stevie's left leg. A hot pain shot up his calf muscle.

"Aargh, aargh I've been hit!" he screeched clutching his leg.

Suddenly the front windscreen shattered into a thousand pieces, showering them in glass as another bullet smashed into the car.

"Drive, drive, fucking drive!" screamed a hysterical Stevie at Scott.

To their right a horrific scream sounded from up high in the tower. Everyone stopped. The crowd, Kaiser, Stevie and Scott, everyone. They all looked up. The boys peered up as a figure appeared on the balcony of the flat, now fully ablaze and spewing thick black smoke. The figure leapt off the balcony plunging to the ground screaming all the way until the hard concrete silenced him forever. Scott was frozen in place as his brain tried to decipher what was going on and what he had just seen. Stevie screamed again as his eyes met with Kaiser who had just witnessed the horrific death of one of his crew. His thin lips turned into a sneer as he strode towards the car, shortening the distance to the targets, making sure that he would not miss again. Stevie desperately tugged at Scott's arm in attempt to get him to move but he was paralysed with fear and shock. He looked back again at Kaiser who was now within 20 metres his arm outright pointing straight at Stevie. His smile broadened as he turned the gun away from Stevie towards Scott, eliminate any chance of escape and dispense a small sliver of payback.

Scott was pulled out of his trance-like fog as Kaiser began to appear in his peripheral vision. He jumped in his seat as he saw the black hole of the barrel of the gun being pointed directly at his head.

"Nooooo" screamed Stevie as Kaiser squinted before pulling the trigger.

'Click'

Kaisers face changed from a look of evil glee and concentration to a look of surprise as the gun failed to discharge. Scott his mouth still wide open in panic finally acted slamming his foot down hard on the accelerator speeding forward as fast as he could towards Kaiser now busily trying to clear the gun. They hit him hard. Kaiser emitting a dull groan as he flew up through the air and straight into the gap where the windscreen used to be. Kaiser smashed into Scott breaking his wrist. Stevie realised Kaiser was very much alive and still in the game and quickly started laying into him with his fists, punching him hard in the face. Kaiser's face was pure bone and he did not seem to be doing much damage. The car sped forward towards the crowd now swelled by huge numbers of residents fleeing the burning tower. People jumped left and right to get out of the way of the car, many had their phones out filming the action which would later be all over YouTube and Facebook.

Through the flurry of punches Kaiser grabbed Stevie's collar of his polo shirt with his left hand as he began to realise what had happened. His legs were broken but had not let go of the gun still in his right hand. Stevie saw a flash of black instinctively pushing Kaisers hand to the side. The gun went off again with a loud bang the bullet whined off into the side window smashing it to smithereens. He changed position bringing the gun back around into the car as Stevie tried to ward it off again.

The sound of the gun recoiling again in the enclosed space ripped through their ear drums deafening Stevie and Scott but again the bullet missed them both smashing through the roof of the car.

The gun jammed again, that glorious click, click, click sound as Kaiser desperately tried to shoot at them again. The boys knew they were now safe. This gave Stevie confidence as he pummelled Kaiser with his fists smashing him again and again. His hands were bloody and broken but he continued on, screaming at the effort. Finally, Kaiser began to sag under the barrage losing his grip. With all his remaining effort Stevie half pushed half dragged him off the car bonnet dumping him off to the side. Scott slowed down moving away from the kerbside as Stevie jettisoned the unwanted passenger onto the road.

They drove on through the estate both breathing heavily but otherwise in silence. Scott started to pick glass fragments from his hair with his good hand flicking them out of the side window. The silence continued until a small smile appeared on Scott's face.

"So what you been up to then, much?"

"Ah, you know a bit of this, a bit of that, you?"

EPILOGUE

Sunrise at Sunrise 1989

The thud, thud, thud of the kick drum was relentless all night. The DJs, heads down, mixed and pounded out acid house over and over to the thousands inside Fairley Aircraft Hangar at White Waltham airfield. The crowd danced hard all night to each and every one of them.

Unbeknown to the four friends from Woodbridge this crazy, drug and music fuelled night was the point in which they slipped from quasi-innocent adolescents into adults. Independence in the form of The Judges car was the start but the remaining vestiges of childhood seeped slowly from their souls as they danced, sweated, gurned and hugged under the huge hangar roof. Their innocence and ignorance eroded in amongst the crowd as the night throbbed yet gradually ticked away into morning. This night would catapulte them towards towards an uncertain future.

An different yet equally unpredictable change was already bubbling and brewing next to the dance risers and under the glittering blaze of lasers accompanied by the cacophony of the four to the floor sound. The Judge swayed and grinning madly as he looked on at Mollie. He was already hooked, bonafide love at first sight. She leant into him kissing him staring dreamily deep into his eyes. The ecstacy no doubt helping but the love and beginnings of an infatuation crashed into The Judge like a class-A powered tsunami sweeping him away. She released him from their embrace grinning as she danced away from him winking in a way that was all knowing, all seeing and all encompassing. She knew. She knew all right. From that moment on she had The Judge in her grip, she would not let go and he was powerless to stop her. It was gone 4am when Stevie noticed the roof was not completely covered in corrugated metal but was interspersed with plastic panels and the morning light began to glow through. Still incredibly hot inside and although the number of people had thinned it was still packed to the rafters with jerking, grooving party goers. He could not see The Judge or Scott. He guessed The Judge was with Mollie somewhere, they had not left each other's side since they had arrived. Scott was still probably still hunting the hangar for that gorgeous raver that ravished him earlier in the evening.

He felt a hand grip his shoulder as an MDMA rush rippled up his back into his head as he gasped and gurned, screwing his face he turned to be confronted by a very sweaty Craig beaming at him. They hugged and laughed as the chemicals and music washed over them. Craig shouted at him over the thumping music.

"Snout?" beamed Craig offering him a packet of cigarettes.

"Yes please squire."

"Getting light outside."

"Yeah what time do you think it will finish?"

"No idea I think it might go on all morning."

"We should probably think about getting Scott back at some point, his old dear probably lodged a missing person's report already" sniggered Stevie.

"Ah fuck her, we're all old enough to do what we want now."

Stevie made a quizzical face as though not believing him. Craig maybe, left to his own devices for a long time, coming and going from his house as he pleased. His dad not really registering or caring what was happening, he had his own problems and demons to deal with, most notably his chronic back pain and associated painkillers plus a fondness for Irish Whiskey. His brother, Shaun, looked out for Craig but he was also young and off out doing his own thing, mostly in London and Manchester following bands.

It was too difficult to talk so they carried on dancing next to each other. The DJ, Paul Trouble Andersen, dropped *Yaah* by D-Shake, a brooding chugging techno laced house track with clacking snares with hypnotic voices and synths. It most definitely was not a hands in the air track and demanded some serious heads down dancing. Craig left Stevie's side to continue dancing with a tall girl with a mad straw hat, its rim pinned back. She wore white dungarees with a boob tube underneath. Stevie looked up at the raised dance platforms, a giant inflatable ball in the background hung from the ceiling where visual effects were being shown from a large projector. The lasers were still firing out across the dance floor but were diluted by the morning light that was beginning to fill the room. Those more prepared than others, such as the older Bromley boys, pulled out their sunglasses hiding their enlarged pupils. Stevie began to see the state of everyone, all off their heads, jaws nashing, wide eyed, arms flailing. He danced for another hour or so but he could feel the drugs wearing off, his lower back began to ache and complain. He turned to look for Craig but could not see him. Someone pointed outside.

Squeezing through the crowd he headed towards the hangar doors which had now been fully opened. Near the opening people were dancing everywhere but as he walked further outside savouring the cooling fresh sweet tasting air he saw dozens of groups of people sitting down, some asleep, some foot tapping but most just chatting away merrily sharing stories and adventures of the night just passed.

Stevie then caught sight of The Judge who was sat upright wearing a pair of sunglasses looking towards the hangar looking very pleased with himself, mostly because Mollie was leant into him sat between his legs. Scott and Craig were also there nattering away with Bromley Ben and a few others laughing at a story being told. He sat down exchanging handshakes before fishing around his pockets for a pack of cigarettes, he had been saving his last one. He screwed up the packet throwing it at The Judge. It hit him on the forehead before bouncing into the lap of Mollie whose eyes were like giant saucers.

"You alright there fella?"

"All good, all good, fucking amazing night mate, still rushing off them thingies. Had a good one?" he replied dreamily with a lazy looping smile on his lips.

"Mate that was something else, never danced so much in my life, seven hours non-stop. The DJ Jules with your name was incredible, didn't look much older than us really. He was properly having it as well behind the decks."

"You boys going to come to another one then?" quizzed Bromley

Ben. The Judge was nodding furiously squeezing Mollie's shoulders, Scott looked a little less enthusiastic and Stevie was the same, he was not sure about the pills and powders aspect of it all. It was a bit heavy even though he loved the feeling but what had him hooked was the music. Some of the tunes he had heard were incredible and was convinced house music was the way forward. Craig was laid out on the grass, Stevie could not see the girl he had been dancing and snogging anywhere and he did not seem to care which wound Stevie up. Craig was the only one who had been laid out of all of them, ridden by Natalie Dorrell from the year above after he gave her his last Rollo.

"Unbelievable. That old fucking trick, a fucking advert tag-line; 'Do you love anyone enough to give them your last rollo?' actually got him laid, the fucker! Here Natalie look, I saved you my last fucking chocolate encased caramel sweet. What the fuck! She fell for it hook line and sinker dragging him into the woods over Ash Hill Park and sat on his prick."

"The best 20p I ever spent" Craig used to brag. Secretly Stevie and Scott had both tried the same trick at school and got nowhere, a toffee down and that was it.

"I really need to get fucking laid!" thought Stevie as he looked at the dozens of girls everywhere, all far too old for him.

One of the lads sat in the circle started arguing with Bromley Ben about the acid house scene.

"Mate it is all a load of bollocks really, you bang on about peace, love and unity, freedom to dance, everyone is equal under one roof, freedom to take drugs blah blah but what's it all about really? As you so rightly pointed out earlier all the London clubs except for maybe Clink Street is getting all snobby about who it lets in based on how they are dressed, walk and talk. But these big scale raves things are no different, it's all about money, nothing else. Profit and greed masquerading as peace and love. Probably a bunch of Thatcher Tory boys running things behind the scenes. Not only that, have you not seen all those dodgy cunts lurking around? These things aren't gonna last, too much money is being made, the violent, nasty element is already here. You're too pilled up to notice, people getting skanked, girls getting touched up and violated in the darkness. That plus the Tory cunts don't like it, they are not gonna put up with it plus they don't get a piece. There are two ways this scene is headed. Licensed festivals and clubs with a 3am limit and alcohol restrictions. The other is underground...YEAH BOY! I met these lads last month, call themselves the DiY sound system, Nottingham lads. They do stuff in clubs and that but they are going to be putting on these sort of events but intimate, not too big. No funfairs, no big flashy flyers. Low key, intimate, word of mouth. Parties in secluded woodland, the valleys of Wales, old quarries where the steep walls keep the sound from travelling. That's where it's at, a bit crustier, a bit more of a traveller vibe. Not my scene, lurching around the countryside living in a Transit van, shitting in a ditch but I will be at the parties man, fuck yeah!"

He continued unable to stop.

"And another thing, then I will shut up ha, ha. The summers of love and these parties are all well and good but there are some weak deluded people out there who will get into the scene a little too much than what is good for them. There has to be the realisation that you have to hold down a job and that. Going out for days on end isn't going to help anyone in the long run. Well unless you're one of them crusties but they are all secret trust fund kids anyway! You said it yourself some of the best nights these days are mid-week up in town, fuck that! Going to Heaven on a Monday night and getting pilled off your box, not exactly a good recipe for holding down a regular job is it?" He finally ran out of steam, seemingly now out of things to say, no more energy to continue.

"Fuck me Dave, how to get everyone to come down that little bit quicker? Fucking hell!" replied Bromley Ben as he looked over at The Judge quizzically.

"Oi! Why do they call you The Judge anyway?"

ACKNOWLEDGMENTS

I recall the idea for these books was during one of my many commutes into London. I had always loved Trellick Tower near Westbourne Grove, which is obviously the inspiration for 'Trentstone Towers' where Stevie and Craig have their safe house. I remember looking up at the looming distopian hulk of a building thinking it would be an awesome location for the grand finale of an action movie. Maybe Arnie or The Rock absailing down the side as baddies try and shoot at them from the upper floors.

I grew up in a place called Woodley, just outside of Reading in Berkshire. It is not a new-town like Luton or Basingstoke so has a bit of character and history. I still live nearby and have a fond spot for the place. I met the love of my life there (in playgroup actually!) and now have two beautiful daughters with her. There is nothing much more I can say about her other than she is simply awesome. How lucky am I to have met my soul-mate who grew up no more than a couple of streets away. Much of the character Stacey is based on my wife, muck-mouth being one of her amusing attributes after a few bevvies.

As for the likes of The Judge, Craig, Scott, China, Tanner etc. they are all amalgamations of all sorts of people from in and around Woodley. So a big nod to all my friends from our little playground of a town, many still in the area, others that have flown the coop and those sadly no longer with us. RIP. The stories from this motley group were another inspiration to write this book but a novel of constant 'bloke gets pissed and does something stupid' would never be a decent read so tried to weave in a story of 90's excess getting out of hand which culminates in a big action finale! For those that like to be picky; I know the London Riots were in 2011 and not 2010 but I needed to get the World Cup vuvuzela story into the mix (yes this actually did happen! Well the horn up the bum bit not the attempted murder although there was a massive ruck down the local!).

Shouts, obviously, to my wonderful parents and in-laws. I really bloody hope they don't read it! I am not sure if my mum could take reading an entire chapter about a bloke being wanked off!

I have always loved electronic music; one of my first records was a 7 inch of *The Jack that House Built* by Steve 'Silk' Hurley (after Spandau Ballet, Howard Jones and Alsion Moyet!). However, it was a holiday to Ibiza in the summer of 93 with my best mate that was the revelation. One of the mix tapes we took, in amongst the rave ones by Top Buzz, Grooverider, Dr S Gachet, Ellis Dee and others, was DJ DK Live at Obsession. He is a DJ from the DiY sound-system crew from Nottingham. We listened to that tape non-stop after cutting our house-music teeth at Love Dove Club at Es Paradis Terrenial and the espuma parties at Amnesia (when there was only one room and a lovely outdoor area; now the excellent Terrace room). So next acknowledgement is to DK who I was proud to have DJ, with DiY Digs & Whoosh (RIP October 2020), at one of our club night in 95 called Moist (very 90's!). You can listen to that Obsession mixtape on Mixcloud and still holds up even with some channel bleed on the mixer and some very on-the-fly alterations to the mix going slightly off. Nice to listen too compared to some of the sterile, auto sync mixes nowadays.

Thanks also to Ben for the initial edit and encouragement. The phonecall we had discussing the big Stevie and Stacey sex scene remains a highlight. Originally I really went for it! No holes barred explicit sexy time; purple headed warriors, throbbing dongs, moist wet pussies! He said it read like a story in a *Readers Wifes* grot-mag so suggested I toned it down. Hope it reads better in the final cut!

Shouts to Brandon Block, whom Stefan Stockdale is loosely based, plus Danny Gould from Clockwork Orange. Reading both Brandon's and Danny's autobiographies gave me a kick up the arse to get it out there after years of writing, tweaking and sitting on it making vague noises about publishing it.

FURTHER INFORMATION
AND READING

Tales From Woodbridge: Part I - All Back To Mine (2020)
Tales From Woodbridge: Part II - All Back To Yours (2020)
Tales From Woodbridge: Part III - Tanit's Revenge (ETA 2022)
  * What happened to the Woodbridge lads between 1989 and 1994?
  * Who is in the boot of Kaisers car?
  * Why is The Judge called The Judge?
Tales From Woodbridge: Part IV - The Peacock Angel (ETA TBC)
Tales From Woodbridge: Part V - Burning Swallow (ETA TBC)

For further information and contact details please visit my socials:
  https://www.facebook.com/roberthellierofficial/
  https://twitter.com/RobertHellierDJ
  https://instagram.com/robert_hellier_official

Mixes and own productions:
  https://www.mixcloud.com/roberthellier/
Search "Robert Hellier" on Spotify, Apple Music, Amazon Music etc.

Printed in Great Britain
by Amazon

81313605R10150